MYSTERY

Gill, Bartholomew
The death of a Joyce scholar.
6/89   18.95

THE DEATH OF A JOYCE SCHOLAR

Also by Bartholomew Gill

THE DEATH
OF A
JOYCE SCHOLAR

A Peter McGarr Mystery

BARTHOLOMEW
GILL

WILLIAM MORROW
AND COMPANY, INC.
NEW YORK

Mystery

Gill

Library of Congress Cataloging-in-Publication Data

Gill, Bartholomew, 1943–
    The death of a Joyce scholar : a Peter McGarr mystery /
Bartholomew Gill.
        p.   cm.
    ISBN 0–688–08713–2
    I. Title.
    PS3563.A296D43   1989
    813'.54—dc19   88–38560
                                                                CIP

Printed in the United States of America

First Edition

1 2 3 4 5 6 7 8 9 10

BOOK DESIGN BY WILLIAM McCARTHY

For

HUGH GILL McGARRITY

publican • beloved brother • *Mensch*

"We Irishmen think otherwise."
—BISHOP BERKELEY

PART ONE

1

It began during an unprecedented period of June heat. After a cold, wild spring that saw force-eleven winds fell ancient beeches and hail showers shatter double-glazed windows, the clouds parted suddenly and bathed an unbelieving Dublin in a strong hot sun.

For the first few days people rejoiced and celebrated. Newspapers reported traffic jams on roads leading to Howth and other nearby beaches, and farmers, ever quick to exploit good weather, worked late into the night making hay with dried grasses. But for those who remained in the city to work, the reaction was different.

By the fourth day they were stunned. Looking up from a telephone or a desk at a sparkling pristine sky, they asked themselves why they had thought late July or early August, when they had arranged to take their holidays, had ever offered better weather. They mused and wandered—hands in pockets, voices vague—until the sixth or seventh day, when the collective mood changed from a tentative acceptance of what life might be like in another clime to downright anger that they had chosen badly.

It was then that Peter McGarr, the senior-most civil servant in his section, decided that—schedule be damned—he would defer to the elements and to a prerogative of his rank. Just half-century now, he asked himself how many more weeks of sunshine he might be able to enjoy in the tranquillity of his back garden. He could remember whole summers of cool breezes and forbidding skies, and with so many of his neighbors and their bands of bawling brats—God bless them—having taken to the coasts, he would have virtually all of Rathmines or at least Belgrave Square, where he lived, to himself.

At home he took the phone off the hook.

Once he'd made the mistake of leaving his phone number while on holiday in Portugal. He didn't get a moment's peace until he instructed the hotel management to say he'd moved on. In the minds of many of his colleagues and much of the press, McGarr had become so equated with his operation that, though much of substance could and often did occur during his several yearly absences, little of the reality of those occurrences could be acknowledged without his presence.

It was a dynamic that cut both ways, and from time to time McGarr regretted being perhaps too much the chief operative and too little the chief administrator of his agency. Yes, he had become a kind of institution, and was therefore more secure. But when, as was now the case, the work load increased dramatically with little hope of relief, it was he himself who bore the brunt of public scrutiny, not the bureau.

At his kitchen sink McGarr now filled the kettle and looked out through tall Georgian windows on the green wonder of his garden, burgeoning in the near tropical heat. It was almost as if he could actually see the plants growing; he easily convinced himself—listening to the flame drum on the bottom of the copper pot—that the wide, rubbery cabbage leaves that were glistening in the morning sun had actually gained inches since he had last seen them through the same window only a few hours earlier.

McGarr's house sat on a corner lot in Belgrave Square, a cluster of mainly Georgian row houses that looked out over a small, planted green area which was bounded on two sides by major through streets. Since McGarr's arrival some six years earlier, the neighborhood had declined from shabby genteel to tatty to near-slum before being rescued by several rent moguls who divided the gracious, eighteenth-century spaces into as many as ten tiny studio apartments.

But at least they had repainted crumbling exterior brick and replaced sagging windows and doors. In such a way, Belgrave Square—unlike some Dublin squares of the same vintage that had been gentrified beyond approachability with new, ornate fanlights and brass nameplates and door knockers—had remained familiar, accessible and democratic, which was how McGarr preferred things. And if prices declined again, he might plunge in himself and restore at least the dwellings immediately surrounding his own. His wife's picture gallery in Dawson Street had been doing nicely in recent years, and McGarr did not plan on being a wage slave all his life.

In the basement, the garden rooms of which he had converted to a kind of hothouse, McGarr changed into his work clothes, a pair of patched, twill trousers, an open-neck, short-sleeve shirt, and an old pair of boots heavy enough to punch down the top of a spade. A man a few inches shy of medium height, McGarr was sturdily constructed with firm, once-quick legs and strong arms and shoulders that he kept fit by means of what he called Chinese exercise. By that he meant daily bouts of vigorous, manual labor, usually, as now, in or around his house.

Bald on top, McGarr kept long the light red hair that remained, sweeping it back on the sides of his head so that it curled at the nape of his neck. He now fitted on a worn panama hat. He had a freckled face and a long nose, which had been broken often and was now bent to one side. His eyes were pale gray, and in all, dressed as he was with dried mud on his boots, he looked like a Dublin navvy from the building trades whose specialty was poured concrete.

The meringue on McGarr's boots consisted, however, of aged chicken manure and compost. Combined in the proportion two to one, it was the secret to his garden and such a fillip to growth that his neighbors and the few friends whom he had made privy to his hobby admired his handiwork in terms that he always found distressing. Having dismissed all the standard explanations for digging in the earth from reestablishing touch with his ecology to taking direct part in the cycle of birth, growth, harvest and rebirth, McGarr believed, and insisted, that he gardened for simple pleasure. Everything from journeying the forty miles down to Kildare for the magic chicken droppings, which clung like glue to his boots and made his eyes water and his nose sting, to enjoying the snappy crunch of fresh vegetables and herbs in all seasons, regaled him in a way that was beyond words. He did it because he did it, he once told his wife, for whom all urges required some explanation, and he couldn't think of anything else that would provide him with such . . . pleasure. There was no other word for it.

✿   ✿   ✿

Thus McGarr worked nearly to noon on the first day of his unplanned, midsummer retreat from things tiresome and worldly, turning over and wetting down his several compost heaps and weeding and tickling his raised beds that differed from traditional Irish "lazy" beds in their width of six feet and their depth of four. The sun, contained by the tall garden walls, became torrid, and in looking up from his hoeing to move the sprinkler from his rows of lettuce, chicory, endives, watercress, and spinach to the beds of nearly ripe asparagus, McGarr noticed a richly bearded face at the top of the wall that he shared with his only truly contiguous neighbor.

It was that of Rabbi Viner, who had lived next door for nearly a decade now and become a particular friend of McGarr's. He too was a Dubliner by birth and sensibility, and their minds often met with a felicity that McGarr considered soothing.

"Grand day, but a bit hot, wouldn't you say? Particularly in your predicament."

"Which is?" McGarr asked.

"Locked in guilt expiation, I have it. Is this the noonday sun?" Having positioned himself in the full, patterned shade of McGarr's gingko tree, he pretended not to be able to locate the source of heat. "We'll have to add Irish civil servants to the lyric, specifically those who phone in ill to pot around in their back gardens. We could then relate it all to the country's unplanned-for and unsolved mortalities."

"Something like the Lizzie Borden jingle," McGarr suggested.

"The very thing," said Viner. "On the charts in no time. Haven't we all a touch of mayhem in our hearts?"

Disregarding his clothes, which were now nearly wet, McGarr moved the sprinkler without turning it off; the fine spray of cold water felt so refreshing that he thought for a moment that he might raise the ring over his head. "But, isn't all mortality unplanned for, or are you intimating that persons known to you—your supplicants, perhaps—plan otherwise? I could send somebody 'round. Preventive mortality, we could call it."

"Something like preventive medicine," Viner chimed in, warming to the crack, as lively conversation or any good time was called throughout Ireland. "It's the coming thing, I'm told. All prohibition and exhortation. Rules. *Dictats.* No smoking, no drinking. Did you hear me, Chief Super or Super Chief, whichever it is they call you down there in the *drum.*"

"Castle," McGarr corrected. "I couldn't imagine myself in a mere fort." McGarr was Chief Superintendent of the Murder Squad of the Garda Siochana, the Irish Police. His office was in Dublin Castle.

"Water. *Mineral* water. And jogging—who, might I ask, ever thought of that abuse of the human body?" Viner was a powerfully constructed man who, much to his family's dismay, had taken on a great deal of weight in recent years, such that he was perhaps the largest man, if not the tallest, that McGarr knew. "Some bloody American, no doubt."

"Wrong there," said McGarr. "He was Greek. Carrying the bad news, he was."

"And suitably dispatched, as I remember the myth. Instant mortality right on the spot and bad cess to all his kind."

There was a pause in which McGarr removed an already damp handkerchief from a back pocket and swabbed his brow. Exactly fifty now, he was beginning to feel both the weight of his years and the injuries that he had sustained along the way. Having begun with the Garda at nineteen, he had chafed under a system that had seemed to reward bureaucratic competence and political pull more than active police work. He had resigned and spent an even score of years on the Continent, first with Criminal Justice and later with Interpol, before returning home to his present post.

But he now had a knee on which both he and a Marseilles thug, who had jumped him from behind, had fallen. It would only take limited lateral movement. His hip—same side—gave off a definite click with each step. The socket had been rearranged in a bomb blast in a Galway disco. And then his back and one arm were riddled with scars that imperfectly concealed damage of which he was reminded whenever he bent too far or reached too quickly. Or whenever he performed any vigorous activity too long.

"Don't you just hate Americans and vegetables?" Viner went on. As with most Dubliners, conversation between them did not always proceed linearly.

McGarr wondered if there were a correlation or a choice. He himself hated neither, and he nearly remarked that he had several good friends who were Americans, but he knew where that would lead. And since much of his garden produce regularly found its way to Viner's table, he imagined Viner himself rather fancied vegetables. He hadn't become that immense on bread alone. "Now what could you possibly have against vegetables? Not to mention Americans, of whom there were on last report a mere two-hundred-and-forty million."

"Oh, nothing. Certainly nothing against *your* vegetables. All organic. No pesticides. No herbicides.
Kosher in the strictest sense and delicious certainly. But
vegetables are best et as an accompaniment, a side dish,
garnish even, to something more toothsome."

McGarr now understood the drift of their conversation and suggested, "Like beefsteak," which was what
Viner wanted to hear. After a series of tests some six
or seven months earlier, Viner's cardiologist had recommended a diet rich in whole grains, fresh vegetables,
and defatted, salt-free potions like consommés and weak
chicken soup. Viner had lost scads of weight and had
admitted to feeling much better. "I don't nod off anymore at three or four in the afternoon. I don't get
angry at little things, goddamn it!" But he couldn't speak
to McGarr, who he knew treasured a solid meal, or look
upon his garden, without conjuring up the entrées with
which those comestibles might be served. They had
gone through this before.

"Smuddered in sautéed mushrooms and lovely green
onions, with a side of bleedin' broccoli hollandaise. No,
no—salmon hollandaise. Forget *vegetables*, dirt-dwell-
ing, lower-life forms that they are, though I wouldn't
ignore fresh asparagus"—Viner's dark eyes turned
toward the rainbow that the full sun was creating in the
mist of McGarr's sprayer—"lightly steamed and dripping
with drawn—"

"Sol!" a voice came over the wall. "Solly! Dinner!"
It was Viner's wife.

"*Bu'ther!*"

McGarr tried to keep from laughing. He half turned
his back. "What is it today?" he asked innocently.

"Twigs and bloody bark, if you must know. What
else?"

"Ach—things could be worse. Consider my situation. I don't have dinner at all."

"And you with a fridge brimming with death." Viner lifted a hand. "Oh, no—dissimulate not. I've seen it: sides of rashers, tubs of butter. Cheeses! Gruyeres, Camemberts, lovely soft, moist Bries that just melt on the tongue," he catalogued as he descended the wall and escaped McGarr's sight. "Pickled herring in cream sauce. The leavings of some highly caloric repast like chicken Française or a pot of Beef Bourguignonne . . ."

"Sol!" his wife called out the open window. "What are you going on about out there? Come in here now while your dinner's hot."

". . . pâté de foie gras on buttered toast points" were the last words of protest McGarr heard for perhaps an hour, until a dog began barking, and, though lame from injuries sustained in a bomb blast years before, in a leap gained the top of the wall, a quarter of which McGarr shared with the dog's mistress.

Somebody was ringing McGarr's front door bell, and the P.M., as the dog was called, wanted to know who. A former member of the Police Canine Corps, the animal had assumed responsibility for the entire southwest corner of Belgrave Square, which very much included McGarr's dwelling; very little occurred there without the animal's blessing.

The tone of his bark, however, said the visitor was not a threat, and McGarr worked on, until the bell continued insistently and the dog came around the wall to find out why McGarr was ignoring it.

Finally McGarr straightened up from his hoeing and swabbed his brow. With the dog by his side he climbed up through the hot sun by a stile in the wall and stared down on a woman who had her finger on the bell.

2

"Sorry," he said, frightening her. "May I help you?"

Raising a hand to her eyes, she tried to look up at him. She was a big woman in her early thirties; her dark brown hair was streaked with gray. Her eyes were also brown, and her skin was freckled and wrinkling on her white neck. "I'm looking for Superintendent McGarr."

"May I ask why?"

She was wearing a plain white sleeveless blouse, turquoise-colored slacks, and white shoes, and McGarr could see that, in spite of her youth and good bone structure, her body had lost its shape from child-bearing. Her breasts had fallen and her stomach was pouchy and distended. To it she was clutching a white imitation-leather purse. "It's about my husband."

"What about your husband?" The dog, meaning to watch for any sign of hostility as she spoke, kept trying to hook its head around McGarr's legs.

She took her hand from her eyes and looked down at her feet, away from the sun. "Look—is McGarr in, or is he not?" She had a flat, Dublin, working-class accent.

He's not, thought McGarr. Definitely. Categorically. But almost in reflex, knowing it was a mistake, he asked, "*What* about your husband."

"Ah . . ." She cast her head to one side. "He's missing."

"For how long?"

"Three days now."

"Is that unusual?"

Again her head went to the side, as if to say not really, but . . .

"And you suspect . . . ?" McGarr looked off into the square, decided once again it was a park. From his vantage point he could see squadrons of fat bumble bees strafing a trellis of roses that was not visible from any other part of his property. Warped in the rising heat, the scene appeared as if through a film of tumbling water, and he blessed its tranquillity and quiet.

"Well, sumtin' happened to him. Otherwise . . ."

"Otherwise, what?"

"Otherwise he'd be speakin' to me," she said impatiently. "Look—are you McGarr? I can't see you standing there like that. The sun—"

"You've been to the Castle?"

She nodded.

"And they sent you here?"

"No—it's not like they did or nuttin'."

"Of course you tried Missing Persons?" Three days was no time for a working-class Dublin man to be gone. He'd probably a drop taken or met up with a mot or both. Given the weather, he might as easily have awakened with some new friends in Wexford or Tralee. Working his way back, he was. On the tides that flow from a tap.

But it also now intrigued McGarr why she should think her husband dead and the Murder Squad the appropriate agency to search for him. And now, in this heat in Belgrave Square.

"I rang them up and they said I'd have to file a report."

"Which you did, I gather?"

She shook her head.

"Relatives. Friends. Any . . ." He looked off again at the roses. ". . . special interests?"

Did she blush? McGarr thought she did.

He waited and again catalogued the inspissated, matronly hands, water-worn and clutching the plastic purse that looked like it was melting in the heat. "It's not like that."

She had something else to tell him, something that had not come out as yet, and she had come for that purpose. How many wives with a husband missing three days would look up the Chief Superintendent of the Murder Squad, bang off, no other calls?

"And then"—she had so turned her head that she appeared to be speaking to the closed door—"I came to you because . . ." There was a pause. ". . . you're one of . . . us."

Really, McGarr thought. In what sense? Obviously in the pancake accent of the great family of Ath Cliath, which he hoped he shared with the woman only on occasion, and then when he was forgetting the best part of himself.

Still, it was an appeal that McGarr had not often heard, and he was enough a creature of his culture that he could not readily turn a stranger from his door. "Your name?"

"Katie Coyle."

It was Dublin, all right, and nothing plainer. "Well, Katie Coyle—would you know how to get to the back garden of this house?" Taking the ring of keys from his pocket, he twisted one off and dropped it at her feet. With the same hand he gave the dog a command. McGarr had saved it from the vet's final needle when, after an explosion in an Irish National Liberation safe house that was being searched, the Canine Corps decided to put the animal down. Its right front leg had been damaged severely, and the dog would only ever move with a limp. McGarr, however, found the nearly nine-stone "personal protection" dog a home with his elderly next-door neighbor, a spinster, and there the creature adopted a proprietorial demeanor that prompted a resident to dub it the "P.M. of Belgrave Square."

The dog now hopped off the wall and on a hobbling gait was soon by Katie Coyle's side. "You needn't be afraid. He'll see that you don't get lost."

And that you get where you're going, he thought, as he waited to hear the door close and the latch catch.

He then scanned the quiet street, checking parked cars for passengers, the square for strollers or others sitting in the shade: anybody he could see in windows, doorways, stoops, side yards. But he saw no one. It was noon, and too hot to go out for those already not out.

Or for work at what was work.

In the back garden, under the deep shade of McGarr's trellised grape vines, Katie Coyle told him that her husband's name was Kevin and that they were from the Liberties, a profoundly working-class area of Dublin that occupied most of a hill between Christ Church Cathedral and the Guinness Brewery. They had nine children ranging from one year and three months to age eleven. They lived in a five-room flat, but were currently looking for something larger, but wasn't everybody else.

And what with Kevin's salary, which wasn't much, and the kids, and the housing grants having been cut off again by the government, there was only so much they could do, him (Kevin) insisting that they stay in the Liberties. "Where we were born and bred, the both of us, before it became the in thing to do for some."

McGarr's eyes met hers for a moment before angling off again. As she was speaking, he had been telling himself how much he needed an iced pint of lager. There were several tall cans in the fridge, but McGarr had a proscription, which he seldom broke: he would not take a drink at home alone before four in the afternoon, except on a holiday. He had almost convinced himself that it was in fact a holiday and that the beer would help him cope with the woman before him, when he chanced to ask, "And what is it that your husband does?"

"For a living? Or elsewise?"

First things first. The *elsewise*—doubtless beer and football; or beer, football, and horses; or (probably better for her, given their numbers) beer, football, horses, and women—they'd get to later, if McGarr tolerated her that long.

But when, with near embarrassment, she said, "Trinity College. He's a professor there," McGarr sat up on the bench they were sharing.

"A what?"

As though to say that she expected better of McGarr, she smiled wryly, and her large, dark eyes that were still a kind of perfection searched his face. "I know I'm not your typical Trinity professor's wife. But nor is Kevin your typical Trinity professor."

McGarr couldn't help but wonder if he had a disturbed woman on his hands. Reaching down to stroke the head of the dog who was lying by his side, he asked, "Of what?" For God's sake, he nearly added. Psychology? *Criminology?* He nearly cracked a smile. He could almost taste that beer.

"English literature, or like Kevin says, literature mostly in English."

"A professor?"

She nodded, then looked toward the perfect rows of vegetables.

"A *full* professor?" he insisted. She would destroy his afternoon only for good reason. But the possible murder of a Trinity College professor of English literature and father of nine, who also curiously hailed from the Liberties, would be in the eyes of the press, which influenced such things in the eyes of McGarr's superiors, the very best of reasons. And only at his peril could McGarr ignore it.

Then he could hardly disregard the fact that nearly nine out of ten homicides were committed by persons either related or known to the victim. And here was the man's wife, who was by her own say-so "unlikely," admitting that she believed her husband had been murdered. How had she put it? ". . . something happened to him. Otherwise . . ." Otherwise what?

Excusing himself by saying "Let me get my notebook," McGarr walked into the basement, where he removed his boots. At the fridge in the kitchen he popped the top of a can of beer and swallowed long until the cold lager bit the back of his throat and brought a kind of satisfying pain to his right eye. He then repaired to the library where, if memory served him rightly, he thought he recalled having seen a volume by one Kevin Coyle, M.A.

And sure enough, there it was among his wife's 90 percent of the library: *Myth-Making: the Personal/Im-*

personal of an Author of Competence. A paperback, the volume had been reviewed in hardcover to what McGarr judged was critical acclaim. Said the *Times,* "Solid, insightful scholarship combined with trenchant wit and graceful prose . . . the book is a minor masterpiece of literary substance and style. As a primer on criticism, it will engage readers on every level."

Said the *Guardian,* "Coyle has observed Pound's dictum to make it new. His *Myth-Making* is so artful an approach to a truly new New Criticism that it often rivals the very works that it treats."

Said the *Observer,* "A brilliant debut. One can only look forward with anticipation to Mr. Coyle's succeeding work, which promises to deal with the entire 'modernist' movement in Irish arts and letters and to be a major publishing event."

The reviews from America were similarly glowing; fanning the pages, McGarr noted that Noreen had actually read the book. It opened readily, and there was a distinct tea stain on page 285.

At the fridge he reached for another pint can, and dialed his Castle office. Glancing out the Georgian window at the end of the kitchen, he noticed that Katie Coyle was now stroking the P.M.'s wide head. A jackdaw kited down into the herb garden but fluttered up again when the dog moved for it.

"Bernie—tell me something. Was there a woman in there a while ago?"

"Jesus, Chief—she *didn't.* When she said she would, I told her don't. He'll eat you alive, shoes, handbag, and all. She had your address and everything."

"Kevin Coyle. From what she said, he's a professor at Trinity College."

"Yah." McKeon's tone was unbelieving.

"Lives in the Liberties."

"Yah."

"The wife seems to think—"

"Ah, Chief. She went through the entire drill when she was here, and Rut'ie nearly threw her out the door. Bodily. Fella's only been gone a couple of days, for chrissake, and from the look a her—"

"Records," McGarr cut in. "On both of them. I want a check on hospitals too. And the Liberties bit. Send Hughie out to interview neighbors."

"You must be *joking*. We don't even know he's *missing*, much less murdered, and in this weather, with what we already have on our plate, and you—"

McGarr hung up blindly as he tilted the can back; he then dialed his wife's shop in Dawson Street. The beer was now giving him a slight, agreeable buzz, and he imagined he must have been dehydrated. It was either that or he was going to hell altogether, which was a possibility now worth considering. He swirled his neck.

The P.M. had returned to Mrs. Katie Coyle's side. The bells of the cathedral on Lower Rathmines Road were ringing. McGarr checked the kitchen clock: three, which was close enough to four, seeing as how it was a holiday of sorts. He allowed himself another gulp.

"Kevin Coyle—what can you tell me about him?"

"What's wrong with your voice?"

"Nothing's wrong with my voice."

"There is, sure."

"Like what?" He tugged again from the can.

"Like high."

It was the proper word. The buzz had turned to a

glow, and McGarr thought that after a bit more gar-
dening, he might dust off his fishing rods and drive out
to Howth for a little late-afternoon fishing. He had
heard there were mackerel running off Puck's Rocks.

"What are you doing?" she went on.

"Interviewing a complainant."

"At home?"

"Why do you think I'm at home?"

"Where else would you be drinking malt where it's
quiet? Early, I might add. Would that we all were civil
servants."

"*Senior* civil servants."

"An adjective all too revealing."

Some twenty years separated them, and he wondered
if Noreen was determined to keep him young through
sarcasm.

"Coyle. I understand he's a professor at Trinity.
You have one of his books."

"And *he's* one of your complainants?"

"Did I say that?"

"You didn't have to. I know the tone."

Like she knew what he was drinking, he thought.
Malt, not beer. "Which tone is that?"

"Coldly official. Your 'state' tone. The tone of the
inquisitor."

"Coyle. Kevin Coyle, M.A."

"Sure, and much more. An utterly brilliant young
chap. Professor, as you intimated. And early. It was
either they promoted him or he was off. Don't you
remember me reading you the article in the *Times*, when
the book came out?"

As far as McGarr was concerned, his ears had been
virginal to the name Kevin Coyle up until a dozen
minutes past, but he conceded. "Vaguely."

"Ah, don't cod me. Yah don't. You never listen. I might as well be speaking to the bleedin' wall."

"Kevin Coyle. The book," he prompted.

There was a pause in which, he imagined, she considered the fate of being married to an older man. Once, when she had complained of his not taking her seriously, she had accused him of thinking of her as "a tootsie, a bimbo, an . . . airhead." McGarr had wondered where she picked up the phraseology, and when he had said, "I'll take you anyway I can get you," she had exploded, "*See!* That's proof."

Finally, she said, "I don't know why I put up with you, but the book, the first one, put Kevin in the spotlight. He had offers from everywhere, England, America. Who knows now when the other takes off."

"*Now?*"

"What d'you do with yourself apart from brief stints at the Castle and early afternoon tippling?" It was another point of contention between them that McGarr's life was too narrowly focused, when in fact trying to perfect him was perhaps Noreen's most enjoyable pastime. "It's been in all the papers for days now. He calls it *Phon/Antiphon.* It's a critical reappraisal of modern Irish literature in English that focuses mainly on Joyce and Beckett. It's out Monday next, I believe, and the publisher is launching it with a big bash at the Shelbourne."

Big bash, for sure, McGarr thought. It wouldn't be much of a party without the main attraction. He wondered what Coyle looked like, what he was as a person, if he could mix with the crowd, introduce his wife around at the Shelbourne, which was Ireland's most socially pretentious hotel. He looked out at Katie Coyle, who was now walking slowly along a path through a rose trellis in the back garden. Dowdy was too mild a term to describe her; she was matronly before her time. Too many children and—could it be?—cares to remember that her appearance might matter.

"What's he like?" Ireland was a small country, and its arts community was truly a little set, of which Noreen and her family, with their picture gallery, had long been a part. It had been there in the shop on Dawson Street that McGarr, while running down a lead in a murder investigation, had met his wife. She had been just twenty-one at the time, a research student at the Cortauld Institute in London. He had been so taken with her radiant red hair and her green eyes and her enthusiasm for her subject, and for life itself, it seemed, that in a vault at the back of the shop he impetuously tried to kiss her. And received a short, sharp slap for his "audacity. And think of it—you, a man old enough to be my father." Only through dogged pursuit had he proved to her otherwise.

"Coyle?" she now asked. "I've never met him, but you see him around now and again. Great walker, and they say he loves the city and knows it as well as Joyce knew it in his time. He even *looks* like Joyce. Tallish. Long, sloping nose a little flattened and off to one side. Wavy, reddish hair. Most of all, glasses."

"Made an impression, it seems."

"Who knows. He might be another, different, more modern Joyce, if you accept the premise that the novel has been both written and therefore exhausted by Joyce, and unwritten and therefore effectively eliminated as an art form by Beckett. What's left then but criticism, which in the future—as begun by Coyle—might become the only genuinely artful possibility for the writer of serious fiction."

McGarr glanced down at the barrel of the cold can that was beading agreeably in the heat and humidity and wondered if he could fiddle with the date of his annual holiday, arranged for four weeks hence. "In other words, Coyle's a man with literary . . ." He rejected the word pretensions, since teaching at Trinity satisfied at least that. ". . . aspirations."

"*Aspirations?*" Another redhead, Noreen's moods could vacillate within mere minutes between elation and despair, and often bore little relation to external stimuli. Six years of marriage told McGarr that at present she was moderating toward the former condition. By nightfall she would be ready for some sort of catharsis. "If the new book is accepted by critics at all like the first, the man'll probably be canonized as our greatest living literary critic. He'll be able to write his own ticket."

If he can write at all, McGarr thought. Katie Coyle stood before McGarr's banks of multicolored lilacs; she was staring up at them as they nodded in the light breeze. Her hands were clasped behind her back, and in spite of the heat, she remained motionless as a statue in the full sun.

"You still haven't told me why you're home."

"Won't be for long."

"*What* about Kevin Coyle?"

"His wife thinks he's a missing person."

There was a pause. "And she came to *you?*"

"She says she thinks I'm one of them."

"Them who?"

McGarr thought of Noreen's explanation of Coyle's new book, which had meant nothing to him, and he said, "Them who aren't the others, I suspect. See you."

"When? And *what* about Kevin Coyle? Why does she think he's missing? Oh, Peter—"

McGarr hung up. His wife was young, beautiful, sensitive, and intelligent, but she had a singular failing. Like most other Dubliners, she could not resist the most insignificant bit of gossip about anybody she even remotely knew, and nothing regaled her more than a certain sort of insider information. He imagined that anything about Kevin Coyle would have a currency among her art and literary friends that would command all ears. At social events those same acquaintances treated McGarr as though he'd just stepped out of the pages of a crime novel.

After a quick shower and a change of clothes, McGarr found Katie Coyle seated at the kitchen table, his second can of beer before her. "Sorry—I didn't think you'd mind."

Of course he didn't; this was more *us* again. "I don't, but you can tell me this." He pulled a chair over and, turning it around, sat down facing her. "*Why* do you think your husband was murdered?"

Their eyes met and hers quickly filled with tears, though she held his gaze. She had heavy, powerful-looking arms, one muscle of which flexed as she swiveled the beer can on the tabletop. "Because people were jealous of him."

"Which people?"

"His . . . 'colleagues,' they called themselves."

"Like who?"

"Well"—her eyes lit on the can—"there was Flood, for one. And Holderness, for another, though he's only a research student still, and not much of that."

"Anybody else?"

"Well"—the eyes flashed off—"there probably was,

though I wouldn't have known, me being tied up with the kids and all."

"This Flood. And Holderness. Where do I find them?"

"Holderness, I don't know, apart from hearing his family has gobs of money and some big estate down in the country. It's summer, and college is closed. And even if it wasn't, Holderness wouldn't be there. Kevin sacked him, and he's not to come back without some committee's say-so.

"Flood is still somewhere about, I'd say. Him and Kevin worked on the Joyce thing Bloomsday. Though in truth the bloody business is Flood's alone and just that—"

McGarr waited, vaguely remembering that Bloomsday was a celebration that involved James Joyce somehow.

"—*business*, as if being a scholar no longer even means being a gentleman, poor pay though it is. 'Summers we must care for our families too, like other people,' Flood said, though by care he meant him and his bitch of a wife in up-market style out in Foxrock, and me and Kevin dodgin' gurriers and bowsies in town. Says him to me one day last year when we had no food in the larder and Kevin . . . off someplace." Her eyes moved toward the garden. " 'What—d'ye think I floated up the Liffey in a bubble? When I got the idea for Bloomsday, I brought it to Kevin, who said he wasn't interested, and I had to go it alone. I put my last pound into the thing.' Joyce's Ireland and Bloomsday Tours, he calls it. He's even got an office and a staff in Nassau Street."

And all on Kevin, McGarr was to conclude.

"And then I'm sure Flood wouldn't miss the party

that Kevin's publisher is throwing for the new book, with all the celebrities he might've sucked up to there. He used Kevin like that, sure he did. Every chance he got."

McGarr again examined her: the wrinkles that extended deep into her neck, her bloodshot brown eyes. He suspected that at one time she must have been a handsome, if large, woman. "You have some problem with Flood?"

"Me? Nar' a bit. It's just him and the likes of him and all the others there at their grand college—fops, swells, and nances, the lot—couldn't hold a candle to me poor husband, and him now dead."

And not them. McGarr said nothing still. Her voice was now laden with emotion.

"Sure, it would be easy to say it was a mistake from the start, Kevin forgetting all he and us were and going in to the college to sit the exams. The moderatorship and later the prizes and such. But what was he to do with all his brains? If he hadn't, wouldn't he have resented me and the kids all the more?" In a small voice she added, "And us *his*, make no mistake about that, sir." She reached for the beer can and drank from it.

Still McGarr waited. The eight-day clock over the fridge wound steadily on, its beat more a springy tink than a tock. A fly buzzed from the hall through the kitchen and out the narrow gap below the raised kitchen window into the garden. With a kind of groan, the P.M. settled himself on the cool flagstones beneath the sink.

"Bloomsday?" he asked to keep her talking.

"That's the day James Joyce's book *Ulysses* was set on. June sixteenth, 1904. And every June sixteenth Flood and Kevin took a bunch of foreigners and Americans around the paths in Dublin. The paths that a fella name of Bloom and Stephen Dedalus, the Joyce characters, traced in the book. Flood acted as guide, Kevin like Dedalus himself, or Joyce maybe. Flood'd bring the group to a place, and there Kevin'd be spouting the words from the book perfect. He had a brilliant memory, he had. He'd need read a thing onc't and he'd have it bang off. It's what earned him all the notice. The memory."

McGarr doubted it. He himself had a capacious memory, and here he was, a policeman. He thought of Noreen's description of Coyle's work and how it had left him cold.

"You wouldn't have another of these on you, would you?" She meant the beer.

McGarr reached over to the fridge and pulled out the last two cans. Placing one in front of his guest, he asked, "*Why* do you think your husband is dead?"

Katie Coyle's strong fingers readily picked back the serving spout of the can. "Because I've got him home with me now. Some miserable fucker stabbed him right through the heart. Bloomsday, I guess. Near the Prospect Cemetery in Glasnevin." Raising the can to her lips, she drank off nearly all its contents. When she lowered it, her face was streaming with tears. "I thought I might keep him with us as long as I could. But he's going off now in the heat. None of the kids know. I sent the older ones down to an aunt in Clare, told her to keep them away from the telly and papers. And the babbies—" She looked away.

McGarr slid the other can toward her. "The address?"

She told him, and McGarr went into the study to use the telephone again.

3

The Liberties refers to a set of trading and tax franchises that the British crown once granted the Archbishop of Dublin. Formerly a wide area that encompassed much of central Dublin, the term now applies only to a small working-class neighborhood distinguished by one of Dublin's tallest hills, several of its major churches, and the great Guinness Brewery.

Mainly, however, it consists of a tight pack of shops, row houses, and commercial buildings and yards, near the largest of which Kevin and Katie Coyle lived in a former warehouse. McGarr at first saw only an open door, a battered lift, and a worn staircase.

Thus he was surprised upon entering the Coyle apartment on the fourth and final floor. It was light and airy and even cool; a westward breeze, sweet with the smell of roasting black patent malt, made the curtains billow out from the windows like wide, white sails.

And if there were but five rooms for this family of eleven—now ten—they were spacious, with tall ceilings and creaky floors that, McGarr imagined, had witnessed the passage of millions of hand trucks. The planks squeaked under foot. The wood had been sanded and varnished to a mirror gloss that allowed two Coyle children, dressed in summer shorts and thick woolen socks, to skate as easily over the surface as across a pool of blond ice.

"Mistar, mistar," said one, tugging at McGarr's wrist. "Are ya a doctor? Me da has taken ill, he has."

And beyond all pain, thought McGarr, finding Kevin Coyle propped up on pillows on a bed which had been turned toward an open window that offered a view of the Liffey and the Georgian perfection of the Four Courts.

"It's like he'll turn to us and say something strange and different about the city, like he always could," said the wife in a tone that was close to breaking.

McGarr thought not. Yes, his eyes were open, but— light blue—they were as opaque in death as shattered agates, and his skin, which was gray, looked soft, like scudding soap. A man in his mid-thirties, Coyle appeared to have been tall, with sloping shoulders and a thin, graceful build. His hair was brown and wavy, and his nose—as Noreen had described—seemed a little off to one side. In all, he looked as much like James Joyce as any photo McGarr had seen of the bard, down to the pair of thick tortoiseshell glasses, one lens of which was now broken and starry.

"I knew it was wrong, but what was I to do with them otherwise. The only time he took them off was in bed, whenever he didn't fall asleep reading, which was seldom. And without them he looked so—" Unnatural, she thought, though she couldn't bring herself to say it.

Her husband was wearing an open-neck linen shirt, stained with dried blood from the first button catch to where a sheet had been pulled up and folded neatly over his torso.

"I didn't know what to do. With him. Treat him like he was alive or dead. But since I'd never been with him dead—" Her voice cracked and she turned to the door, on which one of the children was now beating. "Will ya get out of that, Stephen, or I'll thrash ya sure," she cried.

"You found him where?"

"I didn't, like I said. A mate did. Propped against the wall of gray stones in a laneway at the back of the Glasnevin Cemetery. No life left in him at all. The wound—there—all clotted and thick, glasses by his side, or so he was when I got there and according to a woman whose word you can take."

"And she is?"

"Cat'rine Doyle. 'Catty,' we call her."

And Katie Coyle.

"She lives right there off the Finglas Road. There's a warren of laneways and outbuildings between her back garden and the cemetery wall. Walking her dog, she was, before going off to work. At first she thought he was drunk, it having been in the papers about Bloomsday and all, and her knowing him like she does. 'Get up. Get up out of that now, Kevin, and come inside for some tea,' she said before she saw the wound and the blood. It was then she rang me up."

And not the police. Why? He waited. Out in the kitchen one of the children was crying; through the open windows McGarr could hear the singsong blare of police horns. "And you?"

"I came and got him."

And broke the law. "How?"

"With another of me mates."

McGarr now turned his head from the dead man and watched her closely. What was he hearing here, another revelation? Or a confession? Somewhere off in the apartment—or was it outside the window?—a songbird was trilling a refrain that McGarr had never heard before. It was oddly disjunctive, given the sight before them— it was sweet and complex and filled with celebration for the sun and the summer and the heat.

"Mary Sittonn. She's in antiques in The Coombe." It was a narrow, busy commercial street in the Liberties. "She has a horse and cart, and we went for him."

With a coffin, McGarr reflected. Did they prop him up and put a pipe in his mouth? Or did they just sling him onto the jarvey and throw a tarp over him? A jarvey was not an unusual vehicle for coal men and Travelers, but it was a novelty for a woman in the antiques trade, though McGarr suspected that that explained it. A throwback to a less rushed era, it probably served as a fashionable advertisement.

And they wouldn't have won a second glance at rush hour, apart from the motorist with an oath on his lips, having to swing wide to pass the slow-moving cart: two big, aging Traveling women, anybody would have assumed. Especially on seeing Katie Coyle with her freckled skin and dark eyes. With the dole and housing allowance and the state taking care of so much else, there were plenty of well-fed Travelers around the city these days, living in rubble in the city center or along the green verges of the major dual-carriageways leading out into the country.

"We've a lift here, and it was nothing to get him up."

McGarr looked at her twice. In another context the phrase might have been misunderstood, and he was further put in mind of the wake motif of all she was telling him. What about the kids? Or had the older ones already been sent down to the aunt in Clare?

He scanned her rounded but powerful-looking shoulders. The ambulance and the forensic vans had arrived, each switching off its horn as it entered the laneway. "I need the addresses of your 'mates.' And tell me this— did you kill him yourself?"

Her head went back slightly, and did color now come to her face? It did, he judged. Her eyes strayed to the bed and she shook her head once, but with a resignation that was both judgment and curse—on suspicion or on the police or on McGarr himself. "Good, bad, or indifferent, he was my husband. The father of my children."

"How was he at that?"

"At what?"

"At being the father of your children?"

Another shrug. "He lived here. The children adored him. He was always joking with them. You know— word games, secret phrases for this and that, for a time there they even had their own language."

They? "And as a husband?"

"He brought his money home. Most of it. And then we had the promise of the new book. As for the first . . ." She shook her head. "Kevin wasn't much for trade and sharp practice. He'd read everything but the fine print in a contract, and they took advantage of him there." Tears now appeared on her cheeks.

Like Flood had, McGarr assumed she meant. "Why did you think you could move him?"

She said nothing.

"You're not interested in who might have murdered him?"

"Does it matter? Some low mucker, no doubt. Some drug addict. Some punk. They're all over places like Glasnevin and Finglas. Ballymun's just up the road."

The last was the name of a government-planned, work-ing-class housing scheme that had turned into one of Europe's most crime-ridden communities. "Over and over I told him, 'You think you're immune?' They don't give a tinker's curse who you might be or where you're from or what your prospects are. Or your *credentials*,' as Kevin put it."

She turned to McGarr. "You know—how much a Dub' he was, how gen-u-ine. Half them bastards are foreigners themselves or niggers or worse. But Kevin didn't drive—he *hated* the automobile—and he thought he owned the city, streets and all, after the tons of shite they fed him at Trinity, once his book come out. The first one. The little one."

"And the big one? The new one?" McGarr asked.

"Sure, wouldn't he have moved from reigning deity to interstellar being?"

There was jealousy there. No doubt about it. McGarr considered the notoriety, some of which would now be visited upon his widow regardless of her rough edges. Dublin was a city that loved its artists best (and perhaps only when) dead, and the affection for the Dublin-born and -bred Coyle with his Trinity background and inter-national acclaim might well result in a bit of money now, both from here and abroad. "What would he have been doing in Glasnevin?"

She shook her head. "My thought exactly, when Catty phoned me. 'Glasnevin,' says I. 'What in the name of hell was he doing out there,' though it's in the book, so it is."

"What book?"

"*Ulysses*," she said with a slight twist of the head that was a characteristic Dublin gesture of dislike.

"Overblown bullshit and nothin' more. Glasnevin is in there. The cemetery. It's where Bloom goes with the others to bury Paddy Dignam, the toper who's just died. But Kevin and Flood, they never 'played' the funeral bit, as they called it. 'It's too bloody far,' I can remember Kevin saying to him. 'I get land sick out of sight of the Liffey, and the Phibsborough Road looks like a famous side at football. Of course, we all had to guess which side. Says he, 'The Manchester You Blighted. Then it's life and rebirth that *Ulysses* celebrates, with only a stab at death.' " She again inclined her head to the side and added reflectively, "His very words. Kevin was always punnin', so he was, though how well, he could not have known."

McGarr wondered if she had read *Ulysses*. He hadn't himself. When he had been growing up it was a banned book; called *Useless* by those who claimed to have read it. In the Dublin of McGarr's early years—in many ways the Dublin he could see and hear and smell just outside the windows of the loft in the Liberties—a story wasn't worth telling unless it could be said with convenient haste and, granted, style, to a cozy of friends who were gathered around a few jars. Others had their own tales to tell, and anything tendentious missed the mark.

"What *did* they 'play' then? Kevin and Bloom. From *Ulysses*." Three days before, if her story were true.

The children had begun banging on the door again, reporting that some men had come in. McGarr then heard another woman's voice, shooing them away.

"Ah—they changed every time, since they kept gettin' certain ones back every year. Americans mostly, Germans, and recently some Japs and such. Wanting to appear 'literary' the easy way." She rubbed her fingers together to mean with money. "Which was all well and good for Flood, like I said." Her eyes flashed up to McGarr's. "He never comes up short. Never. Such that he can grant that wife of his her every whim.

"And then Kevin had it all down pat, he did. They'd choose the soft or picturesque spots. The Martello Tower in Sandycove, if the weather was fair. Davey Byrne's or the Ormonde, when the food was better, for a few jars and a bite to eat. Most of the pubs mentioned in *Ulysses* or the ones that have succeeded them they hit year in and year out, both to keep the tourists 'happy,' if you get my meaning, and to keep Kevin 'flowin',' like.

"Beyond all the bluster they pumped him up with at Trinity, Kevin was basically a quiet man, a born scholar and shy, and he needed a bit of courage, so he did. All the more this year, I should imagine." Her eyes again met McGarr's. "With the book and all. He was concerned about how they'd take it, the critics, though he'd been told by them that knew, he didn't have a worry in world."

And you even less, thought McGarr, though that was unfair. No matter how well the new book was received, the woman now had only herself and all those children. And "Cat'rine" Doyle and Mary Sittonn and whatever other mates might appear. Like the one who now announced through the closed door that the 'other' police had arrived.

"Unless you've got something else to tell me?"

"Like what?" Her eyes widened.

"The name of the woman out there with your children, for starters. Doyle, is it? Or Sittonn."

She turned away as Superintendent McAnulty of the Technical Squad pushed open the door and looked around.

❖   ❖   ❖

It was Sittonn. As she quieted the children, McGarr rocked back and forth in a tall wicker chair, staring up at an ornate, matching bird cage hanging at the top of an open window. It was filled with sun and contained two brightly colored tropical birds, the source of the song McGarr had been hearing. Across the bottom of the cage was the advisement: "It is important that we *never* know why the caged bird sings."

It was a line McGarr thought he'd heard or read somewhere, but he was fairly sure that for all her homeliness, Katie Coyle would continue to live in a world where quotes, events, and places from books had a force of fact that not even a dead—no, a *murdered* body— could command. He thought of her ready use of the present tense when speaking of *Ulysses,* while Coyle merited the past alone.

He had been found three days before in a laneway at the back of the Glasnevin Cemetery, where so many of Ireland's patriots and notables were buried, and which also figured in *Ulysses.* The day before the morning on which he was found, a colleague from Trinity had employed him to act as a kind of narrator/actor in the yearly tour that the professor organized for literati and other interested parties. Held on the day that the book was set—June 16, or "Bloomsday," so named after one of the book's principal characters—they had been wont to conduct their guests around *Ulyssean* Dublin, frequenting mainly pubs, by the wife's say-so, though she did not know the itinerary exactly.

She had seemed surprised that her husband had arrived at the cemetery in Glasnevin, which might figure as his final resting place, though rather less so that he had been murdered. Muggers, she had put it down to,

and her husband's hubris at thinking that by birth, background, and predilection he so possessed the city that
he was immune to its darker side. She did, however,
mention the colleague—Fergus Flood—and another former associate, a man named Holderness, who for reasons
that she left vague might have been moved to murder
her husband. Flood had been jealous of Coyle. Holderness had been disciplined by him. Or so she said.

Anybody else? Herself, of course, who had broken
laws that, McGarr believed, were known to all citizens
in regard to destroying evidence, especially in capital
crimes. And Cat'rine Doyle and Mary Sittonn, the latter
of whom now corroborated all Katie had said except for
one word. Katie's "mates" were, according to Mary
Sittonn, "sisters."

Younger than Katie, she was a quick woman, small
and broad, with a round, fleshy, pink face, a button
nose, and hazel eyes so yellow they almost matched her
close-cropped blond hair. In spite of the heat she was
wearing a long black dress and battered, black ankle-
cut boots. With both hands she pulled her dress between
her legs before seating herself on the wicker hassock in
front of McGarr.

They had in fact used a tarp to cover him. "Had
to lie the poor blighter on his side, and him still like
sitting, so stiff he was with death. Back here we could
only sit him in a chair or prop him against the headboard,
which we thought more seemly. Heavy he was for all
his bones, bent up like that, I can tell you."

"But you thought it not unseemly to move him."

For the second time her hand moved to the bristles
of her blond hair, which she ruffled. With her round
features she looked less like a woman or man than a

large, pudgy child of indeterminate sex who had found its way into its mammy's clothes. "In what regard, unseemly?"

It was the wrong word. Unlawful was the correct one, but through long experience McGarr had discovered it was best to avoid the dynamics of confrontation in an interview until the last possible moment, when a sharp question might be used to effect. "In regard to his cause of death."

"Which was?"

"Apparently murder. A single stab wound to the heart."

She blinked. "Are you sure of that?"

"Reasonably. And you're not?" Had Coyle committed hari-kari for some reason . . . literary in nature? Was there a reference to suicide in *Ulysses?* he wondered.

She looked up at the birds in the cage, who had again begun their elaborate duet. "I suppose it doesn't matter, one way or another," she said speculatively. "Dead being dead. Or, rather as you would have it, murdered being murdered."

"Then you found no weapon there as you were examining the site?"

The allusion seemed lost on her, or she chose to ignore it. "I suppose we didn't, and then his wallet and hat were missing. And the ashplant stick and striped blazer that he had begun the morning with. Or so Katie said."

Not to him. "Hat?"

"A boater. Like the Stephen Dedalus character wore in *Ulysses.* In fact it's one of Joyce's own and had his initials monogrammed in the leather of the band. Bought it at auction, Kevin did. Paupered the family for weeks, but what did he care? It was all in the grain, if you know what I mean?"

McGarr did not, and he waited.

"The Joyce grain, man," Mary Sittonn explained, suddenly testy. "You'll have to think Joyce and Beckett and books if you're going to get anywhere with this thing. That's if he was murdered for a 'reason' and not—"

McGarr again waited.

Finally she blurted, "—just murdered."

The wife's first thought.

"You queer?" McGarr asked.

Said Mary Sittonn: "The expression is 'gay.'"

"You gay?"

"None of your fookin' business, Jack."

McGarr liked the sound of that. Jack McGarr. It seemed so much more authoritative than Peter. Like something out of a crime novel.

4

By the time McGarr regained his Mini-Cooper, the small, boxlike car was as hot as an oven, and he got caught in a snarl of homeward-bound commuter traffic along the Phibsborough Road. In the glare of the six o'clock sun —still high on the horizon—the exhausts from the line of great green double-decker buses, lorries, cars, and delivery vans that stretched from Cross Guns Bridge to the corner of Finglas Road rose like a cloud of black sordid steam. The Cooper, which was an antique of sorts, was not equipped with air-conditioning, and the foul fumes that filled its small interior made McGarr want to pull over and walk.

The Brian Boroimhe, an old half-timbered Dublin pub that had been owned by the Hedigan family for nearly a century now, was just across the bridge on the bank of the Royal Canal, and McGarr considered pulling in and washing the sour taste from his mouth with another pint of lager. Instead he reached for a cigarette on the idea that his own pollution, which at least tasted familiar, was preferable to that of an internal combustion engine. But the tie-up broke suddenly, and he drifted by the "Boru" with a longing that was little short of love, one he knew he'd have to satisfy before long.

De Courcy Square sits between the east entrance of the sprawling Glasnevin Cemetery and the busy Finglas

Road. It is a small parallelogram of modest, brick Victorian row houses surrounding a fenced-in common ruled out in individual vegetable gardens. Now, at tea time, with the children indoors, it seemed remarkably peaceful to McGarr. The sun, angling across narrow gabled roofs, filled the nearly peopleless space with a rosy light.

Number 2 lay at the west end of the square, and the aroma from an open bay window netted by lace curtains spoke to him of baking tomatoes and butter and garlic and—was it?—fresh tarragon. Yes. Turning his head to the patch of common that he guessed would belong to number 2, he caught sight of the delicate gray-green leaves of tarragon plants in a bed with other aromatic herbs. But there was another delicious, more complex odor too: fish, and of two types, with anchovies more dominant, though he could not be sure of the second. Trout? No—city folk did not eat freshwater fish by choice. Nor roach. After the exercise of digging in the garden and the distraction of Katie Coyle's news, McGarr had forgotten his stomach; he was now both thirsty and famished. He was about to ring the bell when the door opened and a young thin woman with dark hair opened the door.

"Superintendent McGarr?" She had fair skin and light blue eyes that blinked once, as though snapping his picture.

"None other."

"I've been expecting you and thought you'd get here sooner. I knocked off work a bit early, you see, since I have some friends coming to tea. Won't you come in?"

Cat'rine "Catty" Doyle, McGarr assumed, following her into the house. Her hair, as black as any McGarr had ever seen and cut in a perfect stylish line, spanked on the shoulders of a white sleeveless jumper that revealed an oval of deeply tanned skin on a ruler-straight back. Below, and just the color of her eyes, were blue shorts that swathed what McGarr judged to be comfortable hips. Or, rather, hips that definitely could be comforting.

Her legs, which were also tanned, were thin and shapely, and she wore canvas runners on her feet. They were white, like the jumper and her short, tight, little-girl socks. These last wrapped only her ankles.

In the kitchen she raised herself up after bending to peer in the oven. McGarr noticed that the jumper was slightly transparent, revealing not only the peaks of her nipples but also the hint of dark circles beyond. They were large, about the size of a 10p. coin. Her face was long, the bridge of her nose very thin, and in all she communicated a kind of fragility that McGarr found intriguing.

Mainly it had to do with the way she carried herself, which was nothing if not erect. Her posture was perfect, her movements graceful, and McGarr concluded that Catty Doyle's beauty, which was in a petite way considerable, was overwhelmingly feminine. He also decided that Catty Doyle, who either worked out of doors or who had not worked in some time during daylight hours, had so devised herself and her house that the persons who were expected for tea would have little choice to appreciate that beauty, if they had eyes.

In spite of the elaborate food preparations, no surface in the kitchen seemed soiled, nothing seemed out of place. Herbs, spices, and condiments were neatly shelved. A long cutting board, which had just been scrubbed down, glistened with water. The deep red handles of the knives in a rosewood sheath gleamed as though freshly treated with tong oil.

A table had been set for three in front of the open door to the back garden; the doorway was draped with various beads. The plate was a pattern that McGarr recognized as Belleek, and the crystal Waterford. He then placed the oven aroma that filled the kitchen.

"Plaice Nicoise," he said. "On the bone?"

She seemed startled that he had guessed right.

He stepped past her toward the table and parted the beads, twirling a knobby surface between his fingers. It was a Spanish touch, or Portuguese. Iberian at any rate, and McGarr wondered if they had always hung there or had she put them up especially for the occasion and the heat. The plaice Nicoise was Mediterranean, of course, the wine in the chrome bucket by the side of the table a *vinho verde* from the Minho. What was he seeing here, a little celebration?

"I wonder—could this wait until tomorrow?" she asked pleasantly, her voice feminine and soft, like the rest of her, but surprisingly deep.

McGarr slid the bottle back into the ice water. "I'd lower the heat, were I you. Smells done to me."

"Really," she pressed, half turning to the hall that led to the front door. "Tomorrow I could give you all the time you want." She slid her fingers in the slit pockets of the blue shorts and hunched her shoulders so that her breasts hung loose in the jumper. "Anything."

Was that another sort of offer?

"Tomorrow you'll be speaking to one of my staff." Stepping toward the sitting room, McGarr turned off the

gas and peeked into the oven. The pots were earthen-
ware and Spanish in design, and he was willing to bet
that the second contained a risotto with tarragon, white
wine, and saffron. He made a small, involuntary noise
in the back of his throat. He felt like he could eat a
cow—or a Catty, for that matter—and he had to remind
himself of his purpose. And the fact that he was happily
married to a beautiful woman nearly half his age.

The sitting room, like the kitchen, had been prepared
for company. A coffee table had been set before a love
seat. On it were a bowl of mixed nuts, a wedge of Brie
and another of Stilton. A bottle of Offaly port, 1964,
stood at hand. A trolley held bottles of various spirits
and a shiny bucket, beaded with moisture. With lace
doilies covering the arms and the backs of the overstuffed
chairs and love seat, it seemed a room in which a person
might most pleasantly be pampered by the likes of the
super-feminine Ms. Doyle.

He turned back on the young woman, who was
watching him from the doorway, her cheeks now flushed
in—was it?—anger. "When is your company expected?"

"Half-past seven."

It was seven-ten.

"You understood that a murder was committed."

Her eyes moved off. She nodded.

"And that there would have to be an investigation."

Her eyes fell to the carpet.

"And yet you didn't notify the Guards."

She raised her head to the open window, through
which they could hear heels on the walk of the square.
A man passed by. "Kevin was Katie's husband, wasn't
he? And she's my sister. Look"—the eyes flickered up

at him—"he was dead. I mean, long dead. And"—
another pause—"it's not as though we . . . fancy the
police, begging your pardon, Mr. McGarr. Who *they*—
not *you*—are, if you know what I mean." Her voice
was low and confiding.

"*We?*" he asked in a tone no less intimate. "You
and Katie Coyle are *sisters?*"

She shook her head once and looked away, as if to
say that he just didn't know what she meant.

McGarr had never considered himself unpoliceman-
like. If anything, he struggled to be as complete a
policeman as he possibly could, according to his own
definition of the role, which required that he be a decent
human being first and an official second.

Said Catty Doyle, "We're sisters because of our sex.
You know, *women.*" She glanced at McGarr, and when
he still said nothing, she added, "We discussed it. Mary
said you wouldn't—*couldn't*—understand, and we should
just phone the Guards. The others. The ones here in
Glasnevin. But Katie insisted we take him back to the
house and she would get you. 'Kev would've wanted
it like that,' she said. She also said he used to read
everything he could about you in the papers. 'Pure
Dublin,' he'd say about you."

As was what he was hearing from her now. Soap,
and as soft and sweet as could be had.

" 'He'll find who did this,' she went on."

Again her eyes turned to the sound of footsteps in
the street.

"Which brings me to where and how you found him.
Exactly, Catty. May I call you that?"

She flashed him a quick smile, and with some relief
left the sitting room. She walked quickly into the hall,

through the kitchen and beaded curtains, and out into the full sun of the back garden. McGarr's eyes dropped down on the flat plane that extended from the band of her shorts to the base of her spine and was, he imagined, just the size of his palm. Her step was crisp but graceful, and his urge, following her like that, was to reach out, stop her, and in some way tack her down. He forced himself to look away.

"I have a wee dog. Kinch." She flicked a hand at a doghouse that had been fashioned with some fore-thought into a corner of the garden wall and looked custom-made. It had been raised off the ground; a little ramp led up to its entrance. The style was Swiss, like a chalet, with gingerbread eaves, shutters on mock win-dows, and window boxes with multicolored plastic flow-ers. "Kinch is fixed. It makes it easier that way. And then I can let him out for an hour or two every morning without fear that he'll run off. Between the time I get up and go to work," she went on, opening the back gate and stepping out into the alley.

"And what work is that?"

"I'm in publishing, actually."

"You don't say. In what capacity?"

"Editor." She mentioned a British publishing house, a name McGarr had seen on the spine of Kevin Coyle's book. And she added, "Irish acquisitions and publicity. They fairly well leave things here up to me to make the most of."

Books again, McGarr thought, and he reconsidered Catty Doyle. She seemed rather young and insouciant and all too fey and winning to be an editor in a publishing house. But then McGarr knew little of publishing, and perhaps acquisitions was something to which a person like she might be well suited.

"As I was saying, I had let Kinch out, and I was late and in a hurry. When I opened the gate here and called, he didn't come as usual. And when I listened, I heard him barking down the alley."

Again McGarr followed her, trying to think of something, anything besides the plateau bounded by the crests of her backside. He had even forgotten cold lager beer, plaice Nicoise, and *vinho verde*. He wouldn't know what to do with somebody like Catty Doyle if he had the chance—ultimately, that was.

"It was rapid, worried, sustained barking, the way Kinch barks when somebody's at the door."

McGarr couldn't remember any such barking, but then he hadn't rung the bell.

"And I followed it around the cemetery wall to here. The barking."

As the lane at the rear of De Courcy Square approached Finglas Road, it branched off into another alley, which served Bengal Terrace and was bounded on the other side by the wall of the cemetery.

"Still I couldn't see Kinch, and I walked nearly to that gate"—she pointed to the lane—"before I caught sight of him standing by what I thought at first was some itinerant or tramp. But when he wouldn't come away, and I saw that the man's eyes were open and then recognized who it was, I said, 'Get up now, get out of that, Kevin, and come in the house and have a cup of tea,' " she turned to McGarr, "never thinking—" Her eyes had filled with tears, and her shoulders cupped, then shook.

McGarr's first instinct was to put an arm around her shoulders, but he thought better of it.

"Where?" he asked in a gentle tone.

"There."

"But exactly. Take me to it."

He waited while she gathered herself, noting how much less appealing Catty Doyle seemed to him emotionally stricken and vulnerable than when she exuded the taunt of sexual command. And he decided to exploit the weakness, if only to understand the Catty Doyle who had not prepared herself for guests or the police.

She stepped forward tentatively until they reached an area where the tall grass and weeds beside the granite blocks at the high cemetery wall had been matted down and stained generously with what McGarr imagined was Kevin Coyle's blood. He noted hoofprints and the track of a narrow rubber tire in the soft ground.

"His glasses were there beside him, and I could tell from his"—it took some time for her to get it out—"stare that he was dead. Even before I noticed his chest." Her body spasmed suddenly, as though she would retch, and a hand moved to her mouth.

McGarr looked around and above them. Because of the high walls on both sides of the lane, the site was visible only from either end, and at night—had Kevin Coyle been murdered then—only from the nearer gate, where McGarr could see the top of a streetlight.

"But exactly," he insisted. "It's important that I know how you found him. How he was positioned."

"Why?"

Perhaps to catch you in a lie, McGarr thought, but it was more complex than that. A man who had been stabbed once cleanly through the heart would have gone down limp, like a rag doll, and what she had told him so far did not support that assumption.

With a trembling chin and bleary eyes she tried to look up at him and then at her wristwatch.

"The sooner you show me, the sooner you can get back to your guests."

She pointed at the spot as though to ask if he actually meant that she should. "You mean?"

"There's nothing to worry about. It's just a place like any other. Sure, the ground doesn't remember, nor the wall. And the blood"—he reached down and felt the brown area that now looked like nothing more than some large spot of grease—"is dried. And here . . ." From a pocket he pulled out a handkerchief which he unfolded and spread a few inches from the wall. Fortunately, it was clean. "For those dainty skivvies that match your eyes. We wouldn't want them ruined, sure we wouldn't."

She blinked away the tears and regarded him. "You're not serious."

McGarr kept himself from saying, "Deadly." He smiled slightly and nodded.

"But, I won't."

"Sure you will. You're a lovely young woman who doesn't wish to become involved with the police, unfanciable chaps that we are. Need I remind you that you and nobody else failed to report this murder. That you and—Mary Sittonn and Katie Coyle, was it?—decided to ignore what all three of you knew was the law and the only proper thing to do. Need I say that you compromised this investigation or that I'm struggling desperately—with my conscience, with what *I* know is my responsibility under the law—not to make any of this public. You're a professional woman, you know how things proceed. Others might see you as an accessory to murder."

When she still did not move, he added, "At the very

least it could put your name in the papers. RTE." He meant Radio Telefis Eireann, the state-supported Irish radio and television network. "I should imagine that the murder of Kevin Coyle virtually in your back garden almost"—McGarr had to reach for a word—"contemporaneous with your firm's release of *Phon/Antiphon,* might be construed by some as more than simple coincidence. And then I wonder how it would be taken in London, your involvement in a thing such as this."

He had been guessing, but the flash of her eyes told him he was right. "Who else could publish Kevin's book, I'd like to know," she said flatly, and drawing in a breath, she advanced upon the spot and lowered herself onto the handkerchief. Her back jerked as it touched the wall. She cocked one knee and placed a wrist on that thigh. Gingerly she stretched the other leg out straight and then raised her head until it touched the wall, her eyes looking up over the roofline of the row houses on the other side of the wall. "Like so."

"You're sure."

"As sure as I am of myself," she said defiantly. "I'll never forget it. Never ever. Nor your making me do this."

"His glasses. Where were they?"

"Here—by this hand." She meant the right hand.

"As though he had removed them himself."

"Now that you mention it, yes."

Again he thought of the one thrust right through the heart. Everything would have stopped for Kevin Coyle. Immediately. "Anything else you noticed before you moved him?"

"Not that I can remember."

Tomorrow he would tax that memory.

McGarr offered her his hand, but she ignored it, and he retrieved his handkerchief as she strode past him.

In the house where he followed her—to phone the Technical Squad that would search the murder scene, if indeed it was that, and his office for a team to canvass the neighborhood—McGarr found Mary Sittonn and Katie Coyle in the sitting room.

Mary Sittonn was dressed in a tight black tank top which made her breasts look like they had been wrapped flat, and her arms appear large and outsized, as from a rigorous program of body building. On one was a tattoo of a black cat that was posed coyly, as though undecided whether to pounce or run away. It was grinning, its blue eyes flashing, its tongue protruding slightly between its teeth. Around the young woman's neck was a gold chain with a key. Her short hair had been oiled or greased and was brushed back. By her side was a small, brown Irish terrier that began growling at McGarr until he said, "Kinch? Come here, boy," at which point the dog broke from her and circled McGarr's legs, tail wagging.

Mary Sittonn looked down into the tall glass filled with amber fluid. She raised it to her mouth.

Katie Coyle herself was looking more like Mebdh on the one-punt bank note than anybody McGarr had ever seen. Her long brownish hair had wilted in the heat, and her fleshy face now looked more haggard than ever. Then there was her dress, made of a bleached-out blue color of cotton, which—neither a toga nor a sarong—resembled something meant for classical drama. It billowed around her neck and shoulders and then flowed out in waves, making her appear tented in a robe of

state and only sadly regal, which was, of course, un-
derstandable.

"Kevin wouldn't have wanted us to mourn for him.
He always hated that. 'Dead is dead,' he said both times
his parents died." She was drunk, or at least had been
drinking, though the glass on the coffee table before
her appeared untouched. "How goes it?" she asked in
a voice that seemed so genuinely solicitous of McGarr's
progress that he rejected the conclusion that had been
forming in his mind.

Sisters. Perhaps he truly didn't understand the con-
cept. Or couldn't.

But her *us* was still on his mind. Could *he* be one
of *them,* and in what way?

5

A   t home McGarr's wife Noreen was waiting for him at the kitchen table, which she had set for tea. She had been reading; when he entered, she got up and, raising a palm, said, "Don't bother yourself. Everything's ready, even your *essence du malt.*" From the fridge she drew a can of lager and from the freezing compartment a frosted pint glass, both of which she placed before him. "I'll let you pour that, since I've been led to believe there might be some problem with the bubbles, cold glass and all."

McGarr stared down at the glass, which he had not seen before. Or, rather, which he had been seeing most of his life but never before in his house. It was a standard twenty-ounce draft glass and had probably been nicked from a pub.

"Well?" she demanded.

"Well what?"

"What about Kevin Coyle, of course, and if you toy with me, I won't let you see this." She held up her book, the multicolored dust cover of which read:

Phon/Antiphon
A Work Of Imaginative Criticism

by
Kevin Coyle

"Catty give you that?" McGarr asked.

"D'ya know Catty? Brilliant young woman and"—
Noreen's eyes narrowed and she looked at him closely
before continuing—"it seems that the book-launching
party in the Shelbourne will go on Monday as planned.
Imagine the . . . éclat, the coverage. The international
press. Television, radio. The missus says," and McGarr
chimed in, "Kevin would have wanted it that way."

McGarr scanned his wife's face: her long forehead
and high cheekbones, and her nose, which was perhaps
too straight and too narrow, so that it said more about
class—her maiden name had been Frenche—than about
beauty. And he decided it was her lips that he admired
most. The upper was slightly protrusive and made her
seem forever on the point of breaking into smile, an
illusion which the uncommonly green eyes reinforced.

Early in their marriage McGarr had taken to sharing
some of the information that his investigations generated,
if only to assure domestic tranquillity in his household.
On more than a few occasions Noreen's assistance, which
was usually more informational than tactical, had proved
important, and she was ever discreet. It was as if her
academic background—first honors in modern languages
at Trinity, and later her research study at the Courtauld
Institute—had erected a felicitous blind through which
she saw the world as a kind of shadow play; it was
McGarr himself who from time to time pulled the blind
down and permitted her to see things as they were, or
at least as they appeared to him, which he hoped were
one in the same.

And thus he began telling her what he knew of the
tragedy of Kevin Coyle, author, scholar, narrator/actor,
university professor as well as husband, father, and what

else McGarr had not yet determined. He told her how the wife, Katie, had appeared in Belgrave Square on their doorstep and had taken him to their Liberties "loft" apartment, which Noreen said she would kill to see. "Kevin had every class of arty friend, here and in London and New York. I bet the place is packed with important stuff. I wonder if she'll sell any of it off." From the waves of her deep red locks Noreen drew a pencil and marked *Katie* in the margin of the book. Forever panting, McGarr thought, regarding the faraway look in her turquoise-colored eyes.

And he told her how the first "sister," the attractive and feminine Catty Doyle, whose dog had discovered Coyle's corpse, had chosen to phone the wife and not the police, whom they did not fancy. And how the certainly masculine and perhaps even dykelike Mary Sittonn, owner of an antique shop in the Liberties, had hitched up her horse to her cart, and how, like two tinkers, she and Katie Coyle had crossed the Liffey and climbed the Phibsborough Road, having thought so far ahead as to bring with them a tarp to cover Coyle's dead body.

They found him propped (arranged?) against the granite-block wall of the Prospect Cemetery, behind a neighborhood of working-class row houses. He had been stabbed once, perfectly in the heart, but the murder weapon was nowhere in sight. His straw boater, the same kind that some character had worn in *Ulysses*— "Stephen Dedalus," Noreen supplied; "Don't tell me you, of all people, have never read *Ulysses*?"—and actually a hat once owned by Joyce, was also gone. And his glasses with a shattered lens were found "roughly" by his side, as though he had taken them off with his right hand. *If* the "sisters" who carried him back to the Liberties and allowed him to lay in a kind of state for two or three days before blowing the whistle could be believed. "What do you mean, me of all people?"

"You—the professional Dubliner?"

McGarr's head went back slightly, but he went on. The wife, Katie, seemed to point the finger at a man named Flood—"Fergus Flood," Noreen interjected. "He was at Trinity when I was there. Or, rather, he was *teaching* when . . . Brilliant man, and a good, a solid teacher. Unlike some other lecturers, he gave you the feeling that he truly loves literature." And another man named Holderness. "Holderness. Holderness. Haven't I heard or read his name someplace before? Didn't he write something controversial?"

Said McGarr, "What do you mean *professional?*"

Noreen hunched her shoulders and smiled slightly, knowing she had browned him off. "Well, if you're not the sempiternal Dub', I don't know *who* is. From"— she flicked out a hand, and her eyes scanned his face— "how you look, act, even walk—for Jesus' sake—to who you are and how you"—she now fell to laughing— "think and act. Even what you do—Murder Squad, and good at it—is Dublin. Have you ever listened to yourself? We must get a tape recorder. Say, 'Stately plump Buck Mulligan came from the stairhead, bearing a bowl of lather on which a mirror and a razor lay crossed.' "

McGarr stared down at the half-filled pint glass of lager. *Think?* How could she know how he thought? And what was wrong—or rather, right—with his walk, that it was so much the walk of a Dubliner?

"Go on—say that?"

Trying to smile, he shook his head. Did he need

this abuse after a hard hot day and what promised to be a spate of others no less difficult, at least until public interest in the Coyle murder waned or he solved the crime? But his eyes fell on her shoulders and chest and silky dressing gown, and another promise made him say, "Stadely ploomp Book Molligun—what's the rist of it?"

She couldn't contain herself. Her laughter was so intense, tears came to her eyes. "Admit it, Peter, you—*of all people*—have never read *Ulysses.*" In mock disbelief she put a hand to her mouth and looked away.

McGarr sought relief in the pint glass, which he drained, and considered the disadvantages of having married a much younger, intelligent, redheaded woman who was no less a Dubliner than he, though from the fashionable and Protestant south side. "Slagging," however—as derisive humor was called in Dublin—wasn't limited to any social or religious background, and he waited until she had calmed herself before raising the empty glass. "Interesting item, this. Cost much?"

"Not a penny. *Objet trouvé* on loan from Buswell's Hotel." It was a hostelry near her family's picture gallery in Dawson Street. Noreen frequently entertained clients there.

It was McGarr's turn to raise an eyebrow. "To be returned, I hope."

She looked down at the empty glass. "I suppose you don't want another of those." And when he looked away, she added triumphantly as she rose to fetch another beer from the fridge, "Bernie called." She meant Detective Sergeant McKeon. "He said the preliminary forensic report puts the time of death sometime early in the morning of the seventeenth. The alcohol level in his body was point three three, which made him—"

Locked, thought McGarr. Absolutely drunk. He thought again of the eyeglasses with the smashed lens, which Catty Doyle said were resting on the ground near Coyle's right hand.

"Then the guess is that the knife was plunged in"— she was pouring the lager, but averting her head as she grimaced, splashed some on the table—"and withdrawn immediately, given how much he bled." Placing the glass in front of McGarr, she then glanced down at a note pad. "Otherwise the corpse is unremarkable—how can anybody say that of such a . . . fine man. Or, at least, a fine mind?"

She sat and paused a minute over Coyle's book before addressing herself to what she knew McGarr was waiting to hear. " 'Sisters' bothers me, and that bit about not fancying the police. I would have thought that Kevin Coyle was apolitical. An academic. An artist."

But it was Coyle's wife and her "sisters" who appeared to be political, or at least to possess a perspective that was militant, and gender-relatedly so.

"And then that cart ride—how many miles?"

McGarr was that much a Dubliner that he could say automatically, "Two long miles. Exactly."

"And how long would that take in a cart? An hour in the morning, considering rush-hour traffic? More? You'd think she would have called a cab, him—her husband—dead or not. And would she have taken anybody's word on that?"

Not if she really was one of *us*, McGarr thought. But to give her her due, she might have known how long it would take by any means. McGarr in his little Cooper, which could dodge and jink here and there, had spent about seventy minutes on the road to De Courcy Square, or rather, the rear of Bengal Terrace.

But then traffic would have been flowing the other way when the cart made its trek to the cemetery in Glasnevin.

It was the *us* that was bothering McGarr. He was about as much one of the "sisters" as he was the sort of person who would bother to sit down and piece out the drivel that was *Ulysses*. He'd tried it once and had nearly thrown the book across the room.

Yet after a pleasant repast that featured a delicate prawn salad served with a crisp Montbazillac, McGarr withdrew to the library, where he chanced to pull the volume from the shelf and managed to discover several sections that were nearly intelligible.

But no sooner had he turned back to the beginning and become engrossed, than Noreen appeared in the doorway, catching him at it. "So—it's *now* that he chooses to invest himself in the lore of his beloved city."

McGarr asked himself why now wasn't as good a time as any, until he glanced up from the book and noticed how, silhouetted against the light from the dining room behind her, Noreen's dressing gown had become transparent. And then there was a certain rake to her stance that was suggestive if not downright provocative. She had one leg forward and a hand on the gentle curve of the other hip.

She had decided three months before—arbitrarily, in a *dictat* delivered over dinner at McGarr's favorite restaurant, "My treat. Keep your hand off your billfold"—that after nine years of marriage they would now, in the watershed thirtieth year of her life, have children. "How many?" he had asked. "We'll see," she had answered. "But the way I'm feeling tonight"—she had craned her head and looked off, her pupils dilating— "a veritable hoard."

They had been "trying" now for three months, which

meant precisely timed bouts of strenuous, if draining, activity, to no result apart from the threat that he, not she, would have to visit her doctor for some "coaching."

"I, sir, have been examined. There is nothing wrong with me. You, on the other hand, are—how shall I phrase it tactfully?—a man of a certain age with . . . debilitating habits. You drink, you smoke, you exercise infrequently. And, please, don't give out to me about the garden in which your heart rate is probably never elevated above two strokes per minute. Results are what's called for. I want—"

McGarr had stifled that desire, or rather, the desire of the moment, but he had never heard anything more absurd. Yes, he was fifty, but, yes as well, he had never felt more fit and *able* in his life. "Feeling able and *being* able, my dear, are two different things," retorted his lovely wife, who had tried to schedule an appointment with the damn doctor, who was also a woman, to ascertain—"Scientifically. It's just a simple test"—if he were man enough to get her with child. And the "my dear?" Where had she gotten that, off the telly? Nobody in Ireland said "My dear."

The substantiation had come later, when McGarr had submitted to examination and had been adjudged able. Noreen's doctor was a feminist, and, leaving her office after an exhaustive physical and educational examination/ interview, he had felt nigh on violated.

"You can bring your friend along."

"Who?"

"The bearded one. *Ulysses.* I'll read to you in bed. It ends with a soliloquy that you'll enjoy hearing and'll tell you more than you ever wanted to know about women."

McGarr turned his head to one side, as though to share his anticipation with the aforementioned hero.

And watching Noreen's feline smile of satisfaction broaden as he pulled himself from the chair, McGarr wondered how much light, as opposed to heat, would be shed on the death of Kevin Coyle tonight.

He suspected that *Ulysses*, having waited over eighty years for a "professional" appraisal, could tolerate another few hours of enigma, and on the stairs he reached for his wife's thigh. "What d'ya mean *walk?*" he asked in her ear as she slowed and eased her back into him.

"You know, the trudge. Ah, now Peter—don't do that. I'm going to *read* to you. Janie—" And yet far from moving away from him, she instead reached her arms up over her shoulders and twined her fingers around the back of his neck.

"Trudge?"

"As though, poor things, you've got the weight of an improbable universe on your individual shoulders. Said burden you tot to and put off only in that second most necessary of premises. Fortunately for you, as planning has it, at least one such institution graces nearly every commercial block."

Spinning her around to fireman's carry her to the bedroom—"Now, don't be too rough." There was hope in that—McGarr tried to think of a way of crossing Dublin without passing a single pub.

It was a reflection that a few days later he would find, uncannily, in *Ulysses*, though Leopold Bloom's institution of choice had been the church, not the pub.

It had been a different age.

PART TWO

6

JOYCE SCHOLAR MURDERED

•

TRINITY PROF SLAIN ON JOYCE OUTING

•

WRITER / LECTURER / SCHOLAR
BLOOMSDAY VICTIM
Slain Near Prospect Cemetery

. . . were the headlines in the three morning papers.
McGarr wondered how the last bit got in. Certainly not
from one of his staff, nearly all of whom were seasoned
veterans and understood what any breach of confidence
would mean. Or the Tech Squad, though all of the
papers had their touts.

Sitting at his desk in his cubicle in Dublin Castle
with a brilliant patch of morning sunlight illuminating
the newspaper on his lap, he couldn't keep himself from
thinking of Catty Doyle. How had she described herself?
"Acquisitions editor and publicist. They fairly well leave
things up to me to make the most of."

What was bothering McGarr even more, however,
were the editorials. It was as though all three news-

papers had gotten together and decided to blame the
police for Coyle's death. One attempted to compare
the current level of violent crime with that of 1904.
None seemed as concerned with the actual statistics as
with the details of Joyce's *Ulysses*, as if the characters
in the book of an artist who had spent nearly all of his
life out of the country were real.

"Bloom and Dedalus, the latter worse for drink, were
able to circulate through Dublin and visit the notorious
brothels of Nighttown without so much as a violent
incident or the mention of murder, whereas now a renowned literary scholar has become—after having led
a tour of literati through the city—the ninth murder
victim of the year."

"Wrong on four counts," said Hughie Ward, a young
detective who, like the others gathered in the cubicle,
had been watching McGarr's eyes work down the page.
The second least senior member of the Murder Squad
staff, he was relegated to leaning against some cabinets
just inside the door. The others sat on tables or on the
windowsills. Detective Sergeant McKeon reclined in the
cubicle's only other chair, usually filled by Superintendent O'Shaughnessy, who was now on holiday. "One,
in Nighttown a British soldier knocked Stephen Dedalus
on his arse and bloodied his nose."

"Bully for him," said McKeon. "I only hope Joyce
was writing from experience. I have an idea it's no end
of trouble that fecker's already caused us, and him how
many—"

"Forty-seven."

"Thank you, All-Knowledgeable and Yuppy Inspector
Ward. Forty-seven bloody years in his bloody feckin'
grave"—he looked up—"and where in the name of St.
Surplice, the Papal ponce, did you get that suit?"

Small and dark with diminutive good looks, Ward dressed carefully and well. Today he was wearing a linen suit in an unusual taupe color. His tie was an ochre shade that got on well with his neatly parted hair, the two inches of handkerchief showing in the breast pocket of the jacket, and his woven cordovan leather brogues, the surfaces of which had been polished to a stylishly dull sheen.

Some of the other men began chuckling. One reached out and tried to snatch the handkerchief, but Ward, smiling, dodged and parried his body. He was perhaps a dandy, but he had also represented Ireland successfully in several international boxing competitions. He was popular with the other men, and the smoke of rumor—fanned into a blaze by the Murder Squad staff—had it that he was with the ladies as well.

"Two," he went on, "Leopold Bloom was also accosted in Kevin Street and had to flee a bloke called The Citizen and his vicious cur, Garryowen. The Citizen hurled a biscuit tin at Bloom's head."

"And the cut of it. The jacket," McKeon went on, appraising Ward, "looks like something fit for a cocaine conquistador. Worse, it's the very color of what's left in the bottom of a porter glass."

There was a pause before Delaney—a senior man with a pixyish smile—asked, "Burple?" Sinclaire began chuckling.

"Three, murder *is* mentioned in *Ulysses* at least once, and—"

"Have ya ever read it yerself?" McKeon continued to Delaney, who had assumed the perch on the far corner of McGarr's desk that McKeon himself usually occupied.

"And four, we've had six murders this year and three arrests. One a month exactly. Murders that is." Opening the jacket, Ward flashed its label at McKeon. "Brown Thomas, Sergeant. That's a little shop in Grafton Street." It was Dublin's most fashionable and pricey department store.

"All shite and humbuggery," said McKeon. "On both counts, book and Gook. I have it on report that those two gentlemen emigrated to Hong Kong but can be had anytime mail order for twenty quid apiece." Of course, he meant Brown Thomas.

McGarr was scarcely listening to the colloquy, which was a feature of most morning meetings, as he continued to scan the newspaper commentary. Vague writing, either by design or ineptitude, went on to imply that the Garda Siochana might be partially responsible for ". . . a century-long decline in moral standards" and "an upsurge in capital crime." As if any police force could keep a people from murdering each other.

He closed the paper and placed it on his desk, carefully lapping it over the other two. Believing the mind to be disorderly enough, McGarr loathed a messy desk. He reached for his mug of coffee; he'd spiked it with a liberal dollop of malt before the others had entered the cubicle. Invariably it improved his mood, which was somber of a sunny summer morning with the Castle office looking like a cramped and time-sorrowed relic.

"Then you've read the book," he said to Ward.

"Of course. Hasn't everybody?"

"Not that lout of an editor," said McKeon.

Nor anybody else in the cubicle, McGarr judged from the averted gazes.

Said Bresnahan, "Must've been on his exam for the leaving cert." Ward's junior by a few months and the

Murder Squad's sole woman, she stood in the open doorway so she might more easily tend to any ringing phones or to McGarr's coffee mug. It was the dog's-body post that each new recruit had had to fill, each in his turn, but which Bresnahan resented on sexist grounds. "Then, you know, there's this other article in the *Independent* that tells all about it. The literary angle." The floor groaned under her surprisingly quick but heavy step as she advanced upon McGarr's desk.

There she palmed up the paper, slapped three fingers on her tongue, and began leafing through the pages, her great, reddish-pink body looming over McGarr as he sipped from his cup and tried to place himself on the bench under the grape arbor in his back garden. At this moment a wedge of angling sunlight would be warming his back.

"Dere, dere 'tis," she said in her thick Kerry brogue. "Detective Ward's advice exactly." She stepped back from the newspaper. Two bright patches had appeared in her cheeks, and she was breathing volubly.

Said McKeon, "I have a request. I wonder if Ban Gharda Bresnahan might take to wearing runners. Her tread, now—it's grating, so it is. Day after day of it, you'd think you were living on the Great Plains."

"T'underin' herds?" Delaney asked.

"Horizon to horizon."

Somebody cleared his throat. Somebody else moaned his dismay.

Said Ward in an unconcerned tone, "I only ever read the *Times*." He then adjusted the cuff of his shirt, which was pinned with a gold link. Among Dublin's smart set, the *Independent* was considered the farmers' newspaper.

"Ah Rut'ie," said Delaney, who was the staff conciliator, "don't even try. It's just the boys pokin' a bit of fun."

But her color had turned an alarming shade. "And whoi not? I'm as good as any man here." Her hands went to her hips, and McGarr could see that two dark patches had suddenly appeared on the light blue of her uniform blouse. She glanced from him to McKeon, who had hidden his face in his hand, and back again, as though seeking corroboration.

It was a painful moment, and, when support did not appear forthcoming, she made it worse, "*Better*, in fact. And when true liberation comes to this benighted isle, all you lard-arsed shaggers'll find yourselves workin' for the likes of me."

Sinclaire began chuckling, and the others quickly picked it up. "Lard-arsed shaggers!" he said. "It's a classic. Sure, you would've thought I'd have heard that at home."

Raising the mug and inhaling the hot malt fumes before taking a long, satisfying sip, McGarr could scarcely await the day. As the malt settled in his stomach, however, he suddenly appreciated how much Bresnahan was in fact better than any man in the room. And then Ward too was not without his uses, the most advantageous of which was the possibility that he might keep him, McGarr, from having to tangle with the hydra named *Ulysses*.

Ah, youth, he thought, reaching for a pad on his desk. And inexperience. The lesson? In a meeting with superiors, never volunteer information. Speak only when spoken to, and then to the point raised.

As McGarr wrote, McKeon said, "Coyle's blood alcohol level was point t'ree t'ree. Enough to congelifract a bull rhino. Excuse me, Rut'ie, a neutered bull rhino. Add to that a stab in the heart, and it seems even less likely that he could have melted down a wall into a sitting position, at the same time removing his eyeglasses with his right hand and staring up over the house tops for one last glimpse of dear, dirty Dublin, the city of which he was the buttocks-befriending bard. In that regard I'm t'inking of Ms. Doyle, whose house was nearby.

"The Tech Squad says the soft ground of the site itself was a muddle of prints: men's, women's, a horse, rubber cart tires. The blood was Coyle's or at least of the same type, so that, if he bled to death, he did it there. Dead three days. They'll have the complete written report to us later today.

"The team we put on the Bengal Terrace/De Courcy Square neighborhood found nobody who saw or heard much, apart from a car in the alley leading from Finglas Road into those laneways there at the back of the cemetery. It's an informal thing with two concrete-filled pipes to keep tinker's caravans out. You have to drive up over the sidewalk and over a grass stretch to get in. Man in the house says he was wakened by the sound of a car trying to get up over the curb. He pulled himself out of bed and saw a small white car, something like one'a them little Fiats they had a few years ago. 'Orientals,' we called them."

"A *Cinque Cento*," said Ward.

"That's right. A chinko-chinko. Made a racket, so he said, trying to power up over the rise and then maneuver itself to squeeze between the pipes. Two people in it, or so he thought, and a learner's sticker on the back window. He says he thought it was a

couple'a yokes a little worse for wear, you know, after
hours and—"

"Yokin' around," said Delaney, who shook his head.
"Scandinavians. Blondes. We'll get Ward to round them
all up, and our man or woman'll be among them."

"—until it came back out the same way and had to
yockey around a bit to make the squeeze again. One
person this time, though because of the angle and the
size of the car, he couldn't see who. Man or woman."

McGarr had finished writing, and he reached one
sheet to Bresnahan and the other to Ward, saying to
the former, "Three women, one story. I want you to
interview them in situ. Signed statements—where they
were the night of the murder, with whom, etcetera.
And checks. I want corroborations, where possible, on
everything they swear to. Does any of them own or
have access to a little Fiat? Do they drive? Maybe
Catty Doyle had a date who drove her 'round to the
back door. You know the case. For the moment those
three are yours. See what you can do, and Rut'ie,
remember this: You have the lever. They broke the
law. Use it."

"But—" She looked up from the sheet, her expression at once hopeful, alarmed, and suspicious. "Who'll
do me . . . work while I'm— The typing and filing and
the phone?"

"Ring up clerical. Have them send somebody
'round."

"*Two* somebodies," said McKeon in a tone so neutral
that Bresnahan didn't know if the remark were a com-
pliment or yet another slag on her great size.

"But . . . how long might I take, Chief?"

"As long as you need. Ward . . ." McGarr glanced

over at the young detective. "I want you to go over to a firm named Joyce's Ireland and Bloomsday Tours in Nassau Street and get the itinerary of this year's outing—where exactly they went and with whom."

He thought for a moment, mainly of how much the three-day lapse between the murder and the report of the murder had compromised the investigation. If most of Flood's charges had been foreigners and they had come to Ireland specifically for the Bloomsday event, they might well have already left the country. Others, who were now touring, would be difficult to locate.

"Names and addresses. Once you've got the list, notify the authorities at all points of exit—Shannon and Dublin airports, the boats to England, border crossings into the North. We need written statements from each one of them in regard to Kevin Coyle and what they saw of him that day. Anything . . . extraordinary. Provide specific queries. You know the procedure.

"Then for those who've already left the country, I want you to write them a letter."

Somebody groaned. Another began to laugh. For most of the Murder Squad, reports were bad enough, would perhaps be impossible without Bresnahan or somebody like her. But letters to foreigners explaining what had happened and then asking the proper, specifically worded questions that a barrister couldn't pick apart in a court of law *without* the help of Bresnahan, was a task too onerous to contemplate. And Ward and his wit had long since burned that bridge.

"Also, since you know *Ulysses*," McGarr went on, "I want you to get hold of a recent photo of Coyle. Preferably one in which he's wearing the Joyce boater. The newspapers or Mrs. Coyle should be able to help you with that. Take it around the entire tour. Question anybody who might have had occasion to be with them— barmen, cabbies, shopkeepers. See what you can learn."

When McGarr paused, McKeon said, "Jayz—I hope that's not it, Chief. Just look at the lad, rarin' to go, and with the literary bend and all. Can't we toss in a perk or two—some interviews at the Shelbourne bar around tea time and then on to White's-on-the-Green or the Friars Jacks for a working dinner with Catty? Don't tell me you're going to let him ignore her?"

"The *what?*" Ward asked. Whites-on-the-Green and Les Frères Jacques were the two best restaurants in the city center.

Said McGarr, "Not *it* in the least, Bernie. Ward, why don't we have you ring up the papers and ask them to run a little article for us. We should write it for them to make sure they get it straight. Make it read—"

McKeon cleared his throat and looped a finger at Bresnahan, who stammered, "But Oi-Oi t'ought the Chief Superintendent—"

"Never t'ink when you're around a certain class of man," McKeon advised.

"It's suicidal," said Ward.

McGarr twined his hands behind his head and stared up at a ceiling netted with cobwebs and dangling bits of dust. No wonder he despised desk work, he thought. "Begin with the title: **Gardai Issue Murder Appeal.**

"The Gardai are appealing for information from persons living near the Prospect Cemetery or Finglas Road who may be able to help in the investigation of the murder of Trinity College Professor Kevin Coyle.

"The internationally-acclaimed literary scholar and father of nine is suspected to have been murdered in a lane near the eastern end of the cemetery sometime early in the morning of the seventeenth. Anyone who had contact with Mr. Coyle or who can remember seeing him on the previous evening is asked to notify the police.

"Gardai are also anxious to talk with anybody who observed a Fiat Five hundred with a learner's sticker in the vicinity that night.

"Such persons are asked to call—

"And so forth. Got that, Bernie?"

McKeon hunched his shoulders. "Dunno. Don't think so, and since you and me are the only two in the entire shambles who know how to spell, *you* may be out of luck."

Said Bresnahan, "What was that bit after, 'who saw a Fiat . . . ?'"

" 'Five hundred,' " Ward supplied, " 'with a learner's sticker in the vicinity that night. Such persons are asked—' "

"I know, I know—don't you think I got that?" she snapped.

Ward straightened the knot of his tie and looked away.

Something else now occurred to McGarr—McKeon's playful misuse of the phrase "bullock-befriending bard," which McGarr had read in his brief pass at *Ulysses* on the night before. "You've read the book, Bernie?"

McKeon clutched his chest. "Me? Never say that. Ever, not even in jest. Please, Chief. If it got out, I'd have nobody to consort with who wasn't wearing a Brown Thomas suit."

"And guzzling Perrier," somebody said.

"Ballygowan Spring Water," said another.

The laughter was general, shared even by Ward, and they were nearly out the door when Delaney asked McKeon, "*Congelifract?* How is that spelled?"

"What—do I look like the OED? I got a tenner says it's a word."

Said Sinclaire, who was himself a bit of a toff and on good terms with everybody, including Bresnahan: "Ornery Euphuistic Dick."

"Beats the pants off hard-boiled any day of the week."

"But on Bloomsday." Sinclaire had attended Trinity College for a short time before the need to support a growing family had forced him to emigrate. Only recently returned to Ireland, he had accepted a much less senior post than he had occupied in Australia, and McGarr found him a valuable addition to his staff. He now decided to take him along as companion and witness.

7

McGarr had been passing by, walking through, and in his own way admiring the graceful Georgian buildings at the foot of Dame Street for much of his life. Perhaps because the hubbub of the surrounding city made its way over the tall walls only as a dull roar, perhaps because of the care that had been taken in siting buildings, Trinity College communicated a sense of tranquillity that had often made him take a seat on one of the many walkway benches or to enter the library and browse.

To McGarr it always seemed at first a spacious plane upon which a few academic and dormitory buildings had been placed casually, until their type and number became apparent. Here was a theater and there a chapel and an exam hall, two other libraries, a buttery, a student activities building, tennis courts, a campanile—all arranged with a harmony that rather denied the fact that the urban campus was really quite small.

It had something to do with the scale of the buildings, the insistence upon open green areas, and even with the excellence of its plantings. As Sinclaire and he passed a busload of tourists who were being led toward the library and its *Book of Kells*, McGarr's eyes passed over a noble, ancient oak, a beech tree, flowering shrubs and gardens. Doubtless thinking him a professor, some of the tourists turned for a second glimpse of Sinclaire, tall and thin and regular featured, with silver hair that he let flow over his collar.

"How many years were you here?" McGarr asked him.

"Five terms. A year and two thirds. After we got married I tried to carry on, but Sheila was by then very pregnant and couldn't work, and times then were hard, and—"

McGarr knew. Even though he himself had been a good student and—short and wide, with deceptive speed—an even better footballer, he had had no chance of attending any place like Trinity. With his father a Guinness Brewery worker and happy to be that, McGarr had known from an early age that he would be allowed as much education as the family could afford and that he would work thereafter. The fifth son, he managed to complete school, but he did not know to this day if he would have had the courage to suffer three years confinement in the Trinity library.

In vainglorious moments McGarr liked to think that in his own small way he was a man of action, and he surmised now—following Sinclaire into a dark entry in a mid-campus building—that he had served himself better by choosing a career that satisfied him, if not always totally, then at least continuously for so many years. The prospect of having become a bank manager or a business executive—to say nothing of a university professor, a doctor, or a solicitor—was one he found chilling.

As was the Trinity office that Fergus Flood had shared with Kevin Coyle. It was dark. The interior shutters, designed to block winter drafts, had been pulled nearly

closed. Beyond, McGarr could see stout iron bars strip-
ing the windows.

Explained Flood, "They keep the rugby balls from
shattering the glass, but today I haven't really felt like
switching on the lights."

Beneath the window McGarr could see a rugby pitch
with players at the farther end.

"I will now, if you prefer . . ."

McGarr waited until Flood stood up from behind the
desk before saying that what they had come for required
another sort of light.

Flood was a sturdily-built man of middling height
whose body had begun to run to fat. He was dark with
a dark beard which, closely shaved, made his cheeks
look blue in the dim light. His hair was thinning, and
his forearms, exposed by a short-sleeved shirt, were thick
and hirsute and powerful-looking. In spite of the heat,
he was wearing a bow tie. His face was round, slightly
fleshy, but appeared pleasant.

McGarr sat with his back to the window, in the chair
that he supposed Coyle had occupied. The desk it served
had nothing on it or in it. McGarr opened the drawers
and checked.

Said Flood, "Been like that since I can remember.
An excrescence. Once Kinch—it's what I called Kevin—
tried to have it removed, but they wouldn't let him.
Said they had no other place to store it. Kinch kept
everything in his head. Remarkable mind in every way—
conceptually, analytically, creatively. And his memory
. . ." He cast a hand to a wall that was filled to the
top of the tall ceiling with books. "All mine. If Kinch
had need for a book, there was always the library. One

look as a refresher was all he required, and he had it. Chapter and verse."

Sinclaire eyed McGarr, who, blinking once slowly, cautioned him to wait. He had the feeling that Flood was not a man who should be challenged. He made his living, after all, revealing kinds of mysteries, and it was as though he had been sitting there, waiting for them. As far as McGarr could determine, walking down the hallway, there was nobody else in the building; it was tomblike and funereal in the dim office.

"Three days ago. No, four now," Flood looked up at Sinclaire, whose face could scarcely be seen in the shadow of the bookcase, then at McGarr, who was silhouetted against the room's only light source, as though for corroboration, "Kinch was in great form entirely." It was the cliché for good spirits. Flood settled back in the desk chair and clasped his elbows; he was speaking down at his chest and so appeared jowly and mannered.

"His book would be out Monday next, and already the prepublication reviews that some assiduous editor had made sure all the 'friendly' critics would issue were praising it as a masterpiece. Kinch had always had a problem with reviews—never really believing them when they were good, crediting them all too much when they were bad, which they rarely were. It had something to do with his working-class background. You know about that, do you?"

Neither McGarr nor Sinclaire answered. Flood was speaking, and they'd let him continue until he had no more to say.

"Father was some sort of navvy at the Guinness Brewery. A great pack of kids, and Kinch somewhere in between and ignored and afflicted with a brilliant mind and, I'd say, even a touch of genius that would

have destroyed him, had he remained in that setting."
Flood glanced up, as though having suddenly realized
something.

McGarr wondered if his own father, who was still
alive and had spent forty-seven years in the brewery,
had known Coyle Senior. It did much to explain Kevin
Coyle's having followed McGarr's investigations in the
papers; and his widow's *us*.

McGarr himself had his own us; it included priests
and politicians from his own Synge Street Christian
Brothers School, footballers who wore the colors of his
own former sides, Gardai who had passed through the
Murder Squad before moving on to other positions. He
imagined now that he would have included the young
professor from the Liberties among his own, had he
known him. He now felt a certain pride that Coyle,
who had shared his own background in so many ways,
had been so well regarded by the world.

"Anyway, it was as though Kinch could never quite
believe he was who he had become, or appreciate really
the many good things that kept happening to him. I've
often thought it was what made him such an incisive
critic of Beckett and the novel of incompetence." Flood
looked from Sinclaire to McGarr. "His basic insecurity
could manifest itself destructively in all the . . . women
and in his impecuniousness and periodic drinking bouts.
Some essential self-doubt. Self-loathing."

It was the second time McGarr had heard mention
of the novel of incompetence, and he made note to have
Flood explain it. He also wondered if Flood, like Coyle's
own wife and her "sister," Mary Sittonn, were suggesting
that Coyle in some way had welcomed or encouraged
his own demise. Or had deserved it.

"Shall I go on?" Flood asked. "This isn't the sort

of thing you've come for. You want facts, and I hate to be so lugubrious, so elegiac, but it's just that in my own way I loved Kevin Coyle very much, and I'm utterly shattered that he's dead."

Love? Did one Dublin man say he *loved* another man, even when the subject of that affection was dead? Not in the Dublin that McGarr's *us* knew. "Women?" he asked.

Flood's brow glowered. "Yes—I'm afraid there was that too. It's what I first thought when I read where he had been found, though I believe there's some discrepancy about that as well." Again the eyes tried to find Sinclaire and McGarr. "A woman named Catherine Doyle lives there near the eastern entrance to the Prospect Cemetery," he went on. "She was—*is*—the editor of his new book, as much as anybody might have been Kevin's editor. Actually, I read the book in manuscript form, and it was I who recommended it to her." There was pride in that statement. "The rest you'll have to get from her."

"We'd prefer it from you," said Sinclaire.

"Oh"—from the clasped elbows a hand shot out—"that they were lovers, as much as Kinch could be the lover of anything but his own particular experience, I should imagine. I have no proof, but I think if you ask her, she'll admit it. What with his doubts about his own worth and all the inner turmoil that it brought, Kinch was a man in desperate need of . . . corroboration. I'm only guessing at this, you understand, but from the little he said of it, I gathered that, like most Irish fathers, his own had either been always working or"—he turned his head to McGarr, as though he would understand— "'out,' as it were. If they saw him Sundays, they were lucky.

"As I was saying, since Kinch had only his mother,
who was the one who pushed him, it would follow that
as a man he would turn to women for acceptance. Even
the wife, Katie, is nothing if not matronly. And *was*
from my first meeting her—how many?—fourteen, fifteen years gone now."

McGarr didn't know if what he was feeling was
indignation or something else, but suddenly his ears
were red. Flood may well have been describing McGarr's
own family. Like most Irish families that McGarr had
known at the time, an understanding that amounted
almost to an unwritten contract existed among his father
and mother and the parents of the other children he
knew.

Father went off to a ten-hour workday, six days a
week. His wife or one of his children, when old enough,
would carry his hot dinner to his place of work in a
pail at noon. After work he would return home for tea.
When he arrived, it would be waiting for him on the
table; his wife would serve him. By that time the children had already eaten and been put to bed, or were
otherwise out of the way. Father and Mother would
speak of pressing matters; an individual child might be
called in for censure or praise. Father might then read
a newspaper or visit with his children, but the pub and
the company of his mates claimed the rest of his eve-
nings, which were short five nights a week. The "sec-
ond-most-necessary institution," as Noreen had scathingly
put it, was closed for most of Sunday.

It was also Sunday when the family saw him, briefly,
while attending church, a sports match or race meeting,
then for a sit-down dinner that consisted of a joint of
beef, mutton, or pork. They might venture out together
to the house of a relative or to a park or the strand.

Everybody understood that, given work and the institutions of urban society, this was the way of things. And like a clock, you could have kept time by Father's movements.

Granted the pub was pernicious for some, but it was then, as now, mainly a social institution. Drunkenness was frowned upon, and few who drank heavily held down jobs or lived long. Coyle's father—as McGarr understood James Joyce's had been—might have been one of those, but he suspected not. At the time in Dublin, a Guinness job of any sort had been a respectable working-class occupation that was "husbanded" with respect, especially by any man with a large family.

And finally, if McGarr's own profession had taught him anything, it was that one man's reasons—*if there were any*—for pursuing women, were seldom the same as another's, and could scarcely be reduced to a lecture-hall formula.

But Flood was still speaking.

"I'm sure his wife knew all about it. There's a curious 'sisterhood'—to use their term—among some young women these days. I hear them talking at home—I have a daughter, you see—and my students here in college. Formerly it was 'each woman for herself,' as it were, in pursuit of or"—did he smile? He did "—retreat from a man. Now it strikes me as if they're rather calculating and clinical the way they—women, I mean—get together and . . . divide up a man, or at least look upon men categorically. For . . . *use* and little else."

All from a man who had been speaking minutes before of manly love.

"And then I know Catty Doyle, and Katie herself."

Which was the point of the remark, McGarr suspected, thinking of how most men of his experience had been speaking of women in a categorical manner for as long as he could remember and as recently as the hour before in his Dublin Castle office. He wondered if the battle lines in the war between the sexes were now being more closely drawn, or if Kevin Coyle, independently dependent genius-egotist that he had been, had become the point of a struggle that was at once literary, academic, marital, and sexual.

Plainly they did not know enough, and Flood had said his piece with his thrust at the "sisters." The professor now leaned back in the desk chair.

"Thursday. Bloomsday. Can you tell us what you know of Mr. Coyle's activities?" asked Sinclaire.

Flood's eyes shied toward McGarr, as though he had expected the questions to come from him. "We had every class of thing going on. Jammed, we were, and knew we'd be, right from the ungodly hour of half past six in the morning to closing and beyond, it would seem from what transpired."

Dublin, McGarr was now hearing, and he wondered if Flood, whose surname could be seen on the fronts of shops and pubs citywide, was one of *us* too.

" 'Joggin' for Joyce' and 'The Molly Bloom Marathon' the first event was called. A ten-K hoofing extravaganza for men and women, which because of traffic, had to begin at half past six. It traced much of the route of *Ulysses* through Dublin, ending at the site of the former Nelson's Pillar in O'Connell Street. The newspapers asked if Kinch, who even looked like Joyce, and could play the Stephen Dedalus character from the book better than anybody I've ever seen, could be there for the start. Perhaps you saw the photo—striped blazer, boater, ashplant walking stick in one hand and the starter's pistol raised in the other."

Now that Flood had mentioned it, McGarr realized he had; he had thought the whole thing banal.

"We caught a bit of breakfast at the house of a kindred spirit there in Sandycove, and when we got back outside, we had over five hundred people waiting for us. By my count, which was partial, and did not include the eighty-two on our Bloomsday tour."

McGarr thought of Ward and the letters he'd have to write.

"A carnival it was. But then"—Flood's dark eyes flicked up at Sinclaire and then turned to McGarr— "barristers have their venue down at the Four Courts, surgeons in the Richmond and the Rotunda and in Holles Street hospitals. We, poor word mongers that we are, have only *Ulysses*—thank Homer and Joyce—to make the most of, and 'Shames Choice,' as he called himself in the *Wake*, condemned no aspect of the city. It was all the 'raw clay' of experience to him, to be molded to any purpose including his own. Or mine and Kinch's."

There was a pause while Flood gathered himself. Behind him McGarr heard the thump of a foot on an inflated bladder and the scrunching of cleats through short grass. Somebody shouted, several other somebodies cheered.

"As you know," he began, almost too casually, "*Ulysses* is the story of the peregrinations of two men through Dublin on a June day in 1904. It begins at eight in the morning at the Martello Tower in Sandycove, where the character Dedalus was living with Buck Mulligan and an Englishman named Haines."

"Stadely ploomp Book Molligan," McGarr corrected silently and smiled, thinking of Noreen.

"As usual Kinch began what amounted to his day-long soliloquy there, recanting the opening of the book while perched on a rampart of the tower. But you'll remember the day was stunning, all fair skies and sunlight, and Kinch warmed to his task. Some years he seemed to hate it. Out of sorts and surly, he only mumbled through the day. But this year—maybe it was the new book or something personal or the weather—he was brilliant. He chanted the text. He sang it, pointing out across the bay when he mentioned Howth."

Again Flood paused.

"Others not on the tour demanded that he continue, but we had our schedule to maintain. Into our rented tour bus we climbed and drove up past the house in Dalkey where Dedalus taught on that day in 1904. Then on to Sandymount Strand, where Dedalus strolled and mused with his pocket filled with sovereigns on his way into Dublin. And on to Eccles Street, where we picked up the trail of Leopold Bloom, the book's other main character. But slowly—you know—pulling the bus over so that Kinch, who changed hats to Bloom's bowler whenever the story line demanded, could narrate.

"The bus is a lovely big thing with plenty of windows, soft stuffed seats, air-conditioning—we've used it before—and mostly everybody on the tour was acquainted with the text. Mostly they just sat back and listened. And Kinch—Dubliner, scholar, and (can I say it?) thespian that he was—regaled them. Some, maybe knowing of his new book and half suspecting that, soon famous, he would not again want to perform what (I'll be honest) amounted to an Herculean labor, had tape recorders out. Others asked him to sign copies of *Ulysses*. And still others inquired where they could pick up his new book before returning home.

"To make a long story short"—again Flood's eyes moved from Sinclaire to McGarr, but with a certain twinkle—"we made sure our group was strategically positioned in Davy Byrne's much before lunch. Over the years we've discovered that most of them are used to early hours, and too, given our six-thirty start, Kinch was in need of a wet.

"Which, I must admit"—Flood raised a palm—"was our plan for most of the rest of the day. Without wishing to seem crass, I'll confess that once into jars, our guests are happiest continuing in that vein. The facilities on the tour bus are somewhat limited, and most view the occasion as a literary holiday, with the emphasis solidly on the latter word.

"So—it was on to the Ormond Hotel, after which we visited pubs in Green, North Mount, and Montgomery (now Foley) streets which conform roughly to the pubs that Dedalus and Bloom visited in the 'Cyclops,' 'Oxen of the Sun,' and 'Circe' sections of the book. The original pubs have since been knocked down. There are, of course, surrogates. And we kept Kinch narrating all the while.

"In the last, in Foley Street, I never saw him in better form. As I've said, it's the 'Circe' or 'Nighttown' chapter that deals with Dedalus and Bloom's visit to Dublin's notorious red-light district, and Dedalus plays the piano and sings and dances. Kinch, like Joyce himself—who had such a clear, pure tenor voice that he could have had a career on the stage—was musical. There wasn't anything he couldn't play, and after a kind of intermission he removed the Dedalus boater and his glasses and donned a lady's shift and sleeping bonnet and gave us Molly Bloom's soliloquy which, as you know"—again he looked from McGarr to Sinclaire and back—"closes *Ulysses.*

"But with such verve and vivacity, yet understanding, of what is on the whole of it a complex, multilayered piece, that even I—who have heard him now for over a decade—was impressed.

"The place, McGarrity's—it's new, or at least newly named—was packed, and the crowd nearly brought down the roof."

As though to signal that he had finished his own monologue, Flood folded his hands on the desk in front of him.

After a while Sinclaire asked, "And when was the last you saw him Bloomsday?"

"There in McGarrity's. I'm not as young as he was, and I'm afraid I was done in by the"—his head fell to his chest—"smoke and the noise and, perhaps most, since I don't drink, the relief of having put the entire event by us for the year. I am, I'm afraid, an academic. An unworldly person. And the plethora of detail generated by having to organize an event like this, which is, I should imagine, really quite a simplicity in the scheme of things, entirely exhausts me. And then I could see that Kinch had only just begun to howl, as it were, and if he insisted, I could see I was going to be dragged out to some after-hours club off Merrion Square. I went home to my bed and my wife."

"When was the last time you saw him?"

"Half-eleven. I caught his eye for a moment and signaled that I was leaving. He waved and turned back to the company he was in, and that was it. My last glimpse." Flood paused, then added, "Apart from—

you know—war deaths, I can't think of anything like this happening to any other literary figure like Kinch."

"And what company was Coyle in when you left?" Sinclaire's voice was soft, and in the shadowed room sounded like a conspiratorial whisper.

"A group of Japanese, mostly. Kinch was towering over them."

"Had he mentioned to you or would you know of any plans he might have had for the balance of the evening?"

Flood cocked his head. "He called it 'floating' on his 'Lethe,'—pronounced 'Liffey-float'—which meant that he would allow himself to be carried along by the tides and currents of the night. Mind you, he didn't say that to me exactly. That night anyway. But I knew the look he had well enough . . ."

Sinclaire waited, and Flood explained, "Of . . . beatitudinous bliss, which is probably all-too-clumsily Joycean and redundant. But when he could enjoy himself, Kinch did. It was his working-class upbringing, I should imagine. But he had a way of launching himself into merriment, and when he did, you could read it in his face."

"You seem to have been well acquainted with him. Did he have any known enemies? And please know that we're trying to understand just who Kevin Coyle was. Anything you might mention will be held in the strictest confidence."

"Kinch?" Flood shook his head. "Kinch was exactly what Joyce called Stephen Dedalus in an earlier work— the *Portrait*—a 'priest of external experience.' Kinch was a watcher, an observer, an acceptor, and not in that way alone was he therefore an artist. But he would have made no enemies."

"Did he argue with you?"

Flood's head came up. "Argue in what sense? Academically? My, yes. Often, especially years ago, when he was still just a student and testing his intellectual wings, so to speak. Then we argued interminably, and by that I mean *disagreed* often. But since both of us maintained a studious academic honesty, we—usually he—deferred to the more cogent position. More recently, I found it was I who was deferring to him, though not in all things. But it was always—let me assure you—an *agon* that I found perhaps the most piquant in my life. I am not an outwardly emotional man, but I shall miss Kevin Coyle dearly, and anything I can do to help you discover what happened to him, I will. Anything."

"What about your business? Did you argue about that?"

"*Our* business?"

"Joyce's Ireland and Bloomsday Tours Limited."

Flood shook his head. "*I* own that yoke lock, stock, and the barrel of debts and headaches it takes to get each tour off the ground every year. When I decided to start up the thing, ten years ago, I asked Kinch to join me as a partner, but he wisely declined, saying that he viewed himself more a scholar than an entrepreneur. And then, at the time he was working hard on the new book."

"You paid him, I assume."

Flood nodded. "And well." He reached across the desk and picked up what looked like a bank check. "One thousand pounds, which isn't bad for one day's work, no matter how arduous. This year I've made the check out to Katie. Next year I don't know what I'll do. I've only just thought of it now, with your questions, but I'm not much of a thespian myself, or even a good reader. And as for my memory—I have to keep my home phone number in my billfold so I won't forget it."

When it was apparent that Flood had nothing more to add, Sinclaire said, "Holderness. A research student. We don't have a first name for him, but could he have had some difficulty with Mr. Coyle?"

"David Allan George Holderness, you'll mean. A brilliant chap altogether, but utterly lacking in tact, at least in regard to Kinch. And then they were so much like oil and water—Kinch, the Dub'. Working class. A positivist, let's say, in regard to the world and his work. Yes, he possessed humor and was capable of trenchant sarcasm, the weight of which Holderness himself was sometimes made to feel, but Kinch's great achievement was to have found a way around the aesthetic problem posed by Joyce and Beckett. By that I mean how important novels might still be written in the shadow of their achievements. Holderness was—rather, is— pretty much what Kinch once called him, 'A Beckett clone without Beckett's depth, wit, or sympathy for the human condition.' "

McGarr cleared his throat. He had waited long enough. "Professor Flood—you see in us two plain, poor policemen. Our leisure hours are spent in our garden or with our children. Once, when I was a young man living abroad and feeling . . . bereft of my culture, I picked up a copy of *Ulysses*. The dust jacket said it was Ireland's greatest literary work by Ireland's greatest writer. To be honest, I was mystified. It left me cold. As did—let me add—*Waiting for Godot* and *Endgame*, when my wife dragged me to the theater."

Flood's arms were again folded across his large chest, such that his bow tie appeared fixed to his darkly shadowed jowls. "Well—you're not alone. I sometimes think myself lucky if ten percent of my students actually read Joyce and Beckett and not just the trots of their works. That it leaves most of them cold, I wouldn't doubt. And it's our own fault. Academics, I mean. As Kinch contended, those two are having the last laugh, and it's at our expense. We've played their game, and in so doing, made entirely too much of them. Joyce once bragged that what he was writing would keep scholars busy for years, and here I am over a half century later making literally literary capital from that very prediction.

"Think of him: an odd, acerbic man—half blind, irascible, and impecunious. He quarreled with his best friends and inevitably insulted casual acquaintances. He was a scathing critic, a devastating satirist, and possessed of such boundless egotism that he baldly stated even before he had published much that he was the greatest writer since Shakespeare. Of the *Wake* he bragged that it was the perfect book for the perfect reader, who could spend his entire life reading no other book and still never sound all its depths or understand all its resonances. The problem is, he was right. *Finnegan's Wake* is a masterpiece, the ultimate novel of competence.

"Beckett, who when Joyce's eyesight was failing, took notes for and, it seems, *from* him, played a similarly intricate academic game on his reader. But although always the perfect gentleman personally, Beckett's creation—the novel of *incompetence*—is nasty and cruel and, what's worse, a dead end. A kind of literary black hole.

"Shall I go on?" His eyes twinkled.

"I'd like that," said McGarr. "Especially the bit about the novel of . . . incompetence?"

"Yes—interesting turn of phrase, what? Would you like the short explanation or the long?"

"Well . . ." Sinclaire glanced at his watch.

Flood nodded, folded his fingers together. "It begins with Joyce and the novel of competence. In spite of what I just said about him in a negative way—since we must smash old idols in order to raise new—Joyce was a man of undoubted imminence, great imagination, deep learning, and brilliant intellect, none of it more obvious than in the manner in which he 'plotted'—and I mean that in the strategic, not simply tactical way—all of his works, but in particular *Ulysses,* which, to continue the military analogy, was his breakthrough book.

"About words he once said, 'Why own a thing when you can say it.' And since with his intellect and astounding facility with languages, tongues, stories, and myths, he could say most things, it therefore followed that he— James Joyce, impoverished, emigré son of a Dublin idler—owned not only the things he could name in the contemporary world, but many other things from all recorded time. That was step one in the grand stratagem to become the modern Shakespeare.

"Step two was to analyze the novel. Some critics contend that Joyce decided that the novel was the ideal literary art form of bourgeois society, in which, of course, people define themselves by the things that they own. The novel then is like a container—first word to last, beginning to end, front cover to back cover—that contains things or at least words that are references of things.

"It follows, then, that that novel is best which, within the established limits of the container, includes the greatest number and type of things. Joyce decided he would set the limits of a single day in Dublin and write a book about it. He chose the sixteenth of June, 1904, the day that he first walked out with Nora Barnacle, the shop girl from Galway who later became his wife.

"*But* he would tell *every thing* about that eighteen-hour period, such that he would give (and I quote), 'A picture of Dublin so complete that if the city one day suddenly disappeared from the earth, it could be reconstructed out of my book.' And so he poured the names, places, events, streets, buildings, race horses, tram schedules, tides, prices, advertisements, weather, a dog, a dead man, a birthing hospital, a cemetery, music, the theater, pubs, songs, murder, mayhem—you name it—along with the story of the day for two men who, although only partially acquainted, are like father and son. They are like the hero Ulysses himself, lost and wandering and trying to find their way back to impossible homes. Hence the mythic element.

"Of course, how Joyce wrote the book was also new, an attempt to weave the actual verbal texture of Dublin—the specific whatness of Dublin verbal things—into the container. *Ulysses* is so perfectly constructed that it takes exactly eighteen hours to read aloud, the amount of time that one would have been awake on such a day.

"Joyce said, 'If I can get to the heart of Dublin, I can get to the heart of every city in the world. In the particular is contained the universal.' Shall I go on?"

"Please do," said McGarr, by now wholly intrigued. Flood was making him wonder not only why he had never read *Ulysses*—an omission that he would soon correct—but also what else he had missed in not having attended university. Like many Irishmen, he had a philosophical, speculative bent, which was what had attracted him to police work in general and to the Murder Squad in particular.

"With the *Wake* Joyce decided to write the ultimate novel. Instead of exhausting the possibilities of some other day—or a year or a decade or a century—in dear, dirty Dublin, he expanded the container to its final extension. For setting he chose nothing less than the world entire. For characters all people, speaking all voices, who had ever lived. Time? All time, past, present, and—since there is a belief that certain combinations of words can sometimes serve as prophecy—perhaps even future time as well. In conception, at least, it was an impossible project.

"But he made it all into the simple tale of the dream of a Dublin pub owner. Finnegan, like Jung claimed all of us can, establishes touch with the collective unconscious of the race of man. And his mind, wandering forward and back in time, touches upon all symbol, myth, and history from the hieroglyphics on ancient tombs through Vedic and Norse myths, the Bible in its several forms, sagas and passion plays and verse, and on to modern literature, right up to Beckett himself, who was often sitting across the room from Joyce, and so appears in the *Wake.*

"During the twenty years that it took Joyce to write the *Wake,* he had a team of readers—the literary groupies of his day—scouring the Bibliothèque in Paris, reading all the great books he suggested. They would synopsize each and include a few representative pages of text so that Joyce could then add both statement and word to Finnegan's dream.

"With a few dozen minds and at least one, perhaps two—here I mean Beckett—indisputable geniuses working on the *Wake*, it became the ideally competent novel that the ideally erudite reader might peruse for the rest of his life and still never appreciate in all its ideal complexity. In other words Joyce, within the assumptions of his aesthetic, exhausted the form of the novel of competence. Another novel more complete probably could not be produced, since it would require another Joyce, greater scope, a larger vision, more and better help, a second Bibliothèque Nationale.

"And since the form of the novel as written from Richardson to Joyce was exhausted, Samuel Beckett turned around and attempted to exhaust the form of its 'negative' image, as it were—the novel of incompetence. By incompetence Beckett does *not* mean novels written by incompetent authors. He means that, unlike Joyce, he cannot assume the possibility of communication among human beings, much less between human beings and the collective unconscious.

"For Beckett words don't work. They are an imposition, given us by others after our births; they really can't describe our own particular experiences in our own individual terms. Also, when we speak words, we need somebody else to hear and acknowledge them. A witness. In other words, we can't say *us* in *our own* terms for anybody's ears but *our own*. And if we were to try, say, by speaking out all the words of the Others once and for all, we would find that there's nothing to say, since Western civilization assumes that we are no more than what we were when we were first born—a tabula rasa, a void, *un néant*, a nothing. And nothing can only be described by silence.

"But if the whole point of communication is to confirm

life and existence, then we must try, if only to know we live. With words that are inexact and ultimately unavailing.

"More?" Flood asked.

Sinclaire, who had turned his head to McGarr, said, "Not today, Professor. I think we catch on—Beckett's novels are worse than his plays. Now I know why he won a Nobel Prize."

Flood's laugh was quick and ready.

At the door McGarr looked up at the wall of books. It was *Ulysses* that concerned them at the moment, and at least one shelf seemed to be devoted to nothing else.

"All in the attempt to prove it's not *Useless*," said Flood in a knowing way.

"What would you recommend for the first-time reader of the book? Surely there's a . . ." McGarr searched for a term that was not "trot."

"Key," Flood supplied eagerly. "Dozens of them. The best is this little volume." He handed McGarr a book. "There are others, of course, all the way from long-winded explanations of a single motif to indexes of recurrent elements that merely list the pages on which words are mentioned." Taking another book from the shelf, Flood fanned the pages, revealing what looked like a kind of dictionary. "Take whatever you think you might need."

"This'll be enough for now."

Flood smiled. "Sure—the overexamined book isn't worth reading." And when McGarr's head came up, he added quickly, "Don't take offense. Kinch said that. I'm only quoting."

Said Sinclaire, "By the way, Professor—you wouldn't happen to know who drives a Fiat Five hundred? A

Cinque Cento. It's white with a learner's sticker on the
back."

Flood looked from one man to the other. "Why—
I don't drive it myself, but I own one. It's my wife's,
now my daughter's, car. She's in college here and, you
know, just learning how to drive. Why do you ask?"

"Where is it now?" McGarr asked.

"At home, I believe."

"Which is in Foxrock?"

Flood nodded.

"Are you busy now? Would you mind coming along
with us?"

"Well, I . . ." He turned and looked down at the
desk. "May I make a call?"

"To whom?"

"My wife. I'd like to tell her that we're on our way.
She doesn't fancy being . . . disturbed, you see."

Disturbed at what? McGarr wondered. "I think it
would be better if we just left."

But Flood did not move; his head again turned toward
the desk and the telephone. "Should I phone my
solicitor?"

Sinclaire waited for McGarr to respond.

"I'd be interested to know why you think you need
to." McGarr searched the man's face—the dark eyes,
the fully fleshed bluish cheeks, the slightly aquiline nose.
A few strands of gray had just begun to streak his black
hair.

"Well—this *is* a murder investigation, is it not?"

A refreshing question from an intimate of Kevin, or
rather, *Kinch* Coyle, McGarr thought. He motioned to
the door, and they briskly followed Flood out into the
hall.

8

"You mean you have all eighty-six names and addresses on disk?" Detective Inspector Ward asked. He watched her deep blue, almost violet eyes shy toward the computer terminal at the far side of Joyce's Ireland and Bloomsday Tours office.

"And not only could I get a printout of the names and addresses, but we might also punch in a little letter to those—how many?—seventy-three who live outside the country, asking if they saw the victim after the final pub stop there in Foley Street? Will it do envelopes too?"

She was small and dark, with wavy black hair so thick that it looked kinky and perhaps even rough to the touch. Her face was wide and her cheekbones high, balanced by a long straight nose. And yet for all her Mediterranean features, her skin was fair, and had even taken on a bit of color since Ward had walked in.

And yet it was her body that he most admired, as now with a kind of resignation she rose from where she had been sitting behind a counter and moved toward the computer. Her dress was wide and flowing and made of brilliant yellow cotton; it fell in pleats that both made its volume seem greater and her diminutiveness more pronounced.

But the dress also snugged her waist to a distance

of—Ward estimated—four inches below her hips. A glance from the action of the flowing skirt to her ankles, well-formed and thin, made him draw in a breath involuntarily. He forced his eyes away.

What was it with him, anyhow? he wondered. It wasn't enough that he had passed an arduous night with the head nurse of Surgery at Richmond Hospital, a great blond Danish woman who was at least ten years his senior and had practiced on him the only type of abuse worth praising. Here he was already plotting the corruption, really, of this tiny, exquisite-looking person who was not much more than a girl and probably believed in love and trust and fidelity and all the other emotions that Ward was not willing to consider essential in this life—not yet, anyway.

Yet her skin was nicely and deeply tanned, her back a thin arch that he imagined was interestingly firm but not *too* firm. And he could tell from the perk of her nipples through the soft material of her brown, scoop-neck jersey, that she wasn't a woman in constant need of support, which was one sleazy thought, he thought.

Girl. Girl, he reminded himself, but not too firmly.

He leaned over her so that he could breathe in the scent of her morning shampoo and glance down the open neck of her jersey. "What's wrong?" he asked. "Didn't you tell me Professor Flood said that you were to cooperate with the police?"

"Yes, but . . ."

"But what?"

"Can I tell you something honestly?" The violet eyes flashed up at Ward and nearly caught him staring down the front of her jersey. He wondered if the color was her own or the effect of some tinted contact lenses.

He had once met a girl like that in Greece. There was an also intriguing line across the middle of her chest that separated tanned skin from what looked like the creamiest flesh. It resembled two tightly defined C's, and he couldn't keep himself from imagining how different she would be from his statuesque Dane. Something could be said for quality too, especially in regard to flesh.

Not fully conscious of his smile, Ward waited.

"Truthfully?"

He nodded.

"Well—truthfully, I don't feel very good about any of this at all."

Eye contact was intense now, and he watched her pupils dilate once before dropping down to his lips. His own nostrils pulsed, which was a sure sign that he was leading with . . . well, *not* with his chin.

Then, there was a fringe of tiny blond hair that he now noticed on her forehead and imagined was repeated someplace else on her body. Along her thighs near her kneecaps perhaps, or at the small of her back.

"Because you're taking advantage of me."

Ward's brow furrowed. Tips of his fingers touched his breast.

"Yes, you. Can I be frank about this? Do you appreciate candor in a woman?"

Sometimes, Ward thought. And sometimes not.

"On first sight, from the moment you walked in here, you could tell that I was attracted to you. Physically. And now"—she paused and again their eyes met—"personally. And you're using that to take advantage of me, which I think is wrong.

"Oh, I know," she went quickly on, "you're an older

man, and it's quite obvious you're used to dealing with women. But later, you know, tonight when I think of you, or tomorrow and the next day, I'd prefer to re-member you as a gentleman, and not somebody who merely *wanted* and *got* something from me."

There was nearly a plea in that, and Ward—a pre-cocious twenty-eight—was actually experienced enough with women to know that they sometimes said exactly the opposite of what they really desired. And then her accent, which was mild and fine, with just a trace of a western lilt, appealed to him. Clare, he decided. A country girl. And not long here.

"But I only need what the machine has already got in it—the names and addresses of the people on the tour. And I needed it before we met, A.S.A.P. If we hurry, I can notify the airport and docks, the border crossings into the North, so that those on the list who are touring can be interviewed. This is a murder in-vestigation, and top priority."

She only breathed deeply, raising her shoulders so that the top of the jersey opened a bit more. When she let them fall, her breasts juddered.

Ward added, "The letter is nothing, really. A list of questions. I've got it right here. We could bang it out right now, while I'm phoning the other bit in, and you'd have the eternal thanks of the Murder Squad. My own too, of course."

Still nothing.

Leaning over her chair, Ward's cheek grazed the side of her hair. The shampoo smelled like shikai or jojoba or both; he imagined how pleasurable it would be to run his hands up under all those long and lustrous locks. He was, he now realized, rather tired of blondes. Or at least sated, for the moment.

"Look—if we get on it now, we can have it done by lunchtime."

She turned her head slowly. In profile her face was even more strikingly Mediterranean. Her eyes flicked up to the clock on the wall.

"What's your name, by the by?"

"It's Emer."

"A lovely name. Emer. Have you ever been to Frères Jacques, Emer?" he went on. "It has a cozy second-level dining room and daily specials that are delectable. McGarr—you know, my chief—he dines there regularly. Country French cooking. One day it's Wexford mussels marinière, another calves liver Dijonnaise or salmon en papillotes. Their hollandaise? *Formidable.*" Ward had heard McGarr say something like that to his wife over the phone.

"*Lunch?*" she asked. "Dressed like this? Couldn't we make it dinner instead? I'd feel so"—suddenly the eyes again engaged Ward's—"*special* going to dinner with a man of the world, like you. At Frères Jacques," she added with an inflection that seemed genuinely French. For a moment Ward wondered if she was having him on.

He blinked. Who was he to deny such a lovely young thing the feeling of being special with a—had she actually said—man of the world?

He wondered if he had any credit left on the several bits of plastic in his billfold. Unlike McGarr, with his chief superintendent's pay and a wife with a prosperous business, Ward, whose tastes in most things were inconveniently elevated, operated strictly on the margins of finance. And then, he would not recover from his recent discovery that Danes were costly companions until the end of the month.

The solution, however, was familiar to him. When he picked her up—he now slid her name, address, and telephone number into his billfold—he would claim that Frères Jacques was either closed or booked to the eaves. No place else would do for her; they would go there as promised another time.

And instead he himself would cook dinner for her— fresh salmon steaks; he happened to have them already stocked—in his loft apartment on the quays. Some coaxing might be required, but, armed with a dozen freebie long-stemmed roses from his aunt's florist shop in Dollymount, Ward could sell a woman the Ha'penny Bridge and make her glad she owned it. And then, he had lavished so much attention on his apartment that it virtually sold itself. Or, rather, him.

Which was the point.

Thus Ward left Joyce's Ireland and Bloomsday Tours in high spirits; knowing that at least part of his evening would be filled with a new and intriguing challenge made him glow.

Had she, the "country girl," set him up? He had the feeling she had, which would only make whatever sparring was to go on between them more interesting. In the ring Ward had been noted, after all, for his footwork.

And then, the most difficult part of his present assignment—what would have taken anybody else on the staff days—he had completed at a stroke. Now he had nothing more challenging before him than a leisurely amble through Dublin with the glossy print of Kevin Coyle "playing" Stephen Dedalus, with which Emer— an ancient, hallowed name—had also supplied him, and some phoning to the thirteen Irish residents who had been on the tour.

Granted Ward was new to the Murder Squad, but he had over six years service with the Garda itself, and he now considered himself as much a natural in the streets as he was still—three times a week—on the twenty-by-twenty foot square of buff canvas. Though born and raised in Waterford, Ward loved the busyness of Dublin, its sooty, narrow streets, the rough pace of its commerce and industry.

Living by choice on the quays, he woke up each morning to their hubbub and roar, actually anticipating the morning news that was so much the bane of the others on the staff, including McGarr. Again as in the ring, there was vital action in those pages, with which he was often connected. The editorial jibes were like shots thrown by a tireless and sometimes skilled opponent, neat and cutting here, wild and inept there, but always and ever churning.

It was a small town really, at least in the city center. Year by year Ward was becoming increasingly well known, not merely for his exploits with his fists or for the figure he cut, but also on the level that now meant most to him. By hard, dutiful work, study, and examination he had become a detective as soon as was possible. Partly it had been the police uniform of the Garda that he had found objectionable, but also the uniformity of service. After having distinguished himself in the ring, Ward was not about to settle for anything but a distinguished position in his chosen career.

For two years now he had not taken a holiday, so

that there hardly remained a street or a business or even a church or a government office where people failed to nod or wave or say, "Hello, Hughie, how's the lad" or, "Whipper," which had been his ring name, "when're they bringing you back. Did you see the fight on the telly, those two blokes from America? I was telling the lads how you would've . . ."

Better still were the comments that he heard every once in a while, more frequently in the last year, which made the much-desired equation. Only a fortnight ago at a Garda retirement party he had overheard one man ask another, "What's his name?"

"Who?"

"The detective. The one from the Murder Squad who can handle himself and looks so polished. Little McGarr."

"That's Whipper Ward."

"The pugilist? He's no worse off for it, it seems. Where did McGarr recruit him?"

There was a pause, then, "You know McGarr."

"A likely combination. Let's keep our eye on him," concluded the Minister for Justice, who had been speaking to the Police Commissioner himself.

But there was more to police work than style and availability, and stepping into Davy Byrne's "Moral Pub," as it had been called in *Ulysses*, Ward decided on his strategy.

Since Coyle had last been seen in McGarrity's in Foley Street, it was unlikely that any of the publicans or barmen in the pubs previously visited on the tour would have seen him again. They might have noticed something else, however: some event or argument or altercation.

But Byrne's was already crowded, mostly with tourists, and the barmen, who gathered for a few moments when Ward flashed his I.D., said they had seen nothing out of the ordinary. They expressed their sorrow, as if Ward had been in some way related to Coyle. "A brilliant chap altogether." More selfishly they asked, "Where will we find another the like of him?"

The hotelier at the Ormond worried, "D'you think they'll put it on next year? I mean the tour. They could get some actor or somethin'. Colm Wilkinson." Ward didn't think so. From the snippets of opinion he was hearing, Coyle's had been a singular talent, and passing by a bookstore on his way toward the National Maternity Hospital in Holles Street, he purchased Coyle's first book and attempted to buy the second, stacks of which he could see wrapped in clear plastic behind the counter.

"I'm sorry, but we're not allowed to sell that volume until its official release on Monday."

Ward held out his I.D. "But this is an official murder investigation, and it's important that we understand who Kevin Coyle was as an artist and a scholar."

The woman's eyes rolled once. "Really. I can't. If his publisher even learnt of it . . . and look, there's a queue for the book." She raised a clipboard on which there was a long list of names. "We're already sold out. What you see here."

The surrogate pub in Mount Street that the tour had visited yielded only further eulogies, and Ward began to feel discouraged. Only as he was walking briskly down Westland Row, book in hand, did he notice something that made him hesitate slightly before walking on.

It was a straw boater perched back cockily on the head of a lout in front of Pearse Station, a grimy railway terminus. Four others were with him; the girl by his side was wearing a striped blazer that fit her like a sack.

What to do? Ward looked around. There was a green telephone kiosk across the street, but it would put him directly in their line of vision. Softly he cursed himself for the vanity that kept him from wearing the small radio which clipped on one's belt and was issued to all metropolitan police.

He decided to cross Pearse Street to the pub on the corner and make a quick call from there, when, glancing back, as if for traffic, he saw the band of five move suddenly out onto the footpath. There, the striped blazer and the other girl crossed the street and the three young men walked off the way Ward had come.

He forced himself to wait ten seconds then ten more, until they had a lead of about sixty yards. Ward hoped it was enough, but from the looks of them—all dirty-gray denim and chains, with spiked hair and rings in their ears—they lived on the streets and would know which alleys did not end in cul de sacs and which buildings could lead them to safety in an adjoining street.

They strolled leisurely, the wide, thin shoulders of the tallest—the one with the hat—rolling against those of his mates as he sashayed forward on tall boots with worn heels, doffing the boater to a nun who hurried by, holding the heavy ashplant stick like a cane, then like a military baton, finally like a golf club, the head of which he smacked into a soft-drink can that clattered across Clare Street.

They appeared to be headed for Merrion Square, a fenced park with walkways and gardens; Ward hoped they would veer to the right toward Leinster House, the seat of the Irish government, in front of which he could see several uniformed Gardai. But he was out of luck. Instead they turned up North Mount Street, passing a corner of the square where three artists had set up easels and were painting and displaying their other works.

The tall one cocked the ashplant to his shoulder, as though he would swing it like a bat and knock the legs from under an easel. Alarmed, the woman artist's eyes bulged with fear; the two other louts roared their approval of their mate's daring-do.

"What's the matter?" asked the tall one, again cocking the stick off his shoulder. "You don't fancy sport? *Cricket?*" he bellowed down at the now terrified woman, and Ward nearly rushed forward. But he held himself, stepping quickly toward the park which the others— laughing now—had entered.

"Not to worry, ma'am," Ward said in an undertone, passing the artist.

"Mind yourself," she replied. "They do it everyday, the bastards."

Contained behind a thick stand of shrubs and fence, the garden was a still, sultry vessel of bright sunlight and mounded, fusty beds patterned with bright flowers. At one corner two attendants were at work on a ladder, clipping hedges. Several people occupied benches around the center oval pathway; others strolled the narrow walkways.

Ward decided to act. Here, at least, his advantage in speed could be employed to run down the tall one, the one with the stick; perhaps he might even nab a second, though he knew his chances of that were slight. Slowly he moved his fingers to the button of his taupe linen suit coat and slipped it free. Raising then letting fall his right shoulder, he felt the comforting weight of the Beretta in the holster near his right bicep. Small and light, yet not lacking punch, it allowed the line of his suit coat to remain undisturbed, and was to Ward a kind of equivalent of what he viewed as his own capabilities both in and out of the ring.

He increased his speed as the three approached the oval, where he judged it best to take them. It was the deepest part of the square, with at least a seventy-yard dash to any exit. He flexed the fingers of his left hand and, though still walking, glided now quickly toward them as they approached the widest arc of the central flower bed.

"Sorry," he said. "Excuse me." His left hand darted between the plackets of the suit coat and snatched out the Beretta, which he raised to the level of his left ear, the barrel pointed at the sky. "Hello."

With his right hand he reached out to touch a shoulder of the tall one and then spring back, but, as though on cue, his sidekicks suddenly dropped down on their haunches and, whipping the ashplant off his shoulder, the tall one struck out at the wrist that held the Beretta, which fired before it was slammed into the side of Ward's head, his temple and his ear.

Ward saw stars and went suddenly deaf on one side. Then something was wrong with his wrist; he could no longer hold the automatic. It slipped from his grasp and fell to the footpath as he watched the tall one pivot around, the stick flashing in the sun.

It caught him this time solidly in the ear, which seemed to explode, filling his mind with the whitest light he had ever seen; suddenly he was down on the pavement. The light then took on the color of blood and the shape of a grainy sluggish whirlpool, down which he felt himself slipping.

Fighting it, he forced his eyes open and saw the big one stuffing the Beretta under his belt before they dispersed, each in a different direction. He saw the attendants at the ladder, shouting and shaking fists, begin moving toward him. He saw a woman gaping down, her mouth open in horror.

And he felt his own blood, hot and oily, seeping out of his ear and down his neck along the line of the collar of his shirt.

9

Foxrock, though now somewhat passé as a fashionable address, still had its prestigious neighborhoods. Professor Fergus Flood's was one.

Here the houses were self-contained, set well back from the road, and stylish. With arches over inset doors and windows, and palm trees of two types in the front yard, the house appeared slightly Moorish or Iberian. A Fiat 500 was parked under a narrow car port that looked to have been built especially for it and was attached to the side of a single-bay garage.

There the shadows were deep and cool and the white enamel was pitted and dingy, as though the car had sat long without much care. There was a red L learner's sticker fixed to the rear window.

"As I said, it's my wife's machine. But mostly my daughter drives it. I prefer . . ." Flood motioned to the garage. Through a window McGarr could see a late-model Rover, midnight blue. "When I drive, which is seldom. You've got to be a bit coordinated in this banger. Your arm could fall off, all the shifting that's needed." He reached for the door handle, but McGarr stopped him.

"Please—allow me."

The air inside the car was stale and stank of hot plastic and petrol. Once on assignment while with Interpol, McGarr had been forced to rent a *Cinque Cento*, and now the tiny interior and the stiff bracing of the seat against his back was enough to bring back the stunning headache the machine had given him on the *bianco* mountain roads of the Abruzzi.

He noted the lipstick-stained cigarette butts in the ashtray—Rothman's and some others, which on first glance looked like Disc Blues—the pair of men's mud-stained Wellies below the passenger seat, and the pile of books and papers on the jump seat behind.

"As I was saying, Hiliary's a third-year student," Flood explained to Sinclaire as McGarr continued to examine the car, pushing open the latch of the tiny glove box with the barrel of his pen, flicking up the insurance card and the single road map that it contained. "Literature. Actually, Kevin was her tutor. I'm afraid she's taken all of this rather hard."

A red, felt marker had mapped a route to Dunlavin in Kildare. A curve on a byroad was circled with the advisory, "David's parents' demesne." There was a St. Christopher medal over the rearview mirror, and a sticker of the Sandinista flag and the exhortation NICARAGUA LIBRE affixed to the metallic surface of the dash.

"Maura, my wife's," Flood said, of the medal. "Hiliary's," he indicated the sticker. "Neither of which I support, mind, but the generational disjunction—in belief, in focus—is revealing, wouldn't you say?"

Climbing fully out of the car, McGarr tilted back the seat, all of which rose in a unit to expose a thin-bladed, blue-steel kitchen knife on the rubber mat below. It was something used for specialty filleting—fish, McGarr guessed—and was, with its pale wooden handle, clearly new. With the barrel of the pen, McGarr flipped it over. The stain on the other side of the handle was rust-colored, deeper on the periphery where the blood had clotted. Near the heel was a stamp that said it had been hand-forged by Everdur, Gottingen.

McGarr drew in a breath and let it out slowly, then raised his head to Flood. "Yours?"

Flood's jowls again appeared blue in the shadowed light, and shivered as he shook his head. "I mean, it could be. But—" His head swung to the house.

"Again—tell us who would have used this car Bloomsday night?" Sinclaire asked.

Flood hunched his shoulders and McGarr eased the seat back in place. Without closing the door, he stepped back from the car and glanced at Sinclaire, who turned toward McGarr's Mini-Cooper.

"Perhaps we should go into the house," McGarr suggested. "Would your wife and daughter be at home?"

"Wife," said Flood.

Maura, thought McGarr. Of the medal.

Maura Flood was a large woman whose surplus of flesh appeared to have pooled in the proper places. With wide shoulders, her upper chest—exposed in a flower-print summer dress—was a tanned expanse of smooth skin that attracted McGarr's eye and looked— in the shade of a back garden wall where wrought-iron furniture painted white had been grouped—cool to the touch. Yet when she stood to draw a chair for him, he noted that her waist was still thin; the pleats of the skirt fanned over the radical arcs of her hips.

On one was a palm frond, on the other a red shape that suggested some large tropical fruit. Sitting again, she crossed her legs, and McGarr believed he heard the lubricious glide of thigh across thigh. There was a cigarette between the fingers of her right hand; a crystal tumbler with ice and a slice of lime sat on the table before her. A dark, handsome woman of at least forty, her eyes were deeply circled, as though she had been crying, or had not slept well recently.

Flood insisted on remaining in their company. "Maura is my wife," he explained when Sinclaire said that they would prefer to interview her alone. "I won't abandon her."

To what or whom, McGarr wondered, watching her draw deeply on the cigarette, her dark eyes drifting up to the scuds of cloud that were drifting across the summer sky.

"It's either I'm allowed to remain by her side or I forbid this to continue without our solicitor being present."

Said Sinclaire, "You mentioned that before. Is it a threat? If you think you need a solicitor, Mr. Flood, it's your option."

Maura Flood allowed her gaze to rest on her husband for a bitter moment before moving off. "And you are . . . again . . . ?" she asked McGarr, who repeated his name and title. "You've come about Kevin?"

McGarr nodded.

With the nail of her middle finger she flicked the cigarette butt deep onto the grass of the back garden.

"How many times—" Flood began, but broke off, and, like an oversize retriever, plodded out into the sun to search for the cigarette. He found several and ponderously began collecting them.

His wife raised the glass and drained it. They heard a sound from the house, and Sinclaire pushed himself out of the chair. It couldn't be the Tech Squad yet, their having only just been alerted.

"Bloomsday night. When Kevin Coyle was murdered. Can you tell me where you were?"

"Here."

"With your daughter?"

"For a while. Hiliary left around seven for the cinema."

Flood, still out in the grass, now noticed that Sinclaire had left, and holding what he had found in a cupped hand, moved toward the house.

"And you?"

In a movement that reminded McGarr of the swing of a gun carriage, she redirected her shoulders and eyes. She was a pretty woman with a long, slightly retroussé nose and a delicate chin that made her wide, well-formed mouth seem pensive. "Me?" There was surprise in that. "Why *me?*"

McGarr hunched his shoulders, and suddenly tiring of the—was it?—preciousness of nearly everybody he had dealt with in the previous two days, said, "Yes, you. Did you know Kevin Coyle, and how well? Did you see him"—again he checked her eyes and her upper chest and the ankle of the leg that was crossed over the other and was tanned and shapely. And he thought of what Flood himself had said of Coyle: his talent, his youth, his charisma and taste for women—"on the night he was murdered? Were you perhaps his lover? Did he return here for a little tête-à-tête? Were your husband and he at each other's throats—for business reasons, for professional reasons, for reasons of the heart, or at least of the body?"

Her eyes widened. McGarr leaned forward in the

seat and twined his fingers. "You or your husband or—
am I guessing, here?—your daughter, or all three of
you, are in this thing right up to your necks. Your car,
the Fiat Five hundred out there in the garage . . ."
He waited until she nodded. He wanted to make sure
he was understood. "It has been placed at the murder
scene, *at* the time of Kevin Coyle's death, *with* Kevin
Coyle in it coming, and out of it going. And the murder
weapon—a filleting knife—happens to have been found
under its seat.

"Now, tell me, Mrs. Flood—do you cook? May I
see your kitchen? Do you own such a knife?"

She held his gaze for a moment before reaching for
the packet of Rothman's on the table before her. There
was a tremor in the hand that snapped the lighter.
Blowing out the smoke, she looked away toward the
farther end of the garden.

McGarr could hear voices in the house: Sinclaire's,
which was angry, and then Flood's in an angrier response. ". . . My daughter!"

Said Maura Flood, "Yes, I know Kevin Coyle. And,
yes, I suppose he was my lover, or rather, I was *one* of
his several. And, yes, he wanted to return here or
someplace Thursday night. He phoned me from
McGarrity's in Foley Street said he would meet me
anywhere I liked. He said Fergus"—her eyes flickered
toward the house where an argument was continuing—
"had told him that he was coming straight home and
that, if I were to leave then, I could be gone before
Fergus got home. We agreed to meet at the Drumcondra
Inn. The owner is—*was*—a friend of Kevin's and made
a room available to us whenever—

"I bathed and dressed quickly, but not quickly

enough. Stepping out the door, I saw lights swinging down the wall of the house across the street. At that hour it could only have been Fergus, and I tried to"— She turned her head away from her husband and Sinclaire, who now entered the garden together from the house—"steal out here and out into the alley. I thought I could walk 'round to the street and get into the car and away before he—

"But then," she lowered her voice, "I realized that he would have already seen the car and . . . I decided instead to walk out to the Stillorgan Road. Perhaps the odd cab might be returning to the city, but after fifteen or twenty minutes I tired of waiting. And then the . . . moment had passed. I only wish—"

Now joining them, Flood asked, "You only wish what, dearest?"

Said Sinclaire in a firm tone, "Keep your counsel, Mr. Flood. The Chief Superintendent is asking the questions." And to McGarr, "The daughter was in the house. When I asked her to join us here, she bolted and yer man here prevented me from detaining her. In the car."

"The Fiat?"

"The same."

McGarr's head went back. He flushed with shame and anger. "Christ!"

Said Sinclaire, "I've already got on to Metro and the Tech Squad, so . . ."

At least their embarrassment would be contained.

"Sure, she's just a wee girl," said Flood. "She's got nothing to do with any of this."

But he did, and the wife too. And why, then, did the daughter run? McGarr struggled to contain his emotions. How far could she get in an automobile that could top fifty miles per hour flat out? And which was conspicuous: There probably weren't a handful of *Cinque Centi* in the entire country.

He drew in a breath and reached for his shirt pocket and a cigarette, which was also a Rothman's. "When you returned, was the car in the drive? The Fiat Five hundred?"

She thought for a moment. "I honestly can't tell you. By that time I was resigned to another stimulating evening." Her eyes flashed up at Flood. "I poured myself a stiff drink and went up to my room."

"And your husband, Mr. Flood here. What was he about?"

On a raised arm, the hand with the cigarette waved dismissively. "I couldn't tell you. Fortunately I neither saw nor heard him."

McGarr turned to Flood. "Did you leave the house after you returned from Foley Street?"

Flood nodded. "I did. When I discovered that my darling wife wasn't in, I went looking for her. It was a *wild* night"—he raised an eyebrow—"and I was worried about her."

"Where?"

"Oh, different venues. Jury's, the Burlington, Sachs Hotel."

McGarr watched Maura Flood turn to her husband for the first time.

"Then you know she was having an affair with Kevin Coyle."

"Affair is hardly the word, sir."

Their eyes were fused now, and McGarr waited. At length he asked, "What *is* the word, then?"

"Well, affair suggests *affaire de coeur*. But knowing

both parties intimately as I do and did, I would char-
acterize it more as a brief, pointed congruence. Or,
rather, a spate of brief and—here I'm only guessing—
ultimately unsatisfying congruences. More in the nature
of appetite gratification, I should imagine. Something
like smoking or drinking." A finger motioned to the
glass on the metal table—

McGarr studied Flood's saturnine face and the glint
of amusement in his eye, and he decided that he did
not much care for the man. He wondered if, after having
been Coyle's tutor, he had attempted to direct him as
well, and if the "congruence" between his wife and
colleague had been spiced by a kind of retribution.
"Which car did you use?"

Flood looked away. "The Rover, of course."

"And the Fiat. Where was that?"

"To tell you the truth, I didn't notice it at all."

McGarr struggled to conceal his disbelief. "Certainly
you must have checked to see if it was there when you
went out to look for your wife. And when you returned.
Wouldn't that have been the first thing you would have
looked for?"

The slight smile was back on Flood's soft lips. "As
I stated, I didn't *notice* it at all."

In patent disgust Maura Flood turned her head away.

Was it a test of semantics that Flood now desired?
McGarr wondered. It was the first love of Sergeant
McKeon, McGarr's resident interrogator. Slowly and
with infinite impatience, with bullying and wheedling
and sly confidentiality, McKeon would discover just what
Flood did and did not notice Bloomsday night. In scru-
pulous detail. "For the moment, Professor Flood, you're
charged with impeding the investigation of a capital

crime, which is a felony." McGarr stood and turned to Sinclaire. "Who'd be on the desk of the *Irish Times* now?"

"Nolan, perhaps. Or O'Malley."

Flood's smile collapsed. "It'd ruin me, it would."

McGarr pointed toward the door into the house. "Somewhat less than Kevin Coyle, I'm sure."

Ban Gharda Ruth Honora Ann Bresnahan felt huge and ungainly and more than a little foolish. She was a large woman with broad, strong shoulders and full breasts. She was also thin of hips and at once a bit bow-legged and pigeon-toed. Thus her feet, constrained in low-heeled shoes that she inevitably bought too small in an attempt to conceal their size, made her rock as she walked; they did so especially here in the warren of small shops and lanes in the Liberties known as the Coombe.

The ancient surface of the footpath was pitched and heaved and made her feel almost drunk, a condition that a vow of abstention, taken in her youth, had never allowed her to achieve. And she blushed with morti-fication to find herself staggering all the same. One shoulder brushed against a lamppost, a foot missed a step, and a knee buckled slightly as she hurried along.

And to think, she thought, people willingly submitted to such conditions, and even—she glanced into a window of one of the several antique shops she was passing—prized the dirt and grime of the city, with its sagging roofs and buckled walls and things old, like that miser-able, frayed chintz ottoman. She stopped to consider who or what it could possibly accommodate—a child or a dog or a cat, but certainly not a decently constructed human being. It was something that in the country she had seen chucked out for the tinkers, but there it stood all cracked veneer and splaying legs with an eighty-pound price on it. EMPIRE, the tag said. Roman, she thought.

No, for Bresnahan it was air and light and open spaces and a house with wide bay windows perched, say, up the side of Slea Head, overlooking Bantry Bay; it was a big, strong Kerryman to tend the fields and get her with a brood of little lads and lassies who would care for her in her old age. It was a dream that she had largely forsaken, given the craven character of most men and their generally diminutive size. Instead she thought she might make a name for herself here in the city, and then with seniority and connections put in for the command of the Dingle or Kenmare or Tralee barracks.

Catching sight of herself out of uniform and in Dublin mufti—a short-sleeved black blouse, collar up and opened to the third button, her flame-red hair pinned up and spraying from the back of her head—Bresnahan panicked. All, every bit of the dream, depended on her professional success now, and she was filled with jealousy and a kind of hatred for little *jackeens*, like Ward and McKeon and even McGarr himself, who had the look and the feel for and even the abrupt swagger of these mean streets. Damn them, she'd pluck up her courage and prove herself equal or better, she vowed, as she turned and plunged on.

Coombe Collectibles and Rare Goods was a long, low building with a slate roof and dingy windows. Inside, the shop was dark and blessedly cool, filled with a stale, sweet smell of old wood and cloth and paper that reminded her of death. At first, thinking it was empty, she decided to look around and get the feel of the place before forging ahead with the questioning. The few times that McGarr had taken her along on an investigation—for cover mostly, she was sure—she'd noticed how he had seemed to survey everything first, his eyes roaming as though some crucial part of what he was seeking could be divined from the details of the scene.

But the shop was packed to the eaves with every class of thing from a wicker baby's pram to old, tin-pot soldier's helmets like her great-grandfather had worn when fighting for the British in the First War. She had seen one just like it at her mother's house outside Kenmare. Then there were crystal wine goblets and old silver and even gold plates in locked glass cabinets, frilly dresses and tuxedos and ball gowns on racks.

Distracted by an array of dated fountain pens, Bresnahan had actually stopped to study their thick barrels—they would be well suited to her large hand—when a curtain of beads across a door leading into the back of the shop suddenly parted and the head of what at first seemed like a chubby boy appeared. "Need help?" Her hair was close-cropped, her face small and full and sallow. On her arm was a small tattoo of a black cat with green eyes and an outstretched tongue.

"Not at the moment." As though surprised in the commission of a crime, Bresnahan flushed with guilt or shame; her heart pounded in her throat, and for all her size and authority, she felt like turning on her heels and fleeing out the open door into the sunlight. How could she go on? It was clear she wasn't cut out for this work.

"If you do, give us a shout," said Mary Sittonn—it could be nobody else—as the beads fell back into place. Before venturing out of the Castle, Bresnahan had memorized virtually everyone in the Kevin Coyle file. She would not be stopped for want of application, and she nearly sighed her relief that the woman had left her alone.

Carrying on with the pretense of browsing, she moved toward the voices that she could hear from that room.

". . . utterly brilliant. We'll make a bomb, so we will. There won't be a bookstore in the country with any left, and here we'll sit with a pile of them at five pounds added, which makes, let me see"—she heard the distinctive click of a computer keyboard, and then—"thirteen quid apiece makes fifty-two-hundred pounds, thank you very much indeed!"

Four hundred, Bresnahan thought. She had gotten a first on her leaving cert. in maths, and was nothing if not quick with figures. But four hundred what?

Another voice now said, "Well—Kevin wouldn't have objected."

"*Much*," said someone else in a soft, sibilant tone.

Books, Bresnahan concluded.

"And then with the eighty—how many?"

"Three," the soft voice answered.

"With eighty-three of the out-of-print volume . . ." Mary Sittonn then uttered what amounted to a mannish coo. "Where shall we go? Spain? Portugal? I hear the beaches in Greece don't have a man on them this time of year."

Said Catty Doyle, whom Bresnahan could now see through the beaded curtain, "Then I'm for Norway or Sweden, where the men are tall and blond and liberated."

"Like your man, David Holderness."

There was a pause before Catty Doyle replied, "Ach,

sure—he's just a boy. An enormously talented boy with a bright future in front of him, but still a boy."

Said Katie Coyle, "I wonder how bright it would have been had Kevin—"

Said Mary Sittonn, "Well—there was only one Kevin, wasn't there. For all his faults."

It was then she glanced up at the beaded doorway; Bresnahan again began to panic. She snapped open the tiny black plastic purse she was carrying, but her hand could locate nothing more in the foolish thing than the automatic pistol that she had had to force into its folds.

"May I help you?" Sittonn asked.

"Yes . . ." Still distracted by the purse and the riot of her emotions, which made her suddenly angry, she pushed through the beads and finally came up with the plastic template of her Garda I.D. "I'm Ban Gharda Bresnahan, Murder Squad, and I'm glad you're all together. Chief Superintendent McGarr has asked me to come 'round and speak with you. One at a time."

"Really now. Isn't that considerate of the Chief Superintendent to send us a *woman* from the Murder Squad. We misjudged him. He isn't the total shite we first thought him, after all. Would you care for a cuppa?" Sittonn asked. "Come, sit down and tell us about yourself. And let me inform you now, so you understand—you'll speak to all of us together or none of us at all. We've got no secrets from each other, and the basis of our sisterhood is honesty. Total and complete. In everything."

Bresnahan's head went back. She would not be toyed with, and she thought about what McGarr had told her—they, the three of them, had broken the law, and that was to be her lever. If worse came to worse, she would do what even McGarr did from time to time. She would haul them down to the Castle and to the clutches of Detective Sergeant McKeon, whom Bresnahan believed could have been a brilliant barrister, had his background been different—his tongue could be venomous. Absolutely lethal. And then there was some reason that they wished to be interviewed together, and Bresnahan wanted to know what it was.

The women made room for her, the tea was poured, and a long, painful silence ensued in which Bresnahan, with the burden of their eyes upon her, struggled to keep herself from initiating conversation. It was McGarr's technique to wait. What was it he had said? "Eventually people will tell you what you want to know, if you listen long and closely enough."

"So," Mary Sittonn finally said, "you're from Kerry? How long have you been with the Guards?"

Bresnahan could feel her face taking on further color. The blood was pounding in her temples, her forehead and upper lip suddenly damp. But far from anger, which required a bit of self-confidence, she was now stricken with embarrassment. How, from the little she had said, had Sittonn been able to tell she was from Kerry? Unfair dumb jokes about her countymen and women—the way they spoke, acted, and even thought—were a national passion among the uninformed and ignorant, and nowhere more than here in Dublin. She wondered if Sittonn were poking fun or simply inquiring to make conversation. Someday, soon, Bresnahan would learn the difference, and the subtle, city way in which that difference was communicated.

She managed a "Foive y'arr-es."

"Really! Not long to have been posted to the Murder

Squad. You'd think they'd have you out in some cow
town, hoofing it. It's what happens to most, I'm told.
You must be good at what you do, which is what, might
I ask?"

Raising her head to study the furrowed brow of the
woman's pudgy face, and then swinging her eyes to the
others, Bresnahan decided that Sittonn was indeed making fun. She knew that position well enough, and understood that there were only two ways to deal with it:
either to give back in kind, jibe for jibe, or to play
along, and become more the ignorant culchie than their
most comical expectations.

Again lowering her eyes to the purse that she was
balancing between her large hands, she admitted, "Typing and steno, mostly. I file some and answer the phone."

"No—don't tell us," said Sittonn. "And does he
make you fetch him his tea?"

Bresnahan sucked in some breath, making a sound
that in the country passed as a yes. "Coffee. Always."

"The bastard," said Catty Doyle.

"The prick," said Sittonn. "And his words—what
are they like? Does he treat you . . ."

"Coldly?" Bresnahan asked, when Sittonn did not
supply a word.

"Well, no. I didn't mean coldly exactly, but . . .
you know, patronizingly. Does he call you—what is
your first name?"

"Rut'ie."

"Ruthie or honey or sweetie, instead of Bresnahan?"

She pretended to think for a moment, "No—to be
fair, *he* doesn't. He always addresses me like he does
the others. Last name mostly, and short. He doesn't
waste words." Or mince them, she might have added.

"But *others* call you Rut'ie?"

Bresnahan, thinking of McKeon, whom she revered only a little less than McGarr, nodded.

"And do they make comments or touch you at all?"

Bresnahan raised her head quickly, so that they might understand that nobody ever put their hands on her without permission. "The former."

"The low-lifes. The scum," Sittonn hissed. "And to think sexists like that are charged with protecting society, over seventy percent of whom are women and children. Did you know that?"

Bresnahan pulled in a little more air, noisily, another way to say no. She widened her eyes. She shook her head.

"And yet it's men that run things and abuse us here in what should be by simple vote our own democracy. And them con-*sarned"*—Sittonn pronounced the word as it was spoken in Kerry—"solely with exploitation and the flesh."

"But hasn't it always been the way? Take Joyce, for instance. He was a typical Irish man." Sittonn waited.

"The writer?"

Sittonn nodded. "A phenomenal masculine egotist who, after twenty-seven years together and two children, condescended to marry a woman named Barnacle who could scarcely read or write. In her youth she was a lovely thing, it was told, with that unlikely combination of deep red hair and dark eyes. His father had said of her, 'Well—at least she'll stick to him.' And she did, through all his artistic and dypsomaniacal moods, waiting on him hand and foot.

"He revealed himself, though, for what he was. Of women he wrote, 'An animal that micturates once a day, defecates once a week, menstruates once a month, and parturates once a year.' He likened Dublin to a woman 'with her skirts raised, a whore and a strumpet.' He called Ireland, 'A sow that eats her own farrow.' "

Bresnahan saw her opening and, turning her head slightly, asked, "Was that your husband's opinion of women as well, Mrs. Coyle?"

Katie Coyle seemed surprised by the question. Slowly she turned dark eyes to Bresnahan. "Never voiced, but there was hardly a woman he knew he didn't bed, sooner or later. And indiscreet. Kevin was a kind of . . . intellectual playboy. An academic swordsman. It was his way of toying with women. A cat-and-mouse game."

"And he knew you, Ms. Doyle? And you, Ms. Sittonn?" Bresnahan went on in the same small voice.

Katie Doyle answered, "Catty, yes, which was acceptable to me. After nine children, I'd had enough of him, if you know what I mean. Mary was more fortunate. She doesn't fancy men."

Bresnahan glanced at the tattoo on Sittonn's shoulder. The tongue of the little cat was too long, and there was a nasty curl on its end. Bresnahan repressed a shudder and thought of how, back home in Kerry, she could shock her friends with the tale of how she had interviewed—no, had tea and a chat with—an avowed lesbian. But she wouldn't; she was beyond that now.

"And your opinion of Kevin Coyle?" she asked the thin and striking Catty Doyle.

"A brilliant and engaging wastrel, profligate of his talent, contemptuous of both body and mind. Often he reminded me of a drunken navvy who would've been better off equipped of a navvy's intelligence. Sober, he was afflicted by that brilliance. He was acerbic and trenchant, an utter bastard to anybody who dared challenge his views. Drunk, he was more the self that he should've been, and he seemed to know it."

"And was that the self he brought you on the night of his death?"

She swapped a glance with Katie Coyle. "*Attempted* to bring me. Yes, I should imagine."

"And had he, how would you have dealt with him?"

"Lovingly, had I not been otherwise engaged."

"With who, may I ask?"

"David Holderness."

Bresnahan's brow knitted. "I don't understand."

"I went out with Mary earlier in the evening, but I had arranged to have David stop by later."

"What time did he arrive?"

"Some time past midnight."

"How long did he stay?"

"All night, I believe. I mean, when I awoke, he was gone."

Bresnahan struggled to accept what she was hearing without divulging her disapproval: the woman had had relations with two persons not of the same sex on the same night, and one of them knew as much. And to look at her you'd think she was as pure as the driven snow. Her fine features suggested perfect innocence, which was probably the attraction—for Coyle and Holderness, and for Mary Sittonn as well. Bresnahan had read of such an attraction in the clinical psychology books that she boned up on at night.

"What time was that—that you woke up?"

"Half past eight. I remember because I had so much to do with the book-launching and the party and all. I let Kinch, my dog, out and dressed as quickly as I could.

When Kinch didn't come to call and I could hear him barking, I—but I told all of that to the Superintendent."

Again Bresnahan pulled in some breath to indicate she knew as much.

Said Mary Sittonn, "Not half bad for a country girl. First interview?"

"Alone," Bresnahan admitted.

"And they sent you down to us. Just what is it they told you they wanted to know?"

Bresnahan decided to continue the ruse. "What I've been asking, mainly. The usual stuff. You know—motive, means, and opportunity. For instance, where you were?"

"Me?"

Bresnahan nodded. "After you left Catty off."

"I dropped in on Katie."

"At her flat?"

"Of course. Katie has the responsibility of her children. After midnight she's at home."

Said Katie Coyle, "Surely they don't think we—"

"And Mary was with you how long?"

"All night, if you must know."

"You didn't leave each other's sight?"

As if distressed by the question, both looked away.

Bresnahan continued in the same even tone, "And why *exactly* did you think you could break the law, once Professor Coyle's corpse was found?"

There was a pause while Sittonn's eyes surveyed Bresnahan's reddish, freckled complexion and her large well-structured face. Although a pleasant-looking person, her appearance on first glance conveyed the impression of certain strength. Once, when she was a uniformed Guard in a country town, she had knocked a six-foot-three-inch farmer on his britches with one blow of her fist. It was a story that had circulated throughout the county. Since joining the Murder Squad, she had begun studying *kemp po,* a martial art taught by an official from the Chinese embassy.

Said Sittonn, "Well—it looks like you'll just have to disappoint them, won't you?"

Bresnahan turned to the other two.

Said Catty Doyle, "I phoned Katie first because Kevin was her husband, the father of her children, and plainly dead. After that, I thought it her decision. To phone you or not."

Bresnahan's gaze shifted to Katie Coyle. After a while she said, "Who in the name of hell are *you* that I should phone *you* when my husband dies? Who do *you* represent, or don't you know? You and that plastic shield of yours front for an agreement made sixty-some years ago by two factions of a gang of fighting men who raped, pillaged, and plundered the country and are now long dead. They made laws that allowed them and their bastard spawn to continue the practice *legally.*

"Ours"—she swept her hand to indicate the other women at the table—"is a more ancient and—I would have it—honorable, humane, and civilized code. It has to do with the positive values of growth, life, and pro-creation. With gentleness, understanding, trust, and love. Not exploitation, greed and fear, intimidation and punishment.

"Does it really matter *who* killed Kevin or *how* or *why?* Will knowing that bring him back or help his wife and family get on in the world? Or solace the bereaved? I think not."

Bresnahan waited to make sure the woman had spoken her piece, then said, "Answer me this—in this ancient, honorable, and civilized order of yours, is it wrong for one person to take another's life? You don't have to be a genius like Kevin Coyle, who would appreciate the point, I'm thinking. Nor the wife of a genius, like you, who obviously doesn't consider the way she's acted since his death. Everybody—even the lowliest of us—knows what's right or wrong, and if we don't, we don't deserve to belong in society. At least on a daily basis. We're not talking about gentleness, or trust, here. We're talking about *murder.* And murder violates everything. It's as wrong as you can get. And when it happens, society—even yours—should reserve the right to know who's responsible for the crime and why, if only to keep it from happening again."

Katie Coyle blinked.

It was nearly the exchange that Bresnahan had had with McGarr when he'd hired her. After questioning her point by point, he had told McKeon to dismiss the other applicants. "We've found our woman," he'd said, leaving the room. "Make sure she can fire a gun," which she could, and well. Her grandfather had been in the IRA and had helped found the Fianna Fail, one of the factions of the gang to which Katie Coyle had referred. In his eighty-sixth year he had taught her how to shoot.

"Now . . ." Opening her purse, Bresnahan pulled out her automatic pistol, which she placed on the table, and the three ballpoint pens and Garda forms that she had brought with her. "Since you believe otherwise, I'd like you to write that opinion on these pages along with the statement of where exactly you were, and with whom, on the night of June sixteenth and the morning of the following day."

The three women did not take their eyes from the

gun and its large plastic hand grip. It was a Glock .38, a light but powerful weapon that Bresnahan had purchased after consulting with McKeon, who knew of such things.

"And sign it, please. If you require more than one page, please initial the top of each sheet."

Still none of them moved. Said Catty Doyle, "I don't understand."

Bresnahan nodded. "Chief Superintendent McGarr has sent me here to obtain signed statements from each of you detailing explicitly where you were and with whom on Bloomsday night and the morning of the following day. He also wants you to state just why it was that you thought you could break the law and move Professor Coyle's corpse, to explain why you waited nearly three days before notifying the police.

"Now—is that too much to ask?" Bresnahan smiled— she hoped—wanly enough to let them understand that, though a large, country girl from Kerry, she was most definitely competent and controlled. She had even managed to make her voice sound professional. "I should imagine here is more convenient than the Castle, it being so hot."

Sittonn let out a little cry of pique. "What balls!"

Yes—*what*, Bresnahan thought, pushing back the chair and raising herself up. Since first sitting down at the table, she had been seeing in the shadows of the next room several bulky items that seemed out of place in an antique shop.

"Where're you going?" Sittonn demanded.

"Just stretchin' me legs. How're you coming with that?" With her palm Bresnahan slid a sheet of paper in front of Sittonn. She handed her a pen. Then, with both hands, she lifted and situated the woman at the table in a position best meant for writing. "Square around there. That's it. Now pen to paper and let fly, but only the truth. As you see it."

"You bitch."

"Me? And there all along I thought you were my *sister*." She moved toward the storeroom.

A head swung to her. "You need a court order to go in there."

"Why get technical—didn't you invite me to tea?" Jasus, she thought, I actually *like* what I'm doing, and she even wished that McGarr or McKeon or even that little smoothie Ward were there to see her *in action*. Well, little wasn't quite the word. Yes, he was smallish, but he was also strong—there was no mistaking that— and he had the class of body that she had more than once imagined herself smothering in a profound and passionately loving embrace.

Really?

Standing in the doorway, Bresnahan in one instant stumbled on two entirely disparate and disturbing facts. First she understood, with an immediacy that made her weak, that she was hopelessly in love with a terrible, adorable—*worshipable*, even—little shite who *dated* (most probably an entirely inadequate description) every class of gorgeous woman in multiple, from all that she could know.

And two, she was looking at a storeroom filled with plastic-bound parcels of books. She moved closer and examined the covers. *Phon/Antiphon*, by Kevin Coyle. On a shelf under glass were—she raised a finger to count them—eighty-three copies of the earlier book.

Turning back to the doorway, Bresnahan nearly staggered. In front of her was the most entrancing vision that could ever appear.

She saw long, glorious nights of erotic *love*-making—clutches, embraces, positions, *orgasms* of which she had only had one complete on her own. Complete was also not the word, she had the suspicion. And then a happy, devoted, totally involved domestic life with a man who could—*would*—be McGarr's successor, and her a kind of bigger, better, perhaps-not-more-beautiful-but-more-official Noreen, given the fact that she was a trained professional.

Could she live with that, playing second fiddle to a man? She sighed. No, she had never been content to be second in anything. But did it need to be *second* fiddle? No, again. They could be equals in everything, even police work, if Hughie dark-little-handsome-darling Ward could adjust to that, and she would see that he did.

But then in the doorway Ruth Honora Ann Bresnahan despaired. How could she ever make that lovely, exploitative, trendy little bastard, who was most probably the shallowest human being that had ever trod a footpath, love her, when foxy chicks (she loathed the phrase) were drooling over his every move?

She remembered the little mole—like a period *in a sentence*—that dotted his right eyelid when he blinked or closed his eyes (usually in pique over something she had said or done), and again she was consumed—destroyed—by her original vision.

Yes, she was hopelessly, irredeemably, catastrophically in love, and with the bravado of a high diver she cast herself upon the winds of Eros, which she believed

she had visited on holiday in Greece. Though she could
be mistaken about that as well.

In any case, she stopped in the doorway. "Sisters—
how go the narratives?"

Sourly, three heads nodded at her.

11

D avid Holderness, erstwhile research student at Trinity, lived in a battered Victorian pile on the sea front in Bray, a tatty, former resort town twelve miles south of Dublin. The house had not been painted in many years, and its stucco was crumbling in the salt air. Whole sheets of exterior dashing had fallen, like scales, from the upper stories, and every window of the west side had been boarded up.

It was just five o'clock, and, although the wide road along the seaside esplanade was crowded, McGarr decided he would not park in front of the house. He was alone, Sinclaire having called for a car and accompanied Fergus Flood to the Castle, and he did not want any repetition of the earlier incident in Flood's house.

That the daughter had managed to abscond in the Fiat 500—which had obviously been used to transport Kevin Coyle to the scene of his murder and had had what McGarr supposed was the murder weapon under the driver's seat—still smarted. It had been a major blunder, albeit abetted by Flood, and he only hoped that it was one Sinclaire had managed to conceal.

And then, McGarr was thoroughly tired of the unusualness of the case, with its triad of prima donnas who had arrogated the law unto themselves, with Flood and his wife—who were either lying or not telling all of what they knew—with the daughter who for some reason believed she should run off with what was presumably the murder weapon, with the clique and its literary pretensions.

Luck was with him, and, finding a safe parking place for the Mini-Cooper along a side street, he approached the building from the laneway, if only to understand more completely the totality of David Holderness's abjection. The house was a wreck. The wooden-frame garage in back had tumbled into the garden, itself a tangle of wild rose bushes and rampant ivy.

And there, under a spray of wisteria vines that had grown into a kind of tunnel, was parked the *Cinque Cento*, its rear-engine compartment still hot. Under the front seat the knife remained, untouched; it was as he had left it, the blood on the handle shiny. Which meant what? That the daughter, Hiliary, either did not know it was there or was waiting for some future opportunity to dispose of it.

And Holderness? Well—other than his name and the report that he had had professional difficulties with Kevin Coyle, McGarr knew nothing of him. Except that he now appeared to be an acquaintance of Hiliary Flood.

Easing the door closed and stepping toward the front of the car, McGarr bent to a tire and screwed off the valve cap. With a thumbnail he let the air out of the tire until it was flat. He doubted Flood would have equipped the car with a pressurized tin of air or that the daughter would know how to use one, but to make sure, he flattened a rear tire as well.

Straightening up, he noticed a path leading through the wisteria and ivy toward the back door; it was open, and he moved toward it.

The interior of the house was cool and damp, the walls white with mildew and cobwebs. He was on the side of the house that had been boarded up, and the kitchen and sitting room he passed through bore signs of having been squatted in and trashed. The sink had been ripped from the wall, and a couch appeared to have been set partially on fire.

Sometime in the past the house had been made into a duplex, and a door with a simple catch bolt led into the stairwell. McGarr assumed that somebody either had let Hiliary Flood into the house or that she herself possessed a key. With the length of flattened spring steel that he kept attached to his key ring, he slid back the catch of the lock and stepped into what was evidently Holderness's half of the house.

The stairwell was a revelation. It was painted a blistering white and rendered all the more severe by a fanlight over the front door. The staircase had been stripped to the wood, a clear varnish applied to bring up the grain. The gracefully curved hand rail and balusters were oak and blond, the stairs a dark, reddish wood, probably mahogany, nearly slick under McGarr's feet.

He kept close to the wall, looking up toward the landing as he ascended—slowly, a step every fifteen seconds. He counted silently, until he heard voices or at least sounds coming from a room at the front of the house. He then moved quickly into the first open door he found.

It was a kitchen that was as forbidding and sterile as the stairwell. The walls were the same stark white; in the center of the room stood a table fashioned in plastic or—was it?—enamel, in a modern design that only emphasized its severity. It was too tall and too straight, as were its chairs.

Otherwise the room contained a single gas ring, a small fridge, and a cutting board on a spare wood counter that had been painted black. Nowhere were any foodstuffs or implements visible; McGarr found not a single can or bottle nor any sign of a bread box, a pot, or a pan. He opened the drawer beneath the cutting board: two knives, two forks, two spoons, all with handles of black enamel, like the table.

McGarr moved back into the hall, into a kind of sitting room. The floor was the same mahogany color as the stairs; here and there sat heaps of formless, black material that looked like bean-bag chairs but were filled with feathers. McGarr bent to feel one. There was nothing else in the room—no tables or vases or ashtrays—apart from factory lamps that exposed bare, clear light bulbs under black enamel shades. They were suspended from the tall ceiling on thin black electrical wires.

In the next room books lined all four walls, floor to ceiling. In the center of the floor, under the room's only light, was a solitary chair that matched those in the kitchen.

McGarr approached the door from which he had first heard the sounds; they were continuing, growing louder now as he brought his ear to the door.

He heard what sounded like a moan and then, "Can't we please go to the bed?"

"No. It's here or nowhere."

"But it's no good for me here." In the same breath, however, came a moan, and McGarr threw open the door.

There on a chair in the center of the room was a young woman in curly black tresses and nothing else. Her back was to him. Her feet were on the floor, and she was obviously sitting on a man who was also naked. When the door struck its stop, his head appeared around her shoulder, and his hands, which were clutching the pale, taut, and obviously young skin of her buttocks, kept her from pulling away from him. She tried to turn her head, but he prevented that motion too.

Her captor was a man with a long face, wire-rim glasses, and thinning blondish hair that had been clipped so close to his skull that he looked nearly bald. He was older by much than the woman, who McGarr assumed was Hiliary Flood.

"Yes?" he asked. Not who are you? Or, what are you doing here? Or even, how dare you?

"Peter McGarr. Murder Squad. If you're David Holderness, I'd like to speak to you. If the"—McGarr had to force himself to say—"woman on your lap is Hiliary Flood, she should know that she's under arrest for hindering a murder investigation." His eyes swept the room: two plain windows without curtains on the second story. He could not see a fire escape; there was little chance that she or he could flee.

And yet when the girl tried to move, she was restrained again, with one hand locking her wrist and forcing her back down.

"Jesus! Let me go." She began to sob. "David, you bastard. Let me go."

McGarr opened his jacket to expose the butt of the Walther that was stuck in his belt. He turned his back and stepped down the hall.

Holderness appeared first, wearing the skimpiest of

briefs, black, like the furniture. He was a tall man with a trim, athletic build. His shoulders were wide, his hips narrow, the muscles of his legs taut, like those of a runner. The hair on his chest was graying, and he was deeply tanned. Unself-consciously he moved past McGarr and entered the sitting room. He reclined in one of the feather futons and looked up, his eyes fixing McGarr's.

Said Hiliary Flood from the room that McGarr supposed was the bedroom, though he had seen no bed, "But my clothes—they're in the pantry."

McGarr turned to Holderness, who did not move.

"David!" she pleaded.

Still he didn't move, nor did McGarr, who cared little for the situation: the curious, sterile ambiance of the house, which was such a shambles externally; the man who seemed to have been content to be interviewed *en flagrante*. And he would tolerate no more mistakes in the case.

She appeared in the doorway, her head down and her hands clasped in front of her so that her breasts, which were substantial and firm, were pushed together. She was tall, with an angular build and classic proportions. She had her mother's definite features but her father's coloring, which was dark. There was a crispness to her step that made the flesh on the flare of her hips tremble.

As the door opened into a pantry, McGarr caught sight of a blouse and brassiere on a countertop, a pair of tennis shorts on the floor, and briefs that looked either to have been hung on a knob of a cabinet or to have snagged there in the heat of the moment. Reaching for them, a breast and nipple were silhouetted against the glare of a window.

Holderness's gaze, to which McGarr now returned, seemed to ask, Wouldn't you like some of that, old man? Or, rather, they *said,* You'll never have some of that, old man.

Yet McGarr said nothing until Hiliary had dressed and seated herself in the sitting room on a futon rather far from Holderness. She folded her legs under her, lowered her head and looked down at her hands. Only then did he say, "Well, so much for introductions."

"Really?" asked Holderness. "Have we been introduced? As far as I'm concerned, you broke and entered. Have you shown us identification? Have you a writ to be here?"

McGarr flashed his photo I.D. "Want a closer look?" He flicked his fingers to let the man know he would have to come to him. Making others cater to you was a game McGarr didn't much fancy, but was good at all the same. "As for the writ or the B and E, you were sheltering a criminal in flight, Mr. Holderness, which makes you a criminal yourself."

"Are you charging me with a crime?"

"That remains to be seen."

"Are you charging Hiliary with a crime?"

The young woman's head bobbed up.

"That depends on how helpful she is." McGarr turned to her. "Bloomsday evening, you were . . .?"

She paused, shrugged. "Out, I guess."

McGarr asked himself how much of his life he had spent waiting and listening, and wondered if one of the secrets of a successful life was perhaps doing nothing well.

Hiliary forked her fingers through her black tresses. It was a gesture that cinema stars employed, and seemed entirely appropriate. McGarr could not keep himself from seeing her as he first had, and then later, as she had walked by him.

Finally she spoke. "I went to a film."

"What did you see?"

She named a movie that McGarr knew to be playing in the Dublin area.

"And afterward?"

"I went for a drink."

"Where."

"I prefer not to say." Her eyes shied toward Holderness.

"Were you with Mr. Holderness?"

Holderness smirked.

She averted her eyes and shook her head. "I was alone."

"At the movies?"

She nodded.

"And for the drink?"

Again, which McGarr found hard to believe, for a woman of her age and beauty. "You find it humorous that I should ask if she was with you?" he asked Holderness.

The corners of his mouth rose in what approximated a smile. "She was most probably *looking* for me. It's a family trait—prowling."

Tears had formed in Hiliary Flood's eyes. "Why— Why do I always let you victimize me?"

Holderness tsked. "Sloppy thinking again? How many times must I tell you that there *are* no victims."

"Then Kevin Coyle was a what, Mr. Holderness?" McGarr asked.

"A human being, minimally defined."

"David! You may not have cared for him or he you, but it's academically dishonest to deny his brilliance, which is just another instance of your—" Her eyes darted at McGarr.

"His what, Miss Flood?"

"His jealousy of Kevin, if you must know. It was"— she cupped a hand—"pathological."

Holderness only maintained the wan smile.

McGarr waited until it appeared that neither had anything else to say. "But Kevin Coyle . . ." he said to Holderness. "His murder. That made him a . . . ?"

Holderness's eyes were clear and very blue. "A dead man."

"And nothing else."

"Not a thing."

"His death was no different from, say, natural causes?"

"Dead's dead."

"Who murdered him, then?"

A shoulder moved. "Isn't that your department?"

"It's the Beckett drivel again," Hiliary Flood explained to McGarr. "You know, sometimes you're a *boring* bastard, David. And so derivative. I wonder if you've ever had an original idea."

"And at other times?"

"Beckett?" McGarr asked.

"*Samuel* Beckett," Holderness said condescendingly. "Perhaps you've heard of him. Novelist, dramatist, man of letters. Won the Nobel Prize a few years ago."

Books again, McGarr thought, and he turned back to Hiliary Flood. "That night, while you were"—he dismissed the word prowling—"searching for Mr. Holderness . . ." He waited for her to deny that, but she only looked away. "Where exactly did you go?"

"His haunts. The Bailey, Keogh's. When he wasn't there, I went out to Drumcondra—"

"To the inn?"

She nodded, "The man who owns the place is a literary sycophant.

"I object to that. Rex Cathcart is—"

"Another crashing bore who can scarcely distinguish between an artist, like Kevin was, and a mere would-be academic, like you, who—"

"And he made a room available to you?" McGarr cut in.

"A gracious man. And a gentle person." A slight smile again curled the corners of Holderness's mouth. "And if Hiliary were herself honest, she'd admit to singing Cathcart's praises, however indirectly. I have in mind everything from moues of carnal pleasure to outright screams of orgasmic delight."

McGarr waited for a response, but the young woman only lowered her head so that her long tresses obscured her face. "Then you drove to the hotel in Drumcondra?"

She nodded.

"In the Fiat Five hundred?"

Again.

"Mr. Holderness was not there?"

"I don't know. By that time it was last call. He wasn't in the bar or any of the public rooms. Cathcart bought me a drink in what I thought was a kind of holding action, and I waited for another half hour or so until the barmen got the others out. And then I left."

"In the Fiat Five hundred?"

She looked away and seemed to come to a decision before answering. "No. When I got outside, it was gone. I assumed the police had taken it, since I had

parked it"—her eyes flickered toward McGarr—"ille-
gally, right there on the Swords Road in front of the
hotel. There's always a taxi around there at that time
of night, and I took one home."

McGarr thought for a moment. Fergus Flood, her
father, had admitted venturing out in search of his wife.
Could he have looked for her at the Drumcondra Inn?
He had not mentioned the hotel specifically. "Did you
see your father at the Drumcondra Inn?"

She did not seem surprised by the question. She
shook her head.

"Or your mother?"

She lowered her head. "No."

"Was the car there when you got home? The Fiat."

Nor that question either. "No, it wasn't."

"You looked for it."

She nodded.

"You thought your father might have fetched it."

"He understands nothing about women. He can be
such a bore."

Thought McGarr: nothing boring about knowing that
both your wife and teenage daughter are frequenting
the same hotel for much the same purpose. He wondered if mother and daughter had ever run into each
other, if they shared "intimacies," as it were. "And the
next morning?"

Again she tried to avoid McGarr's eyes.

"It was there."

McGarr turned to Holderness. "And you? Where
were you then? After midnight."

"I was . . . engaged, I must admit."

The girl's head rose to Holderness.

McGarr waited.

The smile was still on the man's face, but behind the silvery surface of his glasses his eyes glittered with what seemed like playful malice.

"With whom?"

His head turned to Hiliary Flood. "Catty Doyle."

"*Engaged?*"

Holderness actually laughed. "Surely you don't mean me to answer that, sir. In present company."

"The venue," said McGarr, but the derision in his voice was lost on Holderness and the girl, who were still staring at each other.

"Her place."

"In De Courcy Square?" Near the Prospect cemetery, where Kevin Coyle's corpse was discovered, he did not add. "What hours? When until when?"

"Well, I'm presently completing a book, and I worked on that until eleven or so. Since I don't drink—though I understand some do—I decided that on that of all nights it was best to leave here, rather than find myself beset by humors and demands that I judged I'd find distressing. In the particular."

But not as particularly dispensed by Catty Doyle, one could only conclude.

"You got there?"

"Say, midnight or thereabouts."

"And you found Catty home."

"As arranged."

"And you remained."

"Until my interest flagged."

"Which was?"

"In a matter of the heart, Mr. McGarr, I heed no clock. Say, four or five. Catty was—how shall I put it—insistent that I stay, but one needs his sleep."

"And by what door did you leave?"

"Does it matter? The front, of course. Ms. Sittonn may be a large and truculent woman, but she is most definitely a woman. I fear her not."

"And you suspected that she might be waiting outside?"

"As I said, in spite of her appearance, she's a woman."

"Which means?"

"In this setting"—the smile grew somewhat fuller and the glasses flashed—"a kind of huntress, wouldn't you say?"

Considering mother and daughter Flood, Mary Sittonn, and perhaps even Catty Doyle, McGarr could hardly disagree. Of course, a case could be made that Fergus Flood, Kevin Coyle, and Holderness himself had been on the prowl as well, but McGarr found Holderness's characterization of women unusual and interesting, especially in regard to what he had said earlier about there being no victims. "And you therefore are the hunted?"

"As luck sometimes has it."

"By which you mean their willing victim."

"Now *that* I didn't say. I mean the hunt in the sense of a search: one person for another who might through some imperfect means of communication, confirm her existence."

McGarr assumed they were getting back to Beckett again. He summoned up from his uncooperative memory the plays that Noreen had dragged him to. "Then there're two persons in a relationship?"

"I would think there would have to be."

"One dominant—"

"The observed," Holderness cut in.

"—and the other—"

"The observer."

"But isn't it more aggressive than that? I'm thinking of the characters in *Waiting for Godot.* One had a whip and a gun, I seem to remember, and kept the other in traces."

"Theatrics," said Holderness. "Mere posturing. One could make a case for Lucky enjoying the better— because less angst-ridden—part of the bargain. And later in his novels, Beckett refines that position. To know Beckett one must, in particular, read his novels."

The "novels of incompetence"? Not likely. The term was still sitting in McGarr's mind like a kind of— how had Flood explained it?—black hole. He hadn't caught word one of what Flood had said.

He stood. "Where's your phone?"

"Out in the hall."

As McGarr dialed his Castle office and waited, he heard Hiliary Flood say, "Catty Doyle—how could you, David? She is so . . . used."

"As well she should be. Another point to consider is that we need each other. She's my editor and col- laborator."

"As she was Kevin's. In his turn," the girl said tearfully. "You should mind yourself."

McGarr explained the situation to McKeon and asked him to send several somebodies out to pick up Hold- erness and Hiliary Flood, the Tech Squad for the Fiat 500 and what he supposed was the murder weapon.

"For sure, this time?"

"What d'ya mean, *this* time?"

"The car. The murder weapon. We're only after having phoned them and—"

"Not us," said McGarr, and when McKeon objected,

he repeated the advisory. "Must have been a mix-up. Theirs."

"What is this—disinformation?

McGarr wished it were that simple. "Anything from anybody else?" He meant his staff.

"Not a peep, but it's only half-four."

And nearly seven by the time McGarr got back to his house in Belgrave Square. There he found Noreen in his study, in his favorite chair, reading *Phon/Antiphon* by Kevin Coyle.

"So?" he asked.

"It's really quite good. And different. It's as though he pretends to be Joyce—critic, scholar, writer, practicing pedant, rampant genius—examining what was written in his time and since. Defending his reputation, so to speak. He's utterly scathing on the modernists."

"Like Samuel Beckett and the 'novel of incompetence'?"

Noreen lowered the book. "You've read it?"

"The 'novel of incompetence' or Samuel Beckett?"

"They're one in the same. No, this." She shook the volume at him.

"Oh, sure. Between meetings and interviews I gave it a peek. I found it revealing, like a still point in a turning circle."

"That's Eliot, but it reminds me. You're to call Bernie. Hughie Ward got mugged or something and'll be off the Coyle case for a while."

McGarr made straight for the telephone in the kitchen. "Is he all right?"

"Bernie said something about his refusing to enter the hospital, so I suppose—"

Said McKeon when he answered the phone, "Sure, some little gurrier. A punk with Joyce's hat on his head, the one Coyle was wearing, and the ashplant stick in his hands. Whipped around without warning and smacked him. His wrist is broke, and there's some question about the hearing in his left ear, but he refused a bed. Said he couldn't find the fecker and murder him in hospital. I ordered him off the case and put him on sick leave. He lost his weapon, though, the Beretta. I thought it best to wait before putting out the word."

McGarr thought about their earlier blunder. Now this. No—he would not be made fun of twice in one day. It was a chance he was taking, but they would recover the weapon and the punk who took it themselves.

"We'll wait."

"I thought you'd say that. I've put everybody available on it. Liam called just to check in, and he'll be returning from Galway sometime tonight." He meant Detective Superintendent O'Shaughnessy, who was McGarr's second-in-command and as knowledgeable about Dublin and its netherworld as any tout or lout.

McKeon then reported what Bresnahan had discovered: the roomful of Kevin Coyle volumes that she had come upon in Mary Sittonn's Coombe antique shop.

"But murder for a couple hundred quid?"

"Try a thousand, and we've seen it for a fiver. And them three with their bent and all."

"And you don't know the half of it." McGarr told McKeon about the Bloomsday evening adventures of David Holderness and the family Flood: "Mother got a call from Coyle, her hubby's colleague, to meet her at the Drumcondra Inn, where Rex Cathcart—do you know him . . .?"

"Aye—a fop, a toper, a blithering ejit when in his cups, and an innocent man."

McGarr waited.

Said McKeon, "Not three of the two-dozen swivers who frequent his bordello pay him more than lip service. With Rex a soft word carries far."

"David Holderness was also on his cuff, and, although Flood's wife never got there, the daughter, Hiliary, washed up around closing. In the Fiat."

"Puddin' proof of adultery as a family tradition."

"Daughter claims she had a drink in the bar with Carthcart in what she believed was a 'holding action.' And when she got back outside, the Fiat was gone. She says she took a taxi back to Foxrock, which we should check on. Next morning the Fiat was back in the garage, today with what I think is the murder weapon under the seat. No forced entry. No sign of having been tampered with."

"How times change. What thief from the old school would ever have thought of returning a car to its garage unscathed. And the care the driver must have taken, jockeying the thing between pillar and post out near the Glasnevin Cemetery. No harm, no foul. And more to the point, no police report."

"But Holderness was out there too."

"In Glasnevin?"

"More particularly, in Catty Doyle's house."

"Near Bingo Terrace? What hours? Mary Sittonn in her steamy statement right here in me hot little hand claims to have been cuddling Catty at least until midnight."

McGarr's head went back. "Two dates, one night?"

"Well—at least a frig and a date."

"Holderness says he left around four or five."

"The wee-wee hours, but light by then."

"Have we canvassed everybody in the neighborhood?

"All but a young couple who left that morning on holiday. Who knows, they might have risen early for a jump on the highway."

"Am I hearing right?"

"It wasn't clear where they were headed, but we'll put a man on them. You know what they say about three."

McGarr waited.

"Butter then chew."

"Which is one way to *manage*—it's French—a twat."

McKeon hung up.

Before taking the phone from his ear, McGarr heard a second click, and before he could reach the fridge and its icy contents, Noreen appeared in the kitchen doorway.

"What language was that?"

"Pol-leesh."

"Then I'll trouble you for a preprandial translation."

There was the light threat of no dinner in that. Before raising the can of lager to his lips, McGarr turned and noticed for the first time what his wife was wearing: a filmy, lacy dressing gown just the turquoise color of her eyes. "Here or there?"

"There, of course, where we can press on with our project." She turned, the silk whistling as she moved down the hall.

McGarr imagined that *Ulysses* would have to wait yet another night for his "professional" opinion, but he vowed that he would get to it soon. It was beginning to irk him that so much of what seemed increasingly important in the Coyle case came cloaked in literary obscurity. Could the whole world be divided into those who had read and understood *Ulysses,* the rest of Joyce, the *novels* of Sam Beckett, and the works of Kevin Coyle, and those other poor benighted, inconsiderable groundlings who did not?

McGarr raised the can and drained it, then reached for another. For the courage to be still without *Ulysses.* And without child.

PART THREE

12

Bresnahan's heart was in her mouth. Never, not for her leaving certification or Garda exams, even for her interviews for the Squad, had she felt so nervous and discombobulated and just generally . . . sick. That was it. She was so destroyed over the miserable little shite who probably never gave her a passing thought, or worse, hated who she was and what she stood for—herself, mostly, up until now—that, pausing before the ancient, battered, quayside building in which Ward kept his digs, she actually felt nauseous.

How in the name of St. Peter, to whom she prayed every night for strength, had she allowed it to happen? And just when she'd been availed the opportunity of proving herself, and had come back with exactly what the Chief had wanted. McKeon had said, "Well—not half bad, Rut'ie. Your report of the interview in particular; how you led them on with the cute little culchie bit. Mind, it won't work around here." He had pointed to a stack of correspondence, but it was the first kind word she had ever heard from the sergeant, whom she regarded as the second hardest man in the universe.

But when she heard in his next breath what had happened to Ward, she despaired. It was as if the floor had sundered to expose a great, yawning gulf down which she could see the young, dark, darling detective—

yuppy though he might be—falling; it threatened to
consume her as well. "But how?" she asked. Wasn't
he a former boxing champ? And the way he carried
himself was like—well, like a dancer or, rather, a boxer,
his square and well-muscled shoulders swaying, his legs
always seeming to be set to give or receive a blow, his
expression not cocky but quietly confident.

"Got careless, I should imagine. Won't happen again,
I'd hazard. Not to Hughie. But we can only hope—
about the ear. The wrist? That'll mend, like his pride.
But right now he's one sorry soldier." McKeon had
picked him up at hospital and brought the hurting detective back to his flat.

And leaving her in one rush, her sympathy—all eleven
stone of it—went out to him, and she knew what she
had to do.

But the stairs of the building were so old they felt
spongy under her step, and the door, when she knocked,
roared like a drum. She heard what sounded like somebody falling and then Ward's voice asking, "Who is it?"

How to reply to that? Ban Gharda Bresnahan? Ruth
Bresnahan? Or "Bresnahan," which she shouted, sure
it was how the others referred to her, and then was
seized with immediate panic. What could she have been
thinking about, coming out here when he was ill? It
was the worst possible time, and surely not the way to
go about making him aware of her as something more
than a competitor or some poor, pitiable lump of pink
flesh, which was probably more in line with his thinking.
She caught sight of her reflection in the glass door—of
her broad shoulders and her jaw, which was definite;
of the oval of her long face, her surplus of bosom—and
she nearly turned and fled.

But the door opened then, and there was Ward, still wearing the shirt and tie he'd had on that morning, but with the collar and shoulder stained by what she guessed was blood. The side of his head was so swollen that his eye was nearly closed and the ear huge and unsightly. He was obviously having trouble focusing, and he raised his only good hand to block the light from the puffy eye. The other was in a cast held in place by a sling. "Yes?"

"I've come to see how you are?"

"Bernie send you?"

"No, I came on my own."

Silently he turned away, and in stepping back into the shadows, his step faltered and his knee seemed to collapse and suddenly he was down, rolling agilely nevertheless to spare the wrist. Then he was on his back, looking up at her. "Christ."

Bresnahan closed the door and reached for the good arm, raised toward her. "You're a bit dizzy, I suspect."

"I hope."

"What's that supposed to mean?" She was surprised at both the strength in his small forearm and how readily she pulled him to his feet, and she imagined with what ease she might toss him around a bit. She blushed at the thought.

"That my balance—" was all he managed before he began going down again.

"Well, didn't they test you for that in the hospital?" She wrapped a hand around his waist and buoyed him on her strong hip, her fingers curling about the tight muscles on his side. There wasn't an ounce of fat on him, she bet.

"Not for a few days. The trauma—"

"I'll say. And where's the bed?" She nearly gasped at having said that so easily. She wondered what was happening to her. What about her upbringing, her past? Could she could forget it all in such a short time?

With his good arm he pointed down the long room that had evidently once served as some type of factory facility; she moved him in that direction. The bed turned out to be an enormous round affair heaped in pillows and soft, downy comforters, and she wondered what extravagances of the flesh had occurred on its shiny surface that looked like gray, steely silk.

She released Ward slowly, but once out of her grasp he fell roughly back and tried to scrabble some pillows under his head. Only after she had helped him arrange them did she look around.

It was brilliant, really, what he had done with the place: dividers and screens, some made of hand-painted, translucent, Japanese-looking textiles, had been placed here and there to section off rooms. One was a kitchen, another a type of study, and there, as in a Victorian tea room, were an Oriental rug and two wing-back chairs, a long, bolstered sofa, a tea wagon and table, even an ornate brass samovar buffed to a sheen.

Bresnahan turned back to Ward with even greater affection and concern, if such was possible. She could see herself forsaking everything she had ever known and living here with an abandon that made her head spin just to think of it.

"Well, we must get you comfortable first," she heard herself saying. "And then—a little tea and something to eat." And then the goods should be examined. Her own mother had taught her that, forgive her the thought.

Shoes came first. And first quality too. She couldn't conceive how he managed it.

"No—I can do that."

"Sure, but me the more easily. Rest your head. Relax. Do you know I studied nursing?" It was a lie, but she wondered how many unsuspecting girls he himself had lied to and debauched on that silken plane. Agreeably, she was convinced with no need of proof.

"Years and years. Whole decades out in Kerry while waiting me higher calling of undressing Inspector Ward." Did she see him smile? She thought she did, while she tugged at the knot of his tie.

"Really—" he again complained, but he had raised his arms, and she had it off.

Next came the buttons on his shirt. "Do you think they did it?"

"Who?"

The hair on his tanned chest was thick and tinged with blond. The muscles of his pectorals were firm, his stomach was ridged with muscles. "Them punks. The ones who—" She thought it best not to risk an unacceptable term.

"How else did they get the hat? And the stick," he added after a while. His brow furrowed.

"But why?" Sliding one hand across his stomach, under the shirt, and then around him onto the small of his back, Bresnahan raised him; with the other hand she pulled the material up toward his shoulders. Drawing in a full chestful of the scent of his cologne or aftershave, something spicy or tangy, she let her breath out slowly and asked—no, begged—God in His mercy to aid her.

"For Coyle's money, whatever he had. The hat, the blazer, the stick." Again the pained expression. "For the hell of it, who knows? The bastards."

"Amen." Unlinking each cuff, she worked the now

ruined shirt off his shoulders and arms and again was pleased and somewhat frightened at how perfect was the confirmation of his muscles. She wondered how she had missed seeing him knock all those other men flat, which she would have enjoyed immensely. She would commence following sport, so she would, and view every boxing match she could. The telly, *live*. Jesus, Mary, and Joseph, what was happening to her? It was as though she had been seized by everything about her that was *animal*.

"But how would that account for the murder weapon being found under the seat of Professor Flood's wife's Fiat Five Hundred?" she asked. She could read in Ward's expression that he did not yet know about the discovery, and as she explained, she tugged at his belt, his hands falling to her wrists.

"Don't."

"Why not? I'm a nurse, remember?"

He seemed to think for a moment, then loosened his grip.

"You might think I was trying to take advantage of you," she observed before continuing her account. Boxer shorts. She knew she would find them, but not the very same taupe-cocoa color of his shirt. The smoothie.

And thighs; to raise himself up he had to push off on the bed, and they flexed like two powerful engines. She then turned and arranged the pleats of the trousers and looked for a closet to hang the shirt and jacket. "Or do you want me to take these 'round to a cleaners."

There was a pause, and then, "Would you, Rut'ie?"

She liked that Rut'ie. That Rut'ie was very nice indeed, and if that was all that came of her efforts, she would be happy.

And then she had seen enough, she had. Jesus, no wonder the women went mad over the little tyke. He was built like a miniature statue of some gladiator, he was a little Adonis, that was it. Or Pan.

"Now then"—she turned back to pull a coverlet over him—"how about some nice hot tea and a cold cloth for your forehead?"

"Ah, no. Really. You've been great. I can't thank you enough."

But by then Bresnahan had reached the kitchen area with its butcher-block table, restaurant-quality cooker, an immense stainless-steel fridge and freezer, its blessed microwave oven. Could he be on the take? she wondered. Or did his parents have money? "And a bite of something to eat, just to get your strength back." Oysters, she thought.

"Well," said Ward, "maybe I could take something."

And Bresnahan, opening the door of the fridge, was astounded by what she found. Some bachelor digs: every shelf was packed with interesting stuff (how would she ever keep her figure, which she mortified herself to contain, in such a place?), an entire selection of cheeses, a glass box of fresh vegetables and a second one of fruit, a plate of salmon steaks. An entire shelf was lined with nothing but bottles of white wine. Had he been expecting somebody? Of course. She had known about that from the start, which was something she'd have to put out of her mind. He was a bounder, a womanizer, a roué, and more, *only because* he hadn't as yet met the right woman. Or, rather, been convinced of the right—"Some fish?" she asked.

"Oh—the salmon. I nearly forgot. Well—it'd be a pity to let it spoil. And the parsley-boiled potatoes.

You'll find them in a plastic container all ready to go. The lettuce—"

"I see the lettuce."

"The lemons are in the bin. For the salmon."

"I see them."

"Salad dressings—"

"I see those too. I'd offer you wine, but you're probably on medication."

There was a pause, and then, "Well—I don't think a little would kill me."

Nor would a smash in the head with an ashplant stick, thought Bresnahan, carrying in a bowl of cold water and a washcloth she had discovered in the bath. The entire room—tile floors, tile walls, and dashed ceiling—were black. She wondered if, with his experience, he might have a social disease. Sitting beside him on the bed to cut his fish, she decided she didn't care. Obviously he was a man who took pains to mind himself and everything he owned. He wouldn't go out with just anybody.

After washing up and before leaving, she pulled her Glock from her purse. "I'll be back to see how you're mending, but in the nonce you might feel better with this." She placed the large, gray-green handgun in his lap. "Rough country, this," She meant quayside Dublin. "You never know who might be coming through that door."

Turning his head so he could see her with his one good eye, he asked, "But what about you?"

"I have another."

"Really? Do you collect guns?"

"No. I collect tools."

Ward reached her his hand. "Thanks." His grip

was as firm as hers, and it lingered. "You're a gem. Really. I don't know how to thank you, Rut'ie."

Bresnahan had an astounding idea, though it could wait.

There was no morning meeting.

Before McGarr left his house in Rathmines, he got a call from McKeon saying that the sexton of St. Michan's had phoned in a complaint that some young people had remained in the church after it was locked at night and had obviously spent the night there, sleeping in the pews. When he had approached to chuck them out, two had threatened him.

The hair on the tops of their heads had been twisted into spikes; they were wearing denim and leather and metal. One was carrying a stout stick. Another had said he had a gun and pretended to reach for it under his jacket.

By the time McGarr arrived, all exits from the church and the surrounding streets had been blocked off and uniformed police were having all they could do to keep the crowds back.

It was perhaps the worst place in Dublin for any sort of confrontation. At one end of the narrow, shop-lined, laneway was Grafton Street, Dublin's premier shopping district; at the other was Clarendon Street and Powerscourt, an arcade of shops and eateries. Now, in the summer, it was packed with tourists. Behind was Wicklow Street, another commercial artery, and it was into the curb there, where O'Shaughnessy stood, that McGarr swung his Cooper.

He got out, since the superintendent was too tall

and at sixty-four too old to be bending to the low car, and they spoke across its forest-green roof.

"They're still in there. Two girls and two boys." O'Shaughnessy let go the last word hesitantly. "Having done who knows what the night long. Sexton says the place reeks of drink." His clear blue eyes flickered up at the spires of the church. He was a profoundly conservative man, and a muscle was working on the side of his face.

"Sexton locked them in and made the call. He says they've tried to break out and now he can hear them smashing things. Then, we've got Guards." With his broad chin he indicated the cordon of blue uniforms at the end of the street. "I'd hate to . . ." Have to arrest them in the church, he meant. "But . . ." With the other police present, the sort of "interview" that both knew was necessary would be impossible in public, where there might be witnesses. "I've said they're wanted for questioning in the Coyle case. And nobody will doubt . . ." They resisted arrest.

McGarr stepped back from the Cooper's open door. He removed his hat and his suit coat, which he folded neatly on the backseat. He slid his watch off his wrist. He reached below the driver's seat for the weapon he kept there, and he tasted the gall that he had repressed since learning of the attack on Ward.

Raising the Walther to pull back its slide and load the chamber, he saw nothing but its black mate barrel and the V of its sight. Nobody attacked one of his staff with impunity. Nobody could be excused for smashing in an ear or breaking a wrist or stealing a handgun or, for all he knew, committing murder.

And then it had been Ward, whom in many ways

he thought of as a kind of son, who had been assaulted, and McGarr's anger was suddenly high. The thought of some smarmy bastard with a stick spinning around and waylaying a man who McGarr had seen knock men twice his size to the floor while on duty, and the best of Europe in the ring, augered down into the element of McGarr's personality that he knew was a weakness: his temper. Which was fierce and explosive.

But there was no help for it now. Blood pulsed behind his eyes and he felt a bit light-headed. The sky had gone grainy, and the buildings were a blur.

Said O'Shaughnessy, "We could get lucky. They could put up a fight," which didn't help.

A shout went up from the barricade at the end of the street and a man began running toward them, a camera raised before him. McGarr took no notice. He simply closed the car door gently, easily, hardly making it click (for control was now essential), and stepped around the Cooper.

The man was being chased by two uniformed Guards, and McGarr didn't notice him until he was directly in front of them, the camera pushed forward into McGarr's face. The flash exploded in his eyes, and his hand, the one with the Walther, darted out and whacked the man on the side of his head, sending him into O'Shaughnessy, who snatched away the camera and with a foot launched the photographer into the Cooper. He caromed off its slick surface and fell roughly into the street. The two Guards snatched him up.

"*Liam!*" McGarr roared—part curse, part plea—like some Homeric swimmer drowning in the sea of his own emotions. A surge of witless, uncontrollable, irrepressible anger made him think his starred eyes would burst.

"We've got him. Don't worry." With all his force O'Shaughnessy chucked the camera into a brick wall that separated two shops. He bent and ripped the roll of film from its broken back. "Charge that son of a bitch with unlawful conduct, with assault, and with battery. And let that be a lesson to them all." He glared at the other journalists, who were shouting now at the barricade.

McGarr's eyes cleared. He felt as he had years before, after the first hit on a rugby pitch—shocked out of any further concern for himself, and fearless. He would give as well as he got, but he would give first.

There were four uniformed guards with shotguns waiting for him at the side entrance to the church. And the sexton, whose hands shook on the key ring as he asked, "Am I to leave the door open?"

"And get yourself gone," said the sergeant in command of the other three. "Back behind the barricade."

"Try not to bust things—"

With a foot McGarr shoved open the heavy arched door; it squeaked on its hinges. Squatting down with his left arm extended and the weapon in the fist of his right, he scuttled into the shadows, keeping close to the wall. If they had a gun, it was the best place to be. If they had the stick too, or a knife, the raised arm could absorb a blow or a blade without him losing his weapon. O'Shaughnessy, quick for his age and size, followed behind McGarr with three of the Guards.

But the transept was empty. As were the apse and sacristy, which they scoured. The church was cold and dark, and as they passed down the nave toward the choir, they were overwhelmed by the sour odor of damp stone, sweetened only by the altar flowers that had been strewn across the marble floor near the doors to the narthex.

There were other smells there too as he approached the door: cheap sweet wine and cigarettes and urine. McGarr had to step around a wide puddle where someone had pissed. He turned to O'Shaughnessy and to one of the Guards, who wielded a shotgun; holding up three fingers, he counted mutely—one, two, three— before he and O'Shaughnessy, each on a side of the nave, kicked open a door of the narthex and rushed in.

The ashplant stick, falling like a guillotine from beside the door, glanced off McGarr's back and struck the barrel of the Guard's shotgun, which discharged with a deafening roar and splattered shot off the stone floor into the stone wall.

The stick came up quickly and caught the Guard under the chin, knocking off his hat. The shotgun dropped from his hands and another shell went off, the load bucking through the wooden paneling of the vestibule. The guard fell back through the doors into the nave.

The boy dropped the stick and was reaching for the shotgun when McGarr's foot smacked into the side of his head, sending him sprawling. Somewhere a girl was shrieking, and McGarr's other foot had just come down on another hand that was reaching for the stick when he was tackled from behind and driven into the tall church doors in front of him, which cracked under the force of both their bodies.

He went down, rolling to get whoever it was off him and away from the Walther that four hands were now reaching for. His elbow went back again and again, pumping into something soft; the screaming grew louder.

Feeling the grip on his arm loosening, he glanced up to see what looked like a witch—hair frazzled, wide red mouth open, the tongue pulsing with the effort of her scream—rushing toward him until she was brought up short by O'Shaughnessy. He reached out and snagged her hair. Her feet flew out from under her, and he swung her roughly down onto the marble floor. He held another one by the neck, and he threw her on top of the first.

Still down, McGarr spun around and struck out with the butt of the Walther. It thwacked off the temple of the boy beneath him, whose head bounced back into the stone of the wall. Then McGarr was up again, quickly scanning the area to see O'Shaughnessy with his weapon out and pointed at the girls. With the barrel of a shotgun, one of the other Guards had pinned the second boy to the floor by the neck. He kicked the stick back into the shadows, where it clattered against the wall.

McGarr jerked the first boy to his feet and drove a fist deep into his stomach—once, twice. He hit him again and again, driving him back into the door. He was taller and wider than McGarr, and he loosed a single wild punch that passed over McGarr's head and exposed an ear.

It was there McGarr struck him, loading all the force of his body into his left hand. The blow spun the boy around and, like something wet flung against the door, he began to ooze down the paneling, until McGarr stayed him.

The kidneys were next. McGarr would have to lead them through a gauntlet of journalists, and the less obviously pummelled they looked, the better.

"The Beretta," McGarr asked before his punch stapled the sagging boy to the door. "The one you took from the man in the brown suit. Where is it?" If they had had it, they would have used it, he was sure.

"Fook yourself, asshole," one of the girls shouted, and the point of O'Shaughnessy's polished brogue flashed. She cried out. It flashed again, more quickly, and she groaned.

"Where?" McGarr let the boy sink to his knees before his own foot came up and caught him in the arse, launching him into the door. And it was then that the anger he had been feeling earlier, and the pain— in his back, where he had been struck with the stick, in his shoulder and the side of his face, where he had struck the wall, in his knee, where he had fallen with the weight of two bodies—welled up. "Where?"

"Ah, for chrissake, he don't know. It wasn't him, it was Jammer."

"Jammer, who?"

"Just fookin' Jammer, is all."

McGarr's foot lashed out, and the boy howled as he again lunged forward into the door. "And your Jammer has the gun?"

"He gave us the stick when he got the gun."

"Where did he get the stick?"

McGarr moved to kick the boy again, but he swung around and held up a hand. "In Glasnevin. On the Finglas Road. Near the cemetery." His forehead was swollen and raw. His nose was bleeding. His tongue darted out to wipe the blood off his upper lip.

"You were with him?"

His eyes moved away.

"Don't say nuttin', Bang," one of the girls warned. "Not on Jammer."

Said O'Shaughnessy, "One more word—"

"With him when?" he asked when McGarr leaned toward him. He touched a fist to his swelling forehead. The back of his hand was wrapped in a kind of fingerless, black, leather glove, studded with silver spikes.

"The park first. With that stick."

"Fook if I knew he'd do it. Fook if I even knew the cop was there."

"Tout! Stoolie!" one of the girls hissed, and O'-Shaughnessy touched her up with his toe.

"Well—you know yourselves how Jammer is," the boy pleaded with the others. "Never know what he's up to. What he'll get you into."

Not from the way it had been reported: the two others had dropped down when the stick had rounded on Ward. They had known he was there and had waited to reach a deserted part of the park before striking. But McGarr let it pass. The truth would come out later, when they were charged. "Like three nights earlier, when you got the stick, the boater, and that blazer." he said, pointing to the girl in the striped jacket that was too big for her. She had pushed the sleeves up on her biceps; the collar was raised.

"No, Jesus, I swear. None of us was with him. Jammer was alone, goin' home. He's got a little spot there in one of the outbuildings, right over the high wall in the graveyard itself. Abandoned, it is. Or forgotten. And don't nobody visit him there, apart from Sweets." He meant the girl in the jacket. "The bloke was jarred. Couldn't walk, only speak. Some car'd just dropped him off, and he says to Jammer, he says, 'They're yours—the stick and the jacket—if you can just get me to my back door.' He told us that, di'n' he?" Bang implored the others. Then, "He can be like that, Jammer." There was a pause before he added, "Considerate."

McGarr thought of how Ward might describe Jammer. He also thought of the gangs of roving urchins who had infested the city in the last few years, and wondered if in the future there would be only two classes, the haves and the have-nots. Or, rather, the lawmakers, who possessed things, and the lawbreakers, who appropriated whatever they could. And all with the Irish Revolution that was to end all that only seventy years old.

He thought of Coyle and asked himself if—practicing Dubliner and Joyce scholar that he was—the Trinity professor would have voluntarily surrendered the stick and blazer. Perhaps only if he felt threatened, as a kind of bribe. The hat, which was authentic, was another matter, but Jammer had gotten that as well. "Then he was alive, the man with the boater?"

"Oh, aye. So said Jammer." Bang's accent was from the North, and his eyes searched McGarr's face. "Why?"

"Don't you read the papers?"

One of the girls piped her contempt, "Bang? He don't read nothin'. Not a street sign. Not even the names of shops. Can't."

"And yourself, now?" O'Shaughnessy inquired of the girl. "Why would we be asking?"

None of them knew, and McGarr tried to imagine what their lives were like on a daily basis. An odyssey, and doubtless lifelong. A trek from pillar to post, with the future as sustaining as the immemorable past.

"What time was all that?"

Bang hunched his shoulders. "We met him about

two, and he had only just come by them things. We were headed to the cemetery ourselves, though not his place, like I said. Fair night and all."

"Where exactly did you meet him?"

"The botanic gardens. It joins the cemetery there by the lane."

Then it had been roughly two hours and a half between Coyle's having left the pub in Foley Street and having arrived in the lane behind Catty Doyle's house in De Courcy Square. During that time he had phoned Maura Flood and asked for her to meet him at the Drumcondra Inn.

How long would he have waited for her? McGarr would have to find out. Could Coyle himself have driven the Fiat to the lane? By all reports Coyle was well beyond it, and his wife had said that he didn't drive and hated automobiles. It had been long enough for Mary Sittonn to have delivered Catty back home after their "date," and before Catty's assignation with David Holderness.

And certainly long enough for Fergus Flood to have driven out to his Foxrock address and, not finding his "prowling" wife and daughter at home, to have returned to the city to search for them "at the usual venues." Which may have included the Drumcondra Inn. They'd have to check. But it was from in front of that hotel that the Fiat had disappeared, only to appear briefly in a lane at the rear of Bengal Terrace where the body was discovered, and finally to be returned to the Flood driveway with the murder weapon under the front seat.

And then Flood would most likely have had a key for the Fiat.

If what Bang had said about Jammer could be be-

lieved. And Bang hadn't himself murdered Coyle for
the boater, the stick, and the jacket. Why? As the final
"and all" of their fair night?

"*We?*" McGarr asked.

"Mick, me, and . . ." His head moved toward the
girls. "Jammer, he come along."

McGarr considered the numbers: three boys, two
girls; and he tried to guess what all and how long that
might take. "Did you come back through the lane?"

Bang nodded.

"How long after?"

One of the girls spoke up. "Half-three," she said
through a wet smile. "That's Jammer, that is." Which
answered one question.

"Did you notice the man again?"

"He was there, all right. Never made it in. Jammer
points to him, says, 'Old woman must've put him out.
Busted his fuckin' glasses,' says Jammer. He was propped
against the cemetery wall, looking up at the sky. Smiling
like. We left him be."

"Did he have the hat on then?" O'Shaughnessy
asked.

Bang shook his head. "Jammer had it from the start.
From when we met him in the bone yard. Made the
girls wear it, you know, while we were partyin', like."
His eyes flickered up at the girls and he attempted a
thin, prurient smile.

"So, where's Jammer and the gun?"

Bang hunched his shoulders, then held up a palm so
McGarr wouldn't begin abusing him again. "God's trut'.
Honest. He—"

"Moves around, don't he, Sweets?" the other girl
said. "Likes a bit' a this an' that. Mainly that, I'd say."

Sweets went for her, and O'Shaughnessy had to separate them.

Bang used the disruption to say in a low voice to McGarr, "The cemetery—he would've stayed away, after what happened in the park. The cop and the stick and all. But it's been days now, and Jammer, he's different, he is. Likes bein' alone. Private, like."

O'Shaughnessy had by then restored order.

"Right," said McGarr, reaching out to rap on the main door of the church. "All up." He rapped again, harder, and they heard keys jingle beyond the heavy oak panels.

"Where we going?" the loud girl asked.

O'Shaughnessy pulled her to her feet. He explained, "Three parts, like the Trinity, which you so much revere. Delousing. Then an examination—physical—at no cost to you. And finally an interview to ascertain if the truth could possibly reside in any statement you might utter."

Outside the church, the Fourth Estate was waiting, cameras raised. They shouted questions about both the incident and the earlier handling of their colleague. But McGarr said nothing, only ordered one of the Guards to remain with the boater, the stick, and the blazer until the press quit the area. There was no percentage in putting Jammer on notice.

13

When Professor Fergus Flood complained that he was being made to repeat the story of his night of the sixteenth for the umpteenth time, Detective Sergeant McKeon said, "Then make it the humpteenth. The Super Chief has just joined us."

Flood sighed and looked behind him at McGarr, who had just entered the room, and allowed—truly for the umpteenth time—that he really should have a solicitor present, only to be told once again that such was possible, he need only to make a phone call. They would wait.

"Ah, no—sure, it wouldn't change anything, would it?" he said, sounding more like a Dublin navvy than a professor at Trinity College.

McKeon hunched his large, soft shoulders. "You tell us."

"I hope you don't think I've been lying to you."

It was hot in the small interrogation room, and Flood's white shirt was blotched with sweat. He was a man who needed to shave often, and his heavy face was now patterned with shadow. As though in search of an ally, his dark eyes turned to McGarr, who was standing off to one side. In spite of the heat, his bow tie was still tight to his throat.

Daintily almost, he touched it with a large hand,

before laughing to himself with evident resignation. "I must be losing me sense of humor. Which won't do, will it? Where to begin?"

"From your leaving the pub in Foley Street, Professor."

He nodded. "I said my good-byes to Kinch, to those of my clients who were still there, and to McGarrity himself, the publican, and left."

"How was he then?"

"Who?"

"Coyle, of course."

"Locked, as I've said." It was an older Dublin expression for drunk, one that McGarr's father had sometimes used, and it seemed odd coming from somebody like Flood. But then, what little they knew of Flood was odd, from his mixed professions, his marriage and family, to his story and the Fiat 500 and where it had been and what it contained.

"Weren't you worried about leaving him in that condition?"

Flood's slight cough was a laugh. "You didn't know Kinch. There was no reasoning with him in that condition, and I could tell he hadn't finished for the night."

"And so you went home. How, please, Professor?"

"In my automobile, which I had parked in college."

"Trinity?"

Flood nodded.

"You walked from Foley Street to which gate of Trinity College?"

"The Pearse Street gate, as I've said, which is the closest. I knocked and the guard, recognizing me, let me in. I'd parked where I usually do, in front of the English department. I got directly in the car, drove to the back gate, and then on to Foxrock."

"How long did all that take?"

Flood's shoulders rose then fell. "What did we say earlier? Ten or fifteen minutes to walk from Foley Street to the car. Then twenty for the drive out to Foxrock. Throw in another five for the lateness of the hour and how tired I was."

"And when you got home . . . ?"

"I fully intended to go straight to bed, but when I discovered that my wife wasn't there, I went to look for her."

"Without checking to see if she had taken the Fiat."

"I knew it wouldn't be there. My daughter had gone out to the ciney, and I never thought to check."

"How would your wife, then, have gone out herself?"

"Taxi. Bus. Somebody might have picked her up."

"Like Kevin Coyle?"

Flood inclined his head. His eyes flashed at McKeon. "Kinch did not drive."

"Then you're suggesting your wife had other lovers?"

"I knew only of Kinch."

"So—in the Rover you drove out to 'different venues,' as you termed it. You visited Jury's Hotel, the Burlington, Sachs, and the Drumcondra Inn."

Flood's head went back just slightly, but enough. Yet he said, "No—I didn't go all the way out there. I stayed here on the south side of town. After Sachs I came home, and there she was."

"Then, since you didn't visit the Drumcondra Inn, you wouldn't have bumped into Kevin Coyle, who was waiting for your wife, or your daughter, who was on the prowl for David Holderness. Or into your Fiat, half up on the footpath in front of the hotel."

"No, certainly not. As I've just told you, I went back home after Sachs."

"What time was that?"

"However long it takes to drive to those places and look round."

"An hour? Two?"

"Perhaps two."

"Which would have put your time of rearrival in Foxrock at two-fifteen."

"I didn't check the clock, but it seems reasonable."

"You checked that your wife was in her room. Or, rather, that the door to her bedroom was closed."

"Yes."

"But you didn't check to see if that Fiat was in under the car port, there at the side of the garage? Or if your daughter was in her room? Or the clock?"

Flood shook his head. "I was exhausted. Destroyed." Again the working-class touch.

"Do you have your keys with you now?"

"Which keys do you mean?"

"Your personal keys. Any keys. Keys, man—do you have any in your pockets?"

Flood's head turned to McGarr, then back to McKeon. "I don't understand."

"It's perfectly plain," said McGarr. "The sergeant would like to see your key ring." McGarr reached into his own pocket and pulled out the keys to his Cooper, the Castle office, and the several that served his house in Rathmines and his wife's business in Dawson Street.

Color had risen suddenly to Flood's skin, and the dots of sweat on his forehead had begun to merge and track down his face. Slowly he produced his keys, which McKeon allowed to remain untouched on the table between them.

With a pencil he indicated one. "The Rover?" he asked.

Flood nodded.

"The Fiat, I presume?" That key had a large letter F on its side.

Again.

"And these others . . .?"

"College, the office, home."

"Had you these keys or some others with you on Bloomsday evening?"

Flood said nothing. His gaze was fixed on the keys.

McKeon waited for Flood's eyes to rise to his. "May I ask you, Professor—how is it that your Rover was ticketed at three-oh-five A.M. in Drumcondra for illegal overnight parking?"

Flood said nothing.

"How is it that Rex Cathcart, the hotelier there, saw you walk into the bar and look 'round and then walk out to the desk, where you asked if your wife was staying there?"

Still nothing.

"How is it that Cathcart, worried that you might make a scene, followed you to the steps of the hotel where Coyle was waiting for a taxi. He was drunk, had tired of waiting for your wife, and he had asked a barman to phone up for a lift."

Flood's eyes shifted to the grimy window. Now, in late afternoon, it was splashing a hot, milky light across the day-room floor. The blat of a fly on a pane was languid and desultory.

"Question—did you offer him a lift home?"

"Why would I do that?"

"To take him out of harm's way. As you said, you could tell he wasn't 'finished' for the evening, and better that he finish with Catty Doyle than one of the family Flood. After all, your daughter was still inside. She—

like your wife, like you yourself by your own admission—very much admired Coyle. And he was in such great form that night. Your words."

"Then why would I have taken the Fiat and not the Rover? Hypothetically speaking, of course."

"Part punishment, part cure. She had no key to the Rover, which in any case was parked a block distant. She would have to get herself home as best she could. And without the Fiat there was no lift for Coyle.

"Tell me, where did you get the knife?"

Flood sighed, then reached into his suit coat, which was hanging over the back of a nearby chair. From his billfold he drew a small card which he placed on the table between them. On it was the name of a solicitor. "Would you ring that number, please? I believe it's time for me to speak to this man."

Off a fingernail McKeon flicked the card back into Flood's lap. "Ring him yourself, Professor. Around here liars do their own bidding."

It was half-six when McGarr got home, and Noreen had not yet arrived. Without pausing for a lager, he retrieved *Ulysses* from the bedroom upstairs and went right out to the back garden, where the high walls would shield him from the wind. It had brisked up around noon and had been building ever since. Tomorrow the weather would change, and he had spent far too many good days inside, as it was.

He set a comfortable chair in a patch of the brightest sun, loosened his tie, and sat. The heat was intense there and was soon baking him so agreeably that for a while he was not moved to open the book. During that time he heard a noise on top of the wall in back of him, a low whine and some panting, and he was soon joined by the P.M., the Garda veteran from the next house. The dog nuzzled his hand, received its requisite evening greeting, and then settled in the shadow of the chair and dozed off.

In his earlier attempts to read *Ulysses,* McGarr had discovered that the only availing approach for the novice reader was to consult the "guide" often and in depth. But he now found himself forgetting the many allusions to symbol, history, and myth and merely "listening" to the words on the page, much as he would listen to a piece of music.

It was a peculiarly Irish song, he understood from the first page, and a particularly Dublin ditty—now melodic and fine, later rough and raspy, then rambling and vague and what McGarr thought of as ethereal, counterbalanced by a focus as sharp and unsparing as any microscope. From the books that a certain literary martinet of a schoolmaster had forced upon him long before, and from years of recreational reading, he understood that *Ulysses* must have been for its time and was most probably still a tour de force, containing more literary devices than he could name or explain. He couldn't keep himself from concentrating on the "voice," or rather the "voices"; they were whispering and singing and chanting and cursing and praying and now stating bluntly in journalese or implying in ad lingo or slyly insinuating, like a whisper in the ear, propositions, avowals, invocations, promises, directives, observations, and whatnot, all in such a heady, ever-changing concoction that after several dozen pages McGarr decided it was more than mere song.

The novel reminded him of the complex weave of

voices raised in complaint, laughter, song, noise, and lament that he had heard all his life in one or another Dublin licensed premises, which could not have changed since Joyce's era. And it was little wonder that—as Flood had said—the more complete book (*Finnegan's Wake*) was the story of the dream of a Dublin publican. McGarr was entertained mightily and did not stop on page 100, when Leopold Bloom—Dublin Jew man and one of the two major characters—approached the cemetery in Glasnevin and another character pointed toward Bengal Terrace:

> —That is where Childs was murdered, he said. The last house.
> —So it is, Mr. Dedalus said. A gruesome case. Seymour Bushes got him off. Murdered his brother. Or so they said.
> —The crown had no evidence, Mr. Power said.
> —Only circumstantial, Martin Cunningham added. That's the maxim of the law. Better for ninety-nine guilty to escape than for one innocent person to be wrongfully condemned.
> They looked. Murderer's ground. It passed darkly. Shuttered, tenantless, unweeded garden. Whole place gone to hell. Wrongfully condemned. Murder. The murderer's image in the eye of the murdered. They love reading about it. Man's head found in a garden. Her clothing consisted of. How she met her death. Recent outrage. The weapon used. Murderer is still at large, clues. A shoelace. The body to be exhumed. Murder will out.

McGarr read on, even though it occurred to him that such a reference would not have been lost upon (and had not been mentioned by) Fergus Flood or David Holderness or, for that matter, the only literateuse involved in the case: the comely Catty Doyle.

Could she have chosen to reside in De Courcy Square that shared an alley with Bengal Terrace because . . . ? And what motive might she have had to murder Coyle beyond possessing a number of signed, first-edition Kevin Coyle volumes that with the man's death would doubtless increase in value? McGarr did not actually know that the books belonged to Catty; Bresnahan had reported overhearing the three women discussing the situation, as though the books were mutual property, but the fact of the matter was, they were actually in Sittonn's possession.

And then Doyle had been Kevin Coyle's editor, and on that basis had lost by his death perhaps more than anybody save his wife and Maura Flood, who had been another of his lovers and had seemed genuinely saddened by his death. McGarr wondered if Doyle made it a point to know all of her writers *in the flesh,* so to speak, and if such practice was standard to the publishing industry. He would have to take to writing books.

Or might the same feminist triumvirate have tired of Coyle's antics and decreed his end? No, again. They might have attempted to alter his . . . behavior, but would they have done him mortal harm? Sittonn's having dropped Catty off at De Courcy Square after their "date" put her on the scene. Had it been straight home for Sittonn? McGarr would have to find out.

In any case, McGarr was—as he had suspected from the first—solidly on literary turf, and he now found it

passing strange that nobody had mentioned the murder
that was spoken of in the novel and Coyle's death there
nearly in the very same spot: Flood, who taught Joyce
in university; Holderness, who was the research student
in literature; Catty Doyle, who most probably knew
Ulysses, or who would have been informed of the dis-
tinction of her address by either of her male lovers.
Even from the little McGarr knew of academics, he could
scarcely imagine a practicing Joyce scholar resisting the
opportunity of displaying his erudition to the likes of a
Catty Doyle.

Or, fully understanding that eventually the correlation would come to light, could the three women have
so arranged Coyle's demise as to suggest an academic
connection? To implicate Flood and/or Holderness?

It was then that McGarr glanced up from the book
and saw the large, bearded Rabbi Viner peering over
the wall.

"Caught in the act. I should fetch me camera. It's
a shot for the papers, so it is. They could run it front
page: 'Murder Squad Chief Closet Ineffectual.' Given
the errata rife in those pages, people'd think it a trypo.
They'd also get letters from the country, whole barge
loads, demanding your resignation. I quote, 'To think
of the cheek of the man, masquerading as a top Guard,
when in fact he was photographed center forward in his
back garden reading a bloody *boook* of all immarh-al
t'ings. Question: Did it have pictures, and of what, and
of whose anatomy, and don't give me that bull it's about
forensics. Or smutty jokes about aborigines and Ker-
rymen? And finally, was it written, edited, produced,
or printed in the U.K. or the USA?' Pronounced, 'Uck'
and 'Ooza.' "

McGarr smiled. Viner wasn't half wrong: sure, an EEC study had just discovered that the Irish bought and read more books per capita than any other European nation, but McGarr did not doubt that Irish bibliophiles were a narrow elite who indulged themselves heroically. He knew of whole voting districts in Dublin that were virtually book-free. People there never read more than the price of hake. Or porter.

"So, what's the title, and if you tell me it's *Pathological Curiosities* or, rather, *Curiosities of Pathology*, I'll never speak to you again, so help me, Dante."

McGarr sighed. Viner was irrepressible. Worse, he was cultivated, and his roots in Dublin were as long-standing as McGarr's own. McGarr could lie and say he was *re*-reading *Ulysses*, ". . . as I do every so often," but lying wasn't his style, especially to a man of the cloth who was also a good friend and an entertaining neighbor.

Sheepishly he said, "It's *Ulysses*."

"Ah, the Kevin Coyle case," Viner said with an alacrity that revealed his purpose in disturbing McGarr. Like most Dubliners, there was little in the city that was not of interest to him, especially murder, and McGarr could imagine Viner, for all his undoubted discretion, confiding to an intimate, "Peter McGarr is my immediate neighbor. I speak to him daily and—"

McGarr said nothing and kept his eyes in the book.

"To think that Flood would throw away so much . . . position, academic acclaim, his little business there in Nassau Street. What does he call it? Joyce's Ireland, I think. And him with a handsome wife and child. Is it her it was over?"

McGarr tried to raise his head slowly.

"It's in all the papers."

McGarr couldn't keep the surprise from his face.

"I'll go get them if you'd like. Splashed all over the front page of the *Press.*"

"Charged?"

"No—not exactly charged. But they're aware that Flood has been helping you in the investigation, and . . ." Viner's glance at McGarr was expectant and hopeful. "Helping" was the euphemism used to imply that a person, while not charged with a crime, was being interviewed in that connection.

"And to think to have come to a foreign land," Viner went on hopefully, the declining sun making his face look round and moonish over the top of the wall, "and established a brilliant career, only to have such a thing happen in the middle, the very best part of his life." Viner himself was approaching fifty, and mid-life potentialities were a present concern.

But it was the earlier allusion that pricked McGarr's interest. "Foreign land?'

"Sure you knew, Superintendent McGarr, that your helper is an American?" Again Viner tried to read McGarr's face. "From some place out on the Great Plains. Iowa, I believe. Or Nebraska. Don't you like the names they have over there? Listen to the sound of that: *Ne-bras-ka,*" he intoned. "Why, the very sound of it conjures up visions of rolling, windy, treeless hills with solitary farmhouses and immense barns and nothing but an horizon sweep of buffalo dung."

Opined McGarr, "The buffalo has been largely extincted, I hear."

"A progressive people, the Americans. Nobody would say they're not. And a Jew—Flood, I mean. In the beginning here—his at Trinity, mine in my congregation—I saw a good deal of him. But like others who have come to this seductive little isle, he soon became more Irish than the Irish." It was a phrase an historian had used to describe what had happened to the early Normans in Ireland. "And I regret to say I lost him. Entreaties ignored. Cards, letters, the same. He sends me a few quid every year with a little note that we should—"

As Viner spoke on, McGarr reconsidered Fergus Flood—an *American,* he who had seemed so much the urbane, educated Dub, right down to the Ath Cliath dialect he seemed able to employ at will and condescendingly? He had the accent, the gestures, and the mannerisms down pat (or, rather, Paddy), and McGarr wondered immediately what else he might have "adopted" in regard to the death of his colleague and rival, Kevin Coyle. Flood hadn't told them all of the truth. Of that McGarr was certain.

Standing, he said, "Excuse me, Sol—I must use the phone."

Viner gloated, "You mean you didn't know Flood was a tribesman of mine? Or is it the American connection? You know, I bumped into him on D'Olier Street a couple of years ago and was amazed how he carried off the donnish, Foxrock bit without batting an eye. To me *who knew,* mind. But then, I'm but a poor man of God. Trusting, compassionate, believing. You, however, are a nag of another—"

The back door closed. McGarr liked Viner, he enjoyed his company, often sought him out. But, to appropriate an American turn of phrase, Viner could also be a humongous (albeit helpful) pain in the arse, especially when he was right.

McGarr dialed three different numbers and finally

found McKeon at his favorite pub. "Didn't I see the name of an American reporter on the list that Hughie got from Joyce's Ireland and Bloomsday Tours?"

"You did indeed. *Boston Globe.* Goldfarb's the name. He's on assignment in the North. They sent him down here for a contradiction."

McGarr waited. The pub was busy and filled with noise.

"A working breather, he said they called the Bloomsday thing, which reminds me. How dare you disturb me while I'm on orificial business?"

"He still here?"

"Goldfarb? As of this morning. You busy, or is the wife in state? Why don't you pop down here, and we'll—"

"I'd like you to phone him up. Make it sound like a tip for a story, you know, him having been helpful and all. Tell him that it's come to light that Professor Fergus Flood of Trinity College is actually a Jewish American from someplace like Iowa or Nebraska, and you thought it might be a story he'd be interested in. If he's any class of journalist, he'll know about Flood and the Coyle case."

There was a pause, and then, "Flood?"

"None other."

"Christ—I'm slippin'. The bugger codded me. I would have sworn he was one of *us.*"

There it was again. "Me too, but we'll let the press sort him out. Somebody with contacts better than ours."

McGarr had no sooner settled himself back in the chair at the corner of the garden than Noreen appeared. She was wearing a deep orange dress, just the color of her hair, and he could tell from her step as she approached him that she had been drinking. He wondered where and with whom, though he knew better than to ask. She would *not* be questioned on her actions, especially when in her cups.

Hand on hip, she stopped before him, looking ravishing, like flame, in the golden hues of the setting sun. Her green eyes flickered down on the book. "So—I'm glad to see you've gotten to it at last. I'd be mortified to have a husband of mine admit in public that he hadn't read *Ulysses*."

Me? he wanted to say. *I've* been trying to read the thing for days now.

"And you needn't bother me tonight. I must get my rest. Tomorrow's the book launching at the Shelbourne."

Him bother *her?*

"I stopped by and helped Catty arrange the flowers." Raising her chin, she presented McGarr with the profile of her face, which was striking: the aquiline nose; high forehead; a definite, if small, chin below a slightly protrusive upper lip. "An intelligent and talented and beautiful young woman, don't you think?"

McGarr waited until the turquoise of her eyes flashed down on him for an opinion. "Her? G'wan," he said in his most obvious Dublin dialect. "She's a scrawny dark mot, all bone and gristle. Blue veins, didn't you notice? She'll age, so, and fast. Like a quayside mist."

"Blue veins where?"

"Her legs. The side of her neck, which she conceals with her hair."

"Well, it's true that she has fine skin. Today she was wearing a full-skirted dress of exquisite pink crinoline." Pink was a color Noreen believed she could not wear. "It must have cost heaps. She looked like a little . . ." The green eyes searched the top of the wall, her smooth brow glowered. In three months she would be thirty, and already they were in full, if covert, crisis.

"Doll?" he suggested.

"No, not *doll*. Do you think I'd ever say that about one of my—"

"Friends?"

Her nostrils flared and the interesting curves of her chest heaved as she tried to clear the thought through the haze of the wine.

"Acquaintance? Associate? Don't tell me Dawson Galleries, Limited, is actually hanging canvases at this authorless book launching?"

The twilight flared briefly in her eyes. "It's the premiere cultural event of late summer. A coup, really. *Everybody*'ll be there, and the other gallery owners will be green."

Better than pink, he thought. "What's she like?"

"Catty? Most professional. Everything has to be just so and she certainly knows how to build a media event. I suspect that years from now publishing people will speak of the launching of *Phon/Antiphon* with a kind of awe. If, however, you mean from a police perspective, you offend me. How you could suspect such a considerate, intelligent, and tasteful young woman of anything but the highest motives and impeccable conduct, points up what I have long considered perhaps your most distressing flaw."

His baldness? His stature? His incipient obesity? McGarr awaited the punch line, as it were, with no little trepidation.

"Your conception of human nature, which is debased. Warped, I should imagine, from your dealings with the dark side of human experience. This may come as a surprise to you, but not everybody compromises her integrity."

McGarr reflected on the bookcase of Kevin Coyle volumes in Mary Sittonn's antique shop, Catty Doyle's extra-professional approach to Kevin Coyle and David Holderness and her complex relationship with her "sisters," especially with Sittonn, who had tattooed her shoulder with what McGarr suspected was a Catty logo. But he mentioned none of that. "What does one wear to such an event?" he asked instead.

Noreen had begun making her way grandly toward the house, taking precise steps, fanning her dress with her hands. "Oh—stylish, trendy things," which meant that a large box containing at least one extravagantly priced item sat in the hallway.

Pity, for him a poor summer suit would have to suffice.

"Why, are you thinking of attending?"

"Perhaps," he lied. She could count on him.

She stopped and turned. "In what capacity, may I ask?"

McGarr raised the book, "Police artist manqué, what else?"

"What about the suit?"

"Your choice."

She smiled slightly. "But please, Peter, no—"

"Gaffs," he supplied.

"And if you have to play Grand Inquisitor, try not to make it—"

"While you're involved in a sale."

"*No*—to hell with sales. I mean *obvious*." There was another pause before she asked, "Hungry?"

He knew what that meant too. "Not really."

"Good. I'm shattered, really, and there's that roast in the fridge. Would you mind . . . ?"

"Not at all. Get some sleep. I'd like to put a bit of the book by before I come to bed. If I'm hungry, I'll help myself."

But McGarr never got to his roast. From the garden he removed himself to the study, then to the sitting room, where, after midnight, he lit a small fire in the grate to dispel the chill, and finally to a tall, wing-back chair in the bedroom, where Noreen was already in bed and he hoped he would soon doze off.

But he had no luck with sleep. He watched the pale light to the east brighten gradually into a brilliant scarlet blush, until finally a crescent of blinding sun forced him to lower the shade. When he finally checked his watch it was seven, and he abandoned the book a few pages from the end and padded down to the kitchen to make her tea and his coffee. Both would need an early start.

As the water heated, he put his hands in his pockets and turned to his back garden; he thought of how startling he found a book that detailed a day in 1904 but still seemed current and accurate. Joyce could as well have been describing the Dublin that McGarr knew, with all its gossip, lies, tall tales, and extravagances. In short, its search for a truth that wasn't too hard to bear.

Why *hard*? Because of the poverty that was written into every page of *Ulysses*. Dublin society then, as now, was stagnant on virtually every level—economic first, but on social, moral, and spiritual levels as well. Back then, the British and the Church and the loss of central, unifying myths could be blamed. Now it was the 6 percent of the population who controlled over eighty percent of the country's wealth, the crushing, largely foreign-held debt that was three times the per capita debt of Mexico, a powerful Church that intruded into all aspects of life and quashed every social or political reform not decidedly in its interest, and finally the British, who were still with them in the North.

Hence the need to patch over the tatty reality of Dublin with puns, rhymes, songs, riddles, circular arguments, and references to arcane mythological and philosophical systems that seemed to McGarr more form that content. In short, the need for something to help pass time, to distract, to arrange.

Like drink.

That was it. *Ulysses* was a grand—perhaps the grandest—way to pass time. McGarr could imagine himself reading it over and over and over again, forever finding something new and forever only scratching its surface. And then Leopold Bloom, and even more so Stephen Dedalus, were what he thought of as typical intelligent Dubliners. They were cynical and sophisticated—by which he meant they were not naive—but they were essentially charming loafers. Defensive and guilt-ridden about their purposeless but oddly beguiling city, they wandered about, flirting with her tawdry charms. For Bloom it was an advert here, the promise of another there, many and recurrent stillborn ideas, and a balance sheet of small losses at the end of the day.

For Dedalus it was an afflatus, a wastrel's bingey gyre from sobriety, control and frustration through drunkenness, nonsense and violence to the condition of having to borrow from another wanderer a few bob, a blessing and the hope of another day in some better and real place unnamed.

Yet in all it was a Bloomsday better than Kevin Coyle's, McGarr supposed, readying (like Bloom himself, he now realized) a breakfast tray for his wife. He now pulled four slices of toast from under the gas and flipped them over. Think of it: Coyle as Stephen Dedalus, right down to his donning Joyce's (Dedalus's) boater and carrying an ashplant stick. Flood as Leopold Bloom, with his dark features and weight, his bow tie and professional manner, his being foreign and a Jew, his inconstant wife and equally liberal daughter. Granted Bloom had followed his Molly through her assignation only in his mind, and Maura Flood's Blazes Boylan was Coyle (Dedalus) himself. But that was life, not art.

What would Flood have done had he caught them *en flagrante,* as McGarr had found the daughter and Holderness in Bray? Perhaps he had not required direct evidence, and—after having observed the brilliant Coyle awash in his talents the day long, and having returned to discover that his wife's appreciation was rather more intense—he had snapped. Certainly the physical evidence suggested the possibility.

The toast was hot to the touch, and he flicked the slices off on a tray, slathering butter across the crusty tops. The dark, oily aroma of his coffee rose to him, and he thought of Catty Doyle, who would be who in *Ulysses?* Perhaps one of the Nighttown whores whom Dedalus visits near the end of the book. Certainly Catty had merged her romantic and professional interests with Coyle and Holderness. Could she have derived some as yet unknown benefit from her relationship with Mary Sittonn?

Lifting the tray and turning from the stove, he decided he was trying too hard to make Dublin then fit Dublin now. For instance, "Kinch" was what Buck Mulligan had called Stephen Dedalus. But Flood (Bloom) had also called Coyle (Dedalus) Kinch, which in Dublin meant—McGarr stopped short and coffee lapped over the edge of his cup—a noose in a rope, the sort that had been used for hanging.

See? More the fool he for reading the book. Were it indeed a "literary" crime, Coyle would have been hung, not stabbed once, neatly, in the chest.

But a few steps down the hall his imagination was off again: David Holderness, who was he in *Ulysses?* Buck Mulligan? McGarr remembered what Flood said Coyle had said about Holderness: "Beckett without Beckett's intelligence, wit, or sympathy for the human condition." Or here Mulligan's wit. The trot that McGarr had followed in reading *Ulysses* had said that the character Buck Mulligan had been patterned on Oliver St. John Gogarty, legendary Dublin physician and eccentric whose writing McGarr *had* read and who *had* been witty. What was that quote of his, describing an infamous Dublin madame? "She had a face upon which avarice was written like an hieroglyphic, and a voice like a guffaw in hell."

No, Holderness was not much of a Mulligan or a Gogarty, or even much of a Beckett. He hardly stood out in any way; after all, there was not a Dubliner of McGarr's acquaintance who wouldn't have had something humorous to say when having been discovered *en flagrante.* And the way the man then insisted upon clasping Hiliary Flood to him, as though either to further humiliate her or—could it be?—to flaunt his prowess with women, had been cruel. Could he have been trying only to conceal his own nakedness? The erection and so forth?

Perhaps. And, given the name Holderness, he could well not be a Dubliner or an Irishman at all. From the little McGarr knew of him, he could be from Iowa or Nebraska, like Fergus bloody Flood. McGarr shook his head. The man had fooled him. He would have to learn more: about Flood, about Holderness, about literature, which he was now bloody tired of. He thought about the book-launching party later in the afternoon.

With a toe he eased open the bedroom door.

Who else was there? Katie Coyle, the victim's wife. Even though he had not until that night read *Ulysses*, McGarr knew something about Joyce, at least the biographical parts, and it struck him now how much Katie Coyle physically resembled Nora Barnacle, Mrs. James Joyce. Both were large women. Both had dark hair— Barnacle's a deep red—and dark eyes. Both had been *wife* and little else to their husbands.

Wife. His own refused to wake up, moving away from his touch and deeper into the covers and pillows.

"C'mon now—all up. Tea's hot. Buttered toast." McGarr placed the tray on the table between the bed and the wing-back chair, which he turned around so they could breakfast together. He stepped into the bathroom, switched on the hot-water tank and the infrared light to heat the tiles.

There he was himself playing Bloom to his Molly, he again thought, closing the bathroom door behind him. And not for the first time did he, a man of a certain age, wonder if there were any Boylans in her life. Well—"Up now! I've lit the gas for your bath"— that was something you couldn't worry about. But did.

"You sound tired."

"Me? Been up for hours."

He had not quite gotten himself back into the chair when the phone began ringing.

It was Sinclaire. The couple who lived in the flat on the Finglas Road overlooking the murder scene had returned from their holiday in West Cork; he could see them in a half hour, before they went off for work.

"I'll be there," said McGarr.

Noreen had fallen back to sleep, her chin pointed, like a dart, at the ceiling.

14

It was an attic flat in a tall Victorian building, and both policemen were puffing by the time they had climbed to the door. The day was dark, muggy, and hot, and McGarr took the precaution of removing his tan straw hat and swabbing its band before setting it back on his head. Noreen had selected a light brown linen suit for him, and it wouldn't do to arrive at the Shelbourne all damp or mussed.

When the door opened and a face appeared, McGarr nearly asked if the girl's mother were at home. She was young, not out of her teens, as was the boy she introduced as her husband. Behind them, nearly dwarfed by him, the tiny flat was neat and clean and packed with many new things. Both were dressed for office work—shirt and tie for him, for her a tight black dress that flexed over her backside as she moved.

"We're not usually light sleepers, and we sleep here." She meant the room, no more than a large closet, that was closest to the door. "But the sound of the car was so strange. Blatty, like a small tractor or something. Michael got up first and looked out, and when he didn't come back to bed, I followed him here to see what was wrong." She took the boy's arm.

He was tall and had to stoop to look out the window of the back porch that had been closed in to form another small room. "We keep our bicycles in the garden." He pointed to the clip that contained the right leg of his trousers. "And I need mine to get to work."

A careful young couple watching their pennies, McGarr thought. In the nook that was their kitchen he had seen an oatmeal tin and a packet of the least expensive bulk tea. In another room was a sewing machine and a computer terminal; he concluded they'd make excellent witnesses in court.

"The car was a Fiat," the boy said. "One of the first models. I had a toy car like it when I was a child. A Five hundred. The interior stayed dark forever, it seemed, with me hopping from foot to foot in the chill.

"Then the door opened and a heavy-set guy got out. He had a hat on, but when he reached the other side of the car, the light from the street lamps on Finglas Road caught his face. A dark man, fleshy face, maybe forty or fifty, hard to tell which. And steady. Not the other one, who couldn't walk at all. I didn't hear what was said, but the heavy one kept trying to get the slim one up the alley, where the car wouldn't fit.

"Laurel and Hardy stuff. First Laurel dropped the stick he was carrying, but, bending over, the hat came off. When he reached for that he fell and lost the stick. Eventually the other man raised a wrist and looked at his watch. He pulled the slim man over near the wall, seemed to debate taking the hat and stick with him, but then laid them down on the drunk's chest."

"Took him forever to turn the car around and get it back out between the auto stops there at the head of the lane," said the girl. "Motor sounded like it would burst."

"Or the clutch."

Sinclaire traded glances with McGarr, who asked, "Bow tie?"

"Sorry?"

"Was the driver wearing a bow tie?"

They looked at each other. She nodded. He said, "Now that you mention it, he was. Large man. Powerful. He moved the other around like he was nothing at all. It was only the shouting that kept him from picking him up and carrying him. When he tried, the drunk started shouting something like 'old' or 'hold.' I only caught the first part of it.

"After a while I got tired of watching them and went back to bed. I reckoned it was a fair night and nearly over by then, and we were to get an early start on our holidays. If he was there in the morning, I'd try to get him some help. But as we were leaving I heard barking and looked out. A woman who I think lives up the lane in De Courcy Square was out there with her dog, bending over the chap, speaking to him. Jet-black hair, older. You know"—his eyes surveyed McGarr and then shied to Sinclaire's snow-white hair, but it was too late to phrase the thought differently—"in her thirties." He looked away.

"By then my father-in-law had arrived, and he's not a man to be kept waiting. We thought nothing of it until we got home and the landlord told us what had happened."

"The hat and the stick. When you saw the woman leaning over the man, did you notice if he still had those two things with him?"

The boy thought for a moment and shook his head. "I didn't notice, but I don't think he had. At least I can remember definitely that he didn't have the blazer on. With the red stripes, you couldn't miss that day or night. He had gotten himself over to the wall proper and was sitting against it. His shirt was open and the glasses he'd been wearing were off. But . . ." He hunched his shoulders to mean that was all.

Said Sinclaire, "The woman. Do you know her?"

"Only on sight," the boy said all too readily, and the girl looked up at him, her eyes searching his face. "At the bus stop, in the shops. The neighborhood's a small place."

McGarr had stepped closer to the window and looked beyond the immense gray stones of the wall into the cemetery. "You seem to know the area. How about a couple of punks. You know—spiked hair in outrageous shades, like pink and green. All leather and denim and studs. I understand they're living somewhere in the cemetery."

The girl joined him at the window. "Right over there, but there's only one. A fella. Doesn't seem to want to be seen much. Like a cat, he is—out the door and up over that great height of wall as quick as you please." She turned suddenly to her husband. "Michael will tell you that up until five weeks ago I was home during the day. I brought my sewing over here to the window where it's cooler and there's good light." Her eyes flickered down at her dress.

"A work of art," said Sinclaire, who, apart from Ward, was considered the handsomest man on the Squad. "Smashing, really."

She blushed.

"Shaved head but for a patch of blond running down the center," said McGarr. "About six two or three. Thirteen or fourteen stone. A punk?"

Said the boy, "Last I saw, the patch was pink and spiked. His eye shadow was pink too. He's only about six feet and no more than twelve stone." He pointed a finger at his own shoulders, which were broad. "Pads. They're all wearing them these days."

"I wonder if you two would like another sort of holiday?" McGarr asked, turning to them. "Courtesy of the Garda Siochana—"

The boy held up a palm. "Ah, thanks, but we have to work."

"And work you will, but from the comfort of some hotel—the Gresham or the Shelbourne, wherever you like."

They looked at each other. "Really?" she asked. "You've got to be joking. Those places cost hundreds of pounds a night."

"We'd like the use of your flat here, for . . ." He pointed toward the cemetery and the long shed that she had indicated. In the deep shadows glass could be seen, as though somebody had taken old windows and constructed a kind of shelter. "Provided I can be certain of your utter confidentiality." He made sure that their eyes met his. "No parents, no friends, nobody should know of this. You can tell people you hit the lottery and you're blowing it on a little high life."

"Ah, but nobody would be—" she began to say before she blushed and looked away. "I mean, we're saving for a house, and—"

Said her husband, pulling her into him, "We'll think of something."

With Sinclaire in the window of the attic flat, McGarr strolled leisurely along the exterior face of the cemetery wall until he got to the area—roughly fifty yards from

Catty Coyle's back garden door—that he guessed was in line with the shed he had seen from the window above.

There he stepped closer to the wall and allowed his eyes to run over its surface until he found what he sought. Jammer himself might be able to climb like a cat, but Bang had said that all five of them including their women had scaled the wall, and at least one of them had to be as ungainly as a fifty-year-old gardener/investigator in what McGarr liked to think of as not half-bad condition. Chinks, they were, that looked to have been chipped out of the mortar of the wall at easy increments to the top.

Careful of the toes of his woven-leather brogues and of the tan, linen suit, McGarr made his way steadily but slowly to the top of the wall. There he found a rope hanging from the limb of a tree; he let himself down. It was cool on the other side, and damp even on a summer's day, but quiet and still; it was as though he had lowered himself into another world. Few noises from the busy Finglas Road reached here. Above him in the trees two jackdaws were quarreling, and deep into the cemetery he caught the distant whine of a hedge trimmer.

McGarr scanned the rows of stone monuments, the empty drive, and the deep grass near the shed. It was a little-visited corner of the cemetery, and he imagined that at night the watchman shined a quick light on the shed and moved on. From his belt McGarr now pulled his Walther, checking it to make sure a bullet was chambered.

He moved to a side of the shed and with his hat off pressed an ear to the gray weathered boards.

He listened for minutes that seemed like hours, but

heard nothing save the dripping of a tap. No moving about, no cough, no noise from within. He rounded the building and stepped quietly into the shadows that he had seen from the window of the attic apartment across the top of the wall. Sinclaire was there. He raised a hand.

McGarr was surprised to find that the windows had been fitted to a precise frame, with most of the lower runs blacked in. All of the work, with obviously "found" materials, looked professional, with tight joints and not a "holiday" in a painted surface that McGarr could see. He tried the door, which was open, and why not? Anybody wanting to get in to the shed would merely have to break the windows. With the barrel of the Walther he scanned the single, open room. Nobody. Only a table, a chair, a cot, a sink, a towel, a bar of soap, and a stool. On the table was a two-ring electric cooker and a set of dishes, neatly stacked. McGarr stepped farther into the room.

The cot was made to what McGarr judged were army specifications; the covers were pulled taut enough to make any packet of cigarettes bounce on the top blanket. At the foot was a fluffy eiderdown which wore like a badge of honor its Brown, Thomas price tag and plastic cord on an outer seam. It had cost 122 Irish pounds. McGarr was acquainted with the security at the fashionable department store, and he wondered how, given the way he looked, Jammer had gotten it out. Below the bed was a single pair of shoes, perfectly aligned and polished to a mirror sheen. Wing-tipped bluchers, by Church; McGarr would not mind owning a pair himself. Another hundred pounds at least.

But he soon understood how the theft of the eiderdown had been accomplished. A section of the glass-enclosed space had been sectioned off by a curtain, behind which McGarr found a three-piece tweed suit, a Burberry's storm coat and matching fedora, a long umbrella with a heavy straight handle that was meant to fit in a golf bag and, when opened, would shield both caddy and player. In a kind of hat box he discovered a human-hair wig, cut long and sweeping in back and slightly graying on the temples. In all, it was a disguise to make Jammer look like a young, monied blood up from the country for a touch of town.

With such cunning, McGarr wondered why Jammer associated with the others, the three McGarr had rousted from the St. Michan's. He also wondered at his age and background; it was one thing to don the garb of respectability, something again to affect the manner. From appearances, however, Jammer's future was not on the streets. He was too altogether neat and contained and—was it?—tasteful for petty theft. Embezzlement, bank fraud, or some clean scam would be more to the taste of someone dressed in the natty costume that McGarr held in his hands. It was probably only a matter of time or daring. With care McGarr rearranged the wig in its box, let the curtain fall back in place.

And it was in turning back into the room that something struck McGarr's eye. Four pots hung from a rack above the cooker, scaled according to size with their lids over the pegs. Various cooking implements hung on another rack, accompanied by a set of cooking knives in an extended rosewood sheath. McGarr moved toward them.

Brass rivets held their rosewood handles in place; apart from age and use, they appeared no different from the murder weapon that had been found under the seat of Flood's Fiat 500. A stamp at the heel of the chef's knife certified that they had been made by Everdur in Gottingen. The set gleamed in the dim light but was incomplete: the filleting knife was missing.

Suddenly McGarr remembered where else he had seen such knives in exactly the same rosewood sheath— in Catty Doyle's neat kitchen, but there a full set. Coincidence? Perhaps.

Or could Jammer have murdered Coyle? Why? What motive would he have had? Could he have known Coyle? Without Jammer or Coyle, it would be impossible to know.

But, say, if Jammer had murdered Coyle, why hadn't he dispensed with the other knives? He was smart; economy aside, wouldn't he have packed up and fled a site so close to the murder scene? It was just over the wall. And why then would he have given away Coyle's blazer and ashplant stick, which could link him to the murder?

Nowhere in the enclosure could McGarr find a newspaper, magazine, or book. There was a radio, but contained in a large, portable sound system—a boom box, they called it—with a generous supply of audio tapes, again arranged neatly in a plastic credenza designed for that purpose. McGarr flicked it on: the machine was set to play a tape of a Dublin pop group that McGarr had often heard on his car radio. The volume was low, scarcely audible. McGarr rewound the tape and switched off the unit.

A hideout, a bare-bones safe house. McGarr wondered if Jammer enjoyed some understanding with the cemetery personnel. He couldn't imagine their not knowing he was here.

He felt like waiting, but he suspected the boy would by now have questioned why Ward for no ostensible reason had gone after him, which was probably why he had not returned to pick up his things.

And then with the gun, used to full effect in what comprised Dublin's underworld, Jammer could have practically anything he wanted.

Which was?

Hard to tell. Nowhere had McGarr seen any evidence of drugs, and the order of the place implied an asceticism and sense of discipline that rather denied the possibility. Also, the way he had dealt with Ward revealed a certain alertness and daring.

Scanning the room to make sure nothing looked disturbed, McGarr noted that Jammer had even washed two cardboard coasters, the sort that were used in pubs to blot the bottoms of pint glasses. Moving closer, he bent his head to read the logo on the one facing him:

McGarrity's Lounge Bar

BOOZE, BOOKS, BEER
and
BLARNEY

Bloomsday
(with Prof. Kevin "Kinch" Coyle reading from *Ulysses*)

16th June

AN ANNUAL BASH

Could Jammer have been in attendance? Could he have followed Coyle to the Drumcondra Inn and then Flood and Coyle in the Fiat 500 back to his own turf? Or were the coasters merely two more things that Jammer had taken from—or had been given by— Coyle?

Should he interview the cemetery personnel and risk a tip-off? No—that could come later, if Jammer didn't turn up.

And then McGarr had staff to dispatch—support and relief for Sinclaire in the attic apartment—and an artist to interview Bang and the two girls. He needed a mock-up of Jammer's face, and Ward to corroborate the rendering, now that they knew Jammer could and had changed his M.O. They would circulate the picture among all uniformed Gardai in the city center, advising them not to ignore well-dressed young men. McGarr himself would accompany the rendering to McGarrity's.

It was a busy, commercial bar with tall, tin ceilings and a Victorian motif that appeared original but had been corrupted by details that reminded McGarr of bars in New York. Here was a row of fluted sconces over dim light bulbs, there small, shaded lamps on tables that had been wedged into every available space. Plants sprouted from pots hung on walls, set in corners and balanced on the ends of the bar.

From somewhere music issued forth, and each of the waitresses, who now at noon were preparing for the lunch crowd, wore a single rose in the frilly bodice of her black-and-white, peasant-girl's uniform, and a little round white button with chartreuse print.

One button said, YOUR QUICHE IS MY COMMAND, another, SEAL IT WITH A QUICHE, and a third, Q.M.A.

Explained McGarrity, "It's the literary touch. You know, in *Ulysses* one of the characters advises Bloom to K.M.A."

Kiss my arse, McGarr's memory of the night's reading readily supplied.

"We've just dipped it in batter and baked it a bit. Hate the stuff myself. You read the book?"

McGarr blinked. Which book? McGarr was rather tired of books.

"*Real Men Don't Eat Quiche,* which I subscribe to myself. But women like it, and men like women. And men like to drink, 'specially on Fridays, which are paydays. To round it all off—not all Irish eat fish, and eggs are cheap." His blue eyes flickered down on McGarr.

McGarrity was a tall, thin man who was evidently prematurely gray and who, just as evidently, had an eye for the ladies, especially those who worked for him. While he spoke, he kept all in plain view. He handed back McGarr's Garda name card. "Missing something?" he asked in such a way that McGarr was unsure if he meant McGarr's lack of height or hair or the three letters that differentiated their names. The button on his own breast said, QUICHE OFF, JACQUES.

"The international touch," McGarrity now explained. "We get a lot of foreigners in here, and I thought I'd tell 'em a thing or two. From the heart."

He also seemed to know what McGarr was thinking. He reached down and took the police artist's rendering of Jammer from his hands. "Hobby of yours? Curious, I don't see a resemblance. Artists, you know, usually can't resist the temptation to draw or paint or even *write* themselves into their creations. But here"— McGarrity placed a hand over the spiked hair of the drawing, so that Jammer seemed as bald as McGarr— "there's no likeness whatsoever, either to you or to anybody else I've ever seen, but him."

McGarrity lifted his eyes to a client seated at the far corner of the bar. "Trinity fellow. Comes in here off and on. Perrier. Ballygowan Spring Water. He'll eat the odd slice of quiche from time to time, right out in the open where even other men can see him. I'll have to get him a button."

David Allan George Holderness had a double in front of him. A tall pint glass was filled with ice, sparkling water, and a squeeze of lime. On the bar were two bottles of Perrier.

McGarr slid onto the seat next to him and ordered a coffee. "Come here much?"

"Now and then, but you know that." His eyes lighted on McGarrity, who had stepped around the bar to get McGarr his coffee.

"Here four nights ago?"

"Actually, I thought of it, knowing how 'Kinch' would be *in form,* as they say."

There was a derisive note in that, and McGarr asked, "And you would have enjoyed the show?"

"As much as anybody could enjoy the antics of a sot, but for other reasons. May I be candid?"

McGarr tried to penetrate the glare of the wire-rim spectacles, but could see only the tall, frosted-glass front window and the POWER'S sign reflected in it. Holderness was wearing a stylish pearl-gray jacket with a thin, raised collar, wide shoulders, and black satin lapels. His thin blond hair sprayed from the top of his head but had been slicked back along the sides, where it appeared darker. If anything, his tan had increased in a day, and made his perfect-looking teeth seem very white indeed.

"At his best, 'Kinch' was a practicing Byronic hero— either 'seething' or brooding with romantic angst that undergraduates and other pedestrian minds considered literary. At his worst, he was just another loud, boorish, bullying, Behanesque, Irish drunk of the sort that gives the country and—much worse for us—the literature of the country a bad name. Again, among those who don't know much about us or our literature. I'm sure you know the type."

Unfortunately McGarr did. Every "literary" pub, of which the city had several, had its resident, unkempt, boisterous, porter-cadging bard or troubadour who took pains to convey the impression that he could live by the word or the note but certainly more agreeably by the pint, should you spring for its cost. "And watching Coyle in that condition gave you pleasure?"

"Because it exposed his sensibility."

McGarr waited.

"Which was corrupt and passé."

Sensibility. McGarr wondered if somebody would murder for sensibility. He couldn't be sure of that either, but he imagined that, seeing Coyle in his cups in some way made Holderness, who was abstemious, feel superior to the man who had blocked his path in university and who was admired by at least two of his women friends— Catty Coyle and Hiliary Flood, judging from what the latter had said when McGarr had spoken to her in Bray.

Could sensibility extend to women? And what exactly was Holderness's approach to women? He had seemed so cold and distant and even contemptuous of Hiliary Flood on the day before. "Catty tells us she had a date before your—what did you call it?—your late-night 'arrangement' with her on the night Coyle was murdered."

"You mean with Mary Sittonn?"

Said McGarr in a thoughtful tone, "Ever notice the little tattoo on her arm? Around here?" McGarr poked Holderness's arm to see how he'd react.

Offended. He looked down as though to say, That's far enough.

"You know, the cat with the smile and the long, curly tongue. Could you take your glasses off for a moment. I'd like to see the color of your eyes."

"Excuse me?"

"Your glasses. Your eyes. I was wondering if they were the same color as Catty's. You know, the eyes of the tattoo on Mary's biceps?"

Holderness lowered his head, as though having to consider the request before he complied. "Is it an official request, Superintendent? Is this some sort of lineup?"

"Get out—we're only sharing a drink. Don't you ever loosen up?" McGarr waited until Holderness eased the wire bows from his ears. "It's just that your appeal to two beautiful young women, like Hiliary Flood and Ms. Coyle, is lost on me. I thought maybe I was missing something."

With the glasses in his hand, Holderness blinked and squinted myopically. Apart from a certain fullness of the face, and perhaps the length of his nose, his resemblance to the police mock-up was really quite remarkable.

"Nope. It can't be your eyes. They do nothing for me. And then they're the wrong color—too light. Maybe I should see your tongue."

Holderness smiled and fitted the bows back over his ears. "It could be you misunderstand Mary and Catty, or at least Catty. By that I mean it's possible to support aspects of a movement without embracing every plank. Not a few Irish women endorse the social and political

aims of the Gay Alliance without themselves being lesbian."

"And you think that's what Catty was doing with
Mary Sittonn from nine to twelve or so Bloomsday evening? Supporting common social and political aims?"

"I didn't say that. I said, it's possible that one *may*
support those aims. Whatever Catty and Mary were
doing is none of my concern. Nor yours, really."

Perhaps, but Holderness's tone had changed, and
McGarr saw an opening. "You mean, it wouldn't bother
you if Catty cared for women more than men?"

"As I hope I've just implied, I don't think she does,
though if she does, I really don't see how that's any of
my business."

"Or if she cares for Mary more than you?"

His smirk seemed to say that he knew that wasn't
true.

"Or if she cared for Kinch more than you?"

Holderness's nostrils flared, and the same thin, defensive smile that McGarr had seen in Bray appeared
on his lips. "If you're attempting to establish what is
known as a love relationship between Catty and me, I
think you'll be disappointed."

"Then what would you call your relationship? I know
you have a word for it. She's your—"

"Witness?"

"That's it. Your witness. I don't know"—McGarr
tasted the coffee, which had gone cold—"it all sounds
so sterile. You know, 'Great crack last night. I made
love to my witness.' No, no—you probably wouldn't say
that either. What would you say? 'Last night I had sex
with my witness, after she finished with her girlfriend
or girl witness.' Or would it be her *other* witness?"

Holderness's tight smile had sagged, but he nodded.

"Would you consider a wee adjective to particularize the evening's proceedings? How about 'best witness,' as in 'Catty is me best witness.' It'd be something like best girl, with no aspersion implied."

When Holderness still said nothing, McGarr went on, "Well—is she better or worse than, say, Hiliary Flood? Or do they both excite the same level of intensity? Or is that another word that should be allowed to fall into disuse?" Yet again he waited, then said, "Has anybody ever told you that you're a stunning conversationalist? Catty, at least, had her preferences in regard to men. Know what she said about you?"

Holderness's head swung to him. McGarr now had his full attention.

"One of my staff overheard her say, 'Ach, sure— he's just a boy. An enormously talented boy with a bright future in front of him, but still a boy.' "

Said Holderness, "Would that Catty could judge. It's flattering, surely, but wrong on both counts. I'm nearly thirty, and an impartial person would say that my future is nothing but dim, or undecided."

Thanks to Kevin Coyle, now deceased. "About Professor Coyle, she says, 'There was only one Kevin, wasn't there. For all his faults.' "

"Well put. I couldn't have said that better myself."

McGarr felt his own nostrils dilate. He did not care for the arrogance of the young man beside him. Holderness missed no opportunity to flaunt—what was it? His intelligence. Or could it be?—what had happened (or what he had done?) to Kevin Coyle. "Fergus Flood has an opinion of you as well."

"What is this, Superintendent—David Holderness

assessment day? Or are you just trying to draw me out?"

"He said that if Kevin Coyle had been a kind of modern-day James Joyce, then you were like Beckett without Beckett's taste, intelligence, wit, or—"

"Sympathy for the human condition," Holderness completed evenly. "Yes—I've heard that before. In fact, I'd be tired of it, were it not so wrong-headed. Beckett had—*has*—no concern for the 'human condition' in the way that phrase is usually meant. If anything, he has contempt for the human condition, but even that is saying too much. What he has is a basic understanding of the human condition that is so well-reasoned, accurate, and flawless that it makes him the greater thinker, writer, and artist than Joyce by far.

"Shall I continue?"

McGarr glanced down at his coffee and wished he had ordered something more suited to the condition he now realized he was in, inhuman as it was.

"Are you married?"

McGarr nodded.

"For how long?"

"Nine years."

"Do you still love your wife?"

He nodded again.

"As much as you did when you first decided that you should marry?"

McGarr had to think about that.

"Or do you, you know, love the remembrance of having loved her, and all the rest now is merely the comfortable familiarity of knowing the other person will be there as your witness or confessor or partner or companion or, more likely, all of that? Am I right?"

McGarr inclined his head. Asking himself if he loved his wife wasn't something he often did. Noreen was his *wife*, which went beyond mere love. And then, he wouldn't have married her if he hadn't loved her.

But Holderness was more interested in his argument. "What does love mean? What *is* love? Love has been the subject of the novel, which in Italian is called *romanzo* and in French *roman,* since its development as a literary form. If not, you know, an actual love story, which some women still *love* to read"—Holderness allowed a smile to flicker across his lips—"then novels in recent times have been about the failure of love or the absence of love or perhaps the impossibility of the Victorian ideal of love, which one could make a case is central to Joyce's *Ulysses.* Are you still with me, Chief Superintendent?"

McGarr didn't like the condescending note in that, but he nodded.

"But what if love is an illusion and exists only in the mind or 'heart' of the lover, and the sort of love, if any, which the loved one holds for the lover can never be the same, or at least expressed similarly. Then what is love but the central lie in the grand fiction that human beings—who are categorically and unreconstructably singular—*can* communicate and 'become one,' as romantics would have it and the mating process suggests? That process in fact only further fractures the possibility, since it creates yet an other.

"We are born individuals who possess no innate knowledge. We are a void that is filled up with illusions. Love is one, or better, a multiple of illusions. Even the way we express what we feel or think is an artifice, created in words or notes or shapes or gestures that really can't accurately express us in our own terms, since we have none of our own. We are nothing but transitory"—Holderness raised his glass—"holding vessels for those same illusions."

"Like a container," McGarr suggested. Holderness nodded, and McGarr wondered how much Beckett's approach, as stated by Holderness, owed to his acquaintance with Joyce and Joyce's aesthetic of the novel, as stated by Flood/Coyle. Perhaps *Ulysses*, as an object that was filled up with the names of things, was itself a metaphor for man. After all, wasn't it named for a man? Joyce could have as easily titled the book "Dublin" or "Bloomsday" or something else altogether.

And finally, Molly Bloom's soliloquy, which closes *Ulysses*, was for all her talk of loves and lovers, of Bloom and Boylan and her children, a statement of how difficult, if not impossible, it was to know anything definite about life.

Holderness concluded, "And thus Beckett would reject any sympathy for the human condition beyond whatever sympathy we might feel for ourselves, which itself can only be flawed because expressed—'

"In the terms of Others," McGarr completed.

"Yes, those who've gone before."

"Tell me—do you feel *sympathy?*" McGarr asked.

"For whom?"

"Well, let's start with yourself. You're after telling me you think your future is dim, which implies some level of sympathy with your own situation." To say nothing of pity.

Holderness nodded his head once, as though to acknowledge that the quote was correct.

"And Coyle—did you, *do* you feel any sympathy for

him?" To say nothing of pity. "Or is that too impossible?"

The smile reappeared. He turned to McGarr, a single eyebrow arching. "As luck and reality would have it."

"Who's this?" McGarr held out to him the artist's rendering of Jammer, his other hand covering the spiked hair.

"Don't know," he said too quickly. Police sketches were generalized to allow for small errors in perception and recall.

"Never saw him before?"

"Never."

"Doesn't look like anybody you know?"

Holderness shook his head.

"Doesn't look like you?"

"If I were vain, I'd be offended."

He was vain, but it was McGarr who was offended. The man thought him a dolt who could be hoodwinked. "How 'bout now?" He removed his other hand.

"How about it."

15

"Is that you, Rut'ie?" Ward called, when he heard the key in the latch. He was sitting up in bed in a bolster that looked like something chopped from a vintage Citroen, if not a Rolls. It was gray in color, and contained his tanned and bare torso in a plush of velour.

And of course it was Rut'ie—who else?—who was struggling with the "supplies" that he had asked her to bring him: two full sacks of supposed food stuffs, the names of which she had never heard until that morning and still could not pronounce, but which, she also supposed, had helped him heal and stay fit after the beatings he had given and taken in the ring, or at least they should, given the price they asked for such measly amounts in the shop on Great St. George's Street not a spit from the Castle. It explained how the little tyke had slipped out for lunch all those months and been back at work in ten minutes, making the modest brown bag that she pulled from the drawer of her desk in a near faint look like a potato sack stuffed with plunder.

Tofu, one of the things was called. It took the shop girl a good minute to get Bresnahan to pronounce it properly while half of "weedy" Dublin looked on— drawn, gray people with eyeglasses and thin little smiles, as if they knew the secret to some Higher Truth but wouldn't tell—and she still came out with "too-foo," which sounded like a polite attempt to say something dirty. "But what *is* it?" Bresnahan asked, and was told by one of the weeds, who looked at her head to foot as though she had never seen a decent, upstanding, strong, and at that point in the lunch hour, very hungry human being in her life, "Bean curd." Bresnahan had looked down at the pale lump of plastic-wrapped, jelled matter in her hand and nearly dropped it. *"Curd?"*

"Like cottage cheese is to milk, but pressed from soy beans."

Bresnahan tried to imagine how that was done. Ireland—or at least the Ireland that she knew—did not grow soy beans, and all the beans that she had ever known had been on a vine or in a can. She struggled to understand how the contents of the can could be pressed and perhaps then strained and filtered and colored to come out with the look, but mainly—she had shuddered—the fleshy feel of the limp stuff in her hands. And to put such a concoction in your mouth? *Why*, she had thought, when the shops were filled with lovely rashers and steaks and chops and kidneys at half the cost? When Bresnahan was so moved she ate fish, which her people back home in Kerry still considered famine food and never touched. Ever.

Then, at the opposite end of the "feel" scale, was *mochi*. "No, no, no," the shop girl kept saying. "Moshe is the name of the Israeli general, the one with the patch over an eye who won the Six-Day War. This is a hard C. *Mochi*." But Bresnahan had already decided that Hughie Ward or no Hughie Ward, she'd never learn to like such fare. Mochi had the dense look, the hard feel, even the sharp corners and hatched-out brick shapes within the block of some class of building material, and there it was, *rice* all along.

Nori was next, pressed sheets of inky-looking seaweed. In Kerry seaweed was something that was put on fields *for fertilizer*, for goodness sake. "What do I do with this?" she had asked. "Anything you like. You take a scissors and cut it up in strips to add to soups and stews. Or you can fry it. It crisps up and gets sweet as a nut." Now there was something that Bresnahan understood. "How?" "In olive oil, is the way I prefer it. I realize olive oil is high in cholesterol but it tastes so good. It's my treat to myself." Bresnahan had turned away. Olive oil had the consistency, the smell, and almost the taste of the emetic she had been dosed with as a child anytime she had had the bad sense to let on she wasn't feeling well.

After that she had simply loaded the cart with the other half-dozen items on the list. And finally she selected a few frozen, organically grown vegetables and a free-range, organically fed chicken, as if some farm products were not and could not be "organic." One thing Bresnahan knew was farms. She had been born and raised on one, and her father, who was as large as the side of a barn, and as strong too, still worked one. And anything—sometimes unfortunately *everything*—on a farm was organic, right down to the odor in the sitting room when guests were present.

When told organic meant no pesticides or herbicides or growth hormones were used in the production of such things, she was moved to laugh up her sleeve. Perhaps on the big farms in Wexford or the Midlands farmers were moved to use such things, but in most of Ireland, where cash was scarce or hard got and seldom parted with, older truly organic methods that cost nothing were invariably employed.

Thus, piqued with indignation at what she designated

the yuppy life-style, Bresnahan bundled herself out of the shop and fled to the markets of Moore Street, where she purchased new potatoes, leeks, and brussel sprouts. In a butcher shop she asked, "I hope that's not organic," pointing at the largest, best-looking chunk of sirloin steak displayed. "Not a chance," said the butcher. "There's nothing living in that whatsoever. It's all the choicest dead meat."

Well, one thing was certain, she thought, depositing both sets of goods in the yuppy kitchen area of his yuppy loft flat, getting to know Hughie Ward was teaching her a few things about yuppies, the aspiring snobs of her generation. Someday she hoped to arrest and charge at least half of them with . . . *pride*, that was it. They were just too awfully sure of themselves and what they chose, what they blessed, and what they didn't, which was as certainly bad.

And how did they decide such things? Did they meet in committee and review, say, automobiles or perfumes or couturiers? Or—which was what she suspected and what irked her most—did they simply *know*? If so, Bresnahan did not have an inkling of how that knowledge was gained, and she was not a little bit envious of what seemed like a genetic predisposition to elitism, which made her angry.

Until she pulled her purse and jacket off the clean line of her shoulders and turned to Ward in the bed, with the covers about his waist. There he was in his contained perfection, all sleek but well-defined muscle, nut-brown in color, and—what was it?—vulnerable with the side of his face black now, and his wrist in the cast. The adored one, the *loved* one, though he knew (and Bresnahan suspected she must do everything to keep him from knowing) not.

"So—Bernie gave you an extra hour."

She smiled. She would be jolly for him and keep it light. Yuppies did not like heavy, which reminded her that she must go on a diet. She wasn't actually heavy, and in fact had lost a full stone since coming to the Squad, but the svelte image, such as portrayed in certain women's magazines, was something she had always wanted for herself, though how one lost muscle she did not know. "Your hour. The sergeant said, 'If you're popping over to Hughie's, you can take his hour too.' And this—I almost forgot." Turning back to her purse, she extracted the half liter of Red Breast, a choice aged malt, that McKeon had given her. "For strength to get you through the long afternoon, says he. If you feel strong enough after and think you can make it, the lads and he are meeting in Hogan's around half past six for a gargle."

Ward turned his head away.

"I know—I told him you don't touch the stuff, and especially now with your head and all, but—well, maybe it's good on tofu." Jesus, she'd got the word right, and Ward turned to her and suddenly began laughing.

"Did you buy some?" he asked.

"The entire blessed list. You should have seen their faces in the shop. When I appeared in the doorway, they thought for sure it was a reenactment of the film classic *Revenge of the Red Meat Eaters*. All I needed was a cigarette and a bit of booze on me breath to be entirely in caricature."

He laughed louder and then raised a hand to his head. "Ow—that hurts." He had no idea that Bresnahan could be such good company.

"Though I'll give you a choice, sick one," she ranted right on, sliding the whiskey across the counter toward the other liquor, rows of it that, imagine, he never drank. Surely he was a curious Irishman, which was in that way good, and she wondered if he had been a foundling and was really Italian or Spanish or of one of the dark, southern peoples who only drank wine.

Swinging back to him, she straightened up and tucked her light blue uniform blouse into her dark blue uniform skirt; as she did so, she watched his eyes trace the line of her breasts, turned in profile to him. "Tofu or mochi with tahini, miso and tempeh, all in a soup of kefir"— here she began laughing herself—"just to keep it down. Followed by enough evening primrose to choke a horse, polished off by a brilliant dessert of trail mix.

"Or, on the other hand"—she dug into her Moore Street packet and pulled out the steak—"a thorough meal of meat and potatoes with fried onions and brussel sprouts done by a farm girl who knows of such things as strength. Afterward you'll simply sail down to Hogan's with enough ballast in you to float the British navy, if you're of a mind."

"Really?" Ward had still not taken his eyes from her body, which he considered large but fetching, in the way one could admire proportion and strength. Her broad shoulders, which looked to have little knobs on the ends, devolved to a narrow waist and thin but definite hips. Her face wasn't exactly pretty, but with its light gray, laughing eyes, and a smile that pouted high cheekbones, and a strong chin, it was certainly acceptable.

And then there was the way she carried herself, like a boxer dipping to loose a left hook or a rugger who had just been slipped the ball. It had something to do with the fact that she was a bit bow-legged and tended to rock when she walked, as though those shoulders were a burden that took some strength to bear.

And yet her movements were contained and fluid, and Ward imagined—and had heard tell—that she had been a fine athlete in her day, which, mind, wasn't long past. Field hockey, he seemed to recall. And basketball, which Ward had always thought of as a woman's sport. How old could she be now, twenty-six, twenty-seven? Surely not thirty.

The truth was that Ward was now feeling very much better, and suddenly about as horny as he had ever been. Staring at the lovely configurations of her chest— which those shoulders made seem pendulous—Ward felt an actual gut-gnawing ache in his stomach, and it occurred to him that getting Bresnahan into bed for the afternoon was precisely what he most needed, though it would be wrong. They *worked* together and were in a way rivals, for Jesus' sake. One did not go to bed with staff (or at least the staff that Ward one day fully intended to head), and she was just an innocent country girl. What would he do with her afterward, which meant every day for the rest of their careers? Maybe he was just hungry.

She had said, "It's so pretty I know it must look like plastic." She meant the beef steak.

"Give us another look," he asked, if only to get her from behind the counter so he could have another glimpse at her hips and her legs, which were large but long and shapely. As she bent to him, his eyes darted to a mirror and he checked the gentle curve of her well-muscled backside. He hated himself for the thought that she could be, would be, fun. He couldn't imagine that she hadn't in her time: On his several forays into the country he had found the girls quick and ready and rather expert at the sort of dalliance that satisfied all, got them home on time, and raised not an eyebrow the next day in the village.

"Nice?" she asked.

"Nice," said Ward, "and—" His good hand shot out for her wrist. "Crack open the Chablis, would you? It's on ice in the fridge, and you'll like it."

"But I don't drink," she said, almost blurting out that on her Confirmation Day she had taken The Pledge and *observed it faithfully* for fourteen years, of all unreasonable, unfashionable things, before she added, "on duty."

"But you're off." He smiled, and she could have melted.

"For two hours."

"A sip—what could it hurt?"

And there went The Pledge, right out the window on the first suggestion from the little devil.

His good eye met hers and—was it?—color rose to her face. Yes, it was, and suddenly Ward felt the need to release her hand and reach for one of the several newspapers that were strewn about the bed. After a quick scan, he dropped it on his lap and watched her move back toward the kitchen, chatting away now. Happy, he thought.

Was it just the brush he'd had with danger, he wondered? He could have been killed, and he'd read somewhere that the threat of death was a definite aphrodisiac and that more women got pregnant on the eve of battle and shortly after than at any other time.

She returned with the wine. "Just a sip, now. I believe I've a weak head, and how in the world I'll ever return to the Castle—"

Ward raised his glass in toast: "To a good woman from a man in need. I don't know how to thank you."

Bresnahan hated to think she knew how he could, and as she looked down to sip, her eyes fell to the newspaper, which was pulsing slightly. She hadn't spent all those years on a farm not to know what that meant. He liked her. Or at least he'd like to have her, which wasn't really the same thing, though it might be a start, done right. Which was how? She panicked, and in a single gulp tossed off most of the wine in her glass.

Her hand came up to her chest and she forced herself to swallow and was pleasantly surprised. Far from tasting like whiskey or stout smelled, which was bitter and harsh and heavy, the wine actually tasted slightly sweet and mild and light. She turned on her heel and went back to the kitchen with a slight bounce in her step; expertly—and as quickly as she could—she began making their dinner.

Was it going to happen to her here and now, in the middle of the day, for the first time, when she'd taken her first drink and really should be at work with a man whom she secretly loved but was nothing more than a little roué? It had all the—earmarks was not the right word—of a penny dreadful.

The negatives were the hour, which wasn't romantic, the occasion, which was ministering to a sick friend, the possibility that she might nettle the boss (McKeon) returning late (how much late, if done right?) or the big boss (McGarr) if he might need her, and, Jesus, she didn't want that. He was a Turk, that one.

Then there was the further and more important negative that he (Ward) would take her lightly—a boff in the afternoon—after which she wouldn't have even his respect. And finally there was the possibility that he wasn't the roué that rumor painted him, and she might get pregnant. Not having any experience at such things, she didn't know that she would, but she had always imagined that, given the way she looked (healthy) and felt (healthier still), the mere touch of a man would blow her up like a pumpkin.

She reached for the glass, drank off what remained, and poured herself another, saying, "Lovely stuff this. Where'd you get it? Want another glass?"

"Of course," said Ward, stretching. "I feel . . ." He couldn't come up with the right word, or at least one expressible.

And then the steak and trimmings were done, and Bresnahan, loading the plates up the side of her arm, soon had everything laid out on the bed on all the newspapers save one ("Use that like a place mat," she advised, smiling playfully), and they ate.

God, Ward thought, it was just what he needed, and the taste! "What did you put on this steak, Rut'ie?"

"Ah, a bit of this and that."

"Could you write it down?"

"Me? I don't remember, actually." Her head was spinning now, and she felt suddenly like she'd dropped three stone in weight. Rashly, she added, "If you want it again, I guess you'll just have to have me back. You've certainly got a well-stocked kitchen. Cook much yourself?"

His mouth filled, Ward waggled his good hand to suggest that he dabbled but did not cook in the strict sense. Most of what he'd assembled in his kitchen was an attempt to encourage the women who came there to cook for him.

His most successful line was, "Sure, with all this I

bet we could whip up something better than most restaurants. Why don't I do the salad," and then he'd
praise whatever was produced, no matter how unpal-
atable, to the skies. It was called positive reinforcement,
which he'd read about in a book, and it was step one
in getting a woman to bed, and much less expensive
than, say, Les Frères Jacques. He suddenly remembered
the girl at Joyce's Ireland and Bloomsday Tours; he'd
phone her later from Hogan's. Maybe she was free for
the night.

But now with Bresnahan he wasn't joking. True, he
ate tofu and mochi and tempeh and the like more for
what it did for him and how easy it was to prepare than
how it tasted. It gave him less cut, which made his
skin seem youthful, and he could just pull it out of the
packet or apply a little heat and cook some rice—at
which a rice steamer had made him expert—and there
it was. The taste, however, was either bland, bitter, or
queer.

Bresnahan's steak was another thing altogether. He
went into encomiums, saying he couldn't remember when
he'd last had beef so tender and tasty. And the spuds
slathered in butter *with* sour cream and chives and tiny
sprouts. Why hadn't he ever thought of that before?
He hadn't crunched brussels since he'd left his mother's
kitchen in Waterford, and they made him nearly growl
with delight. Maybe that was it all along. He'd been
hungry, perhaps hungrier than he ever knew, and that's
who Bresnahan reminded him of. His mother, another
big, shapely woman.

Ward forced the thought, which was unsettling, from
his mind, and soon had his portion of steak, what had
been left warming in the oven, and even some of Bres-

nahan's—"Really, for a big girl I'm not much with the knife and fork," she lied, being too preoccupied to eat herself. She then cleared the dishes and poured coffee and sat back down at the side of the bed. "I'll do the washing up in a few minutes." She glanced at her watch. "Before I leave."

"Ah, t'anks, Rut'ie," Ward said for at least the third time in the Dublin accent he had appropriated at least two months after having joined the Squad, and there followed a silence in which he felt the definite vibes (something he didn't just believe in; something he understood implicitly) that he knew what she was thinking about, and she knew what he was thinking about, and he knew she knew he knew, and so forth . . . , and they were thinking about the same thing.

Her eyes rose from the lip of the cup and moved to his; they collided for the briefest moment and caromed off.

Whew! Was her breathing as obvious as she thought? Her heart was mostly in her throat, beating so wildly she thought she'd choke.

The newspaper was thumping. He raised his knees.

"Curious how a big meal makes you warm," she hazarded, wondering how he had ever gotten the reputation as a playboy. Perhaps he didn't care for her or had scruples about a cohort. "I mean I'm—" Hot was the exactly wrong thing to say, but she could feel nothing but the blood in her temples, and she thought she was going to explode.

As an antidote she forced herself to imagine how many other women Ward had had on that circular bed that belonged in a bordello, until a little voice told her, Ah, ___ the other women, Rut'ie. As long as he ___ s

you. Exactly, she thought, and turning her head back
to him, she was about to suggest a nice long back rub
for an invalid, when he asked,

"What about the case?"

"Which case?"

"Coyle, of course."

"Ah—the Coyle case." Yes, that was something to
speak about. An update, all business, and she had so
much to tell him. And maybe after a decent interval
she'd rethink herself, which was always the smart thing
to do. They'd have other opportunities, if she had
anything to do with his future.

He already knew that the bloke who struck him with
the stick was called Jammer and that they were running
him down, but much else had happened while Ward
was still nursing the effects of the blow.

Suspects: she spoke about the three women whom
she herself had interviewed. There was possibly something carnal between Catty Doyle and Mary Sittonn
and—who knew?—perhaps between Katie Coyle, the
victim's wife, and Mary Sittonn, or perhaps among all
three of them, "for Jesus' sake," she added.

"How do you feel about lesbians," he asked, fully
recumbent now, head on the palm of a hand.

"Certainly *not* with me fingers," she replied glibly,
and he smiled.

"I mean, really."

She shuddered. "They give me the Willies."

"Better than the Joes."

And then there was the stock of Kevin Coyle books
they had in Sittonn's antique shop, as though they
had put them by against the day Kevin Coyle would
snuff it.

But what reason had Katie Coyle to do in her husband apart from perhaps jealousy, which she had disclaimed saying that she didn't care what he did, just so long as he supported her and her kids and no other babies were made, especially by her? And then by Dublin standards, Coyle had been a good husband, father, and provider who brought most of his money home. Certainly she would benefit from his death, but all the more had he lived to produce further books.

Sittonn? She too might have been jealous of Coyle's attentions to Catty, but then she would have had to have been jealous of David Holderness too, and who knew how many others. Catty was, it seemed—how had the Chief Super expressed it in his elegant, written report?—"predisposed to sexual congress."

"Nice turn that," said Ward.

Bresnahan raised an eyebrow. Jesus, was he that much of a swordsman that he'd done her too? "Catty?"

Ward laughed again, and his hand moved out and touched her arm. "No, no—nice *turn of phrase.*"

She looked down at the hand, and, when their eyes again met with kiloton force, they knew that what they were thinking would happen. It was as much as agreed; the hand did not move back.

Almost breathless now, Bresnahan pulled in what little air her capacious lungs could take. The room was a blur. She decided to concentrate on what she was saying and let events take their course. He was plainly in charge, and she his for the taking.

"Then there's the Floods," she went on rapidly, nearly breathless now. Fergus, the father, had as much as discovered Coyle, and in rapid succession had become his mentor, tutor, and thesis advisor, only to see his student quickly eclipse him in reputation within the academic community of Ireland and throughout the British Isles. As readily, Coyle then established himself as an international literary figure.

Once a year also Coyle would unshamefacedly display the capacity of his memory by reciting whole chapters of *Ulysses*. Then there was his affair with Maura Flood, about which Flood was cognizant to the point of even knowing where they met. Did he mind? He said he didn't. Did he follow them? He did. Had he lied about that and his activities on the night of the murder? Yes.

From as much as they could piece together so far, Flood drove from the final pub to his house in Foxrock and, finding nobody there, to various hotels until, at the Drumcondra Inn, he discovered his wife's Fiat 500. It was the daughter, though, and not the wife who had driven there. She herself was searching for David Holderness, but Flood couldn't have known that, since he met Coyle—who'd tired of waiting for Maura—in front of the hotel.

"It then occurred to Flood—or this is what we assume, since he lied to us—that he'd teach the wife a lesson and drive the Fiat away *with* Coyle, who wanted to be taken to Catty Doyle's house. She—Catty—was Coyle's . . ." Bresnahan searched for a term.

Bottom woman, Ward thought. Port of last resort. "True friend," he suggested.

Bresnahan's head went back in mirth, and Ward said as nonchalantly as he could, "Twist around a bit here and let me loosen your tie. After all, it's summer. Why be so formal?"

Bresnahan turned to him and smiled slightly, raising a single eyebrow in what she believed would approximate a practiced manner. She then leaned back and raised her chin. "But Catty had been spoken for that evening—by Mary Sittonn earlier and David Holderness later on."

In spite of the cast, Ward's fingers were deft with the knot, and he soon had the tie off her. The buttons of the blouse came next. He nuzzled her ear and sent a shiver down her spine. Having it happen like this in the course of what amounted to their business was somehow more acceptable than a more formal arrangement, given how different they were as people. And it would keep everything light, the way he preferred it, she imagined.

"Flood, anyway, didn't stay long in the lane behind De Courcy Square. Catty, for all her unscrupulous behavior—"

In reaching for the fourth button, Ward's arms wrapped her breasts; the edge of the cast grazed her left nipple, and she flinched.

"—probably didn't want her neighbors to see men knocking on her door at all hours of the night, and Coyle had Flood drive him 'round to the back door, or at least as close as he could get in the Fiat, which was halfway down the alley."

Flood was observed helping Coyle out of the car and trying to move him to Catty's back door, which proved impossible. He then left Coyle lying prone in thick grass there, near the wall, with the boater and stick resting on his chest. Flood must then have returned the Fiat to Foxrock, and collected the Rover on the next day. How three days later the murder weapon—a kind of filleting knife, the blade of which had been custom-honed to a fine point—came to be found under the front seat of the Fiat, was another question, unless, of course, Flood, knowing that he was being watched, waited and returned and dispatched Coyle with the knife.

"But that would have to have been between the hour that he was observed, roughly one o'clock—Jesus, you're tickling me so!" Having freed the blouse from the waistband of her uniform skirt and pulled it from her shoulders, Ward had begun to run his lips over the fine, reddish-blond hairs at the nape of her neck while his fingers moved to the snap of her brassiere. ". . . and half-two when the Punks who struck you—" With the brassiere undone, Ward's hands slid across her back, around her ribs, and with a touch so gentle they felt like warm feathers, caressed her breasts. "—returned from the cemetery," she managed.

"The solicitous Jammer, as their story went, inquired after Coyle's condition and was asked by him to help him get to Catty's back door on the promise of the blazer he was wearing, the ashplant stick, and even the boater that had once been owned by Joyce himself and had cost Coyle a pile when purchased years before. All Bang and the others knew was that Jammer and Coyle disappeared down the alley—well away from the place in which Catty and Katie and Mary Sittonn said they found the corpse—and returned not long after with the blazer, the stick, and the boater, and without the man."

Ward's thumbs and forefingers were now gingerly feeling her breasts—circling the aureoles, flicking and squeezing her nipples, which were extended farther than she had ever seen them and which felt like they'd burst. "What about the weapon, the knife?" he said, his mouth cupping her ear, his tongue darting into it so that her entire body spasmed agreeably.

Ward was actually amazed. Yes, he had known that

she was a big, well-built woman, but he had never expected what was now in his hands, and he wished he could cut the cast off his palms to appreciate her totally. He had been with large women before—no more than a few nights earlier with the Dane from the Rotunda operating theater—and without exception they struck him as rather gross, especially their breasts, which were either flabby or too soft, their nipples too large or unresponsive to the touch or kiss.

Bresnahan's, however, had shape and body. Their skin was firm and her nipples taut and elastic, and oh, their *size*. Truth was that, after legs, Ward enjoyed the physical woman—whom he seldom got beyond—most for her breasts, and in Bresnahan he had found what he could only believe was perfection.

His mind, coursing (pulsing?) ahead, imagined how it would be to have her swaying over him and all that was now in his hands facing him, hitting him, abusing him with the softest, warmest weights. Or just to have her around, say, placing glasses on the upper shelves of the cabinet in the kitchen, and to catch her unawares and simply heft the slopes of her mighty tits. And then—

His hands fell to the waistband of her skirt, and, pushing off with her legs, she moved back into him, making sure she pressed up against his lap. Hard. "It's that that's got us." Her voice was now a whisper, as she watched the hands continue to disrobe her. "It's the same knife as the Chief thinks he saw in Catty Doyle's kitchen, and the same as the ones in the boy's digs on the other side of the cemetery wall. In appearance."

The band undone, Ward's good hand now moved down onto her stomach, moving over and back over the bare flesh.

"In kind, though, the specific knife was missing from the sheath in the boy's set but present in Catty's.

"I dunno—" The hand dipped still farther and, as he touched her, Bresnahan's body jerked involuntarily; her legs began moving her up against and into him so he could reach lower still. And in a rush she reached back and actually touched him for the first time. "It's a mystery, so it is."

She grasped the back of his neck, which felt hard like sinew, and pulled his mouth down on hers.

And then they were both fully in the bed with him on top and now her, rolling, wrestling. When they could speak, Ward asked, "But who had the opportunity?" He wasn't going to bother to undress her further. He was above her now and naked, and she looked up on him in his nakedness and smiled. He was gorgeous, she thought, all that she could hope for. A thin, strong little monkey of a man that she could bounce around a lifetime long.

"Catty, of course," she said. "Flood. Then Mary Sittonn, who dropped Catty off, was in the neighborhood for at least some time. And Holderness, who Catty says spent the night there. And Jammer—"

Ward lowered himself to kiss her. "A whole passel," he said.

She nodded, her eyes meeting his.

"Five."

Again.

"And your bet?"

"Who dun it?"

He nodded.

She now reached for him. "Inspector Ward, who is advised not to say another word. At least for a while."

✧   ✧   ✧

An hour ran into two, then three. Another cork was popped, and Sergeant McKeon was phoned up and lied to by Ward. "The hospital says it needs more tests, and I was wondering if Rut'ie could take me there. I'm still a bit dicey on me pins."

"Don't you think he'll check?" Bresnahan asked from the pillows. "God—I could never lie to him like that. You don't know him, if he ever found out he'd never let either of us forget it."

"Who's lying? I'm scheduled." He waved a slip of paper at her.

"Then you're going." And suddenly a pall of guilt fell over her like a leaded curtain, and, love or no love, she felt like an utter slut who had abandoned everything decent in her life for drink and easy sex *in the middle of the bloody afternoon,* for heaven's sake. And she looked for someplace to set the wine goblet and get herself out of there.

But Ward wasn't through with her yet; he was in terror of what he'd do if she just left. He was in fact a lady's man, and like drink or drugs or horses or cards would be to another, women were both his singular pleasure and his bane. And once tasted . . . "Suddenly I feel faint." Ward collapsed into the bed and spilled her wine on her stomach. "And then it's virtually impossible to get a taxi around here at this time of day. Give me a touch of that."

"You have your own," she said, already understanding that she was at her best unmanipulated or, rather, when unmanipulable. "Then I'll just have to take what I can get." His head moved toward her stomach.

But when much later she looked at herself in a mirror in the toilet—an obscene thing, it covered one wall—

she burst into tears. Hardly a square inch of her body remained unscathed by marks and bites. He had been like a little animal, so he had—crawling all over her, throwing her around, making her do this and that. Using her. Abusing her. *Pleasurably*, of course; he was good at all of it. Too good.

And when she thought of what her father or mother would think—it was like the bottom had dropped out of her world or what she had known and valued in it. Overnight. A mere week before, she would have wagered all the money she had scrimped to put in the bank for something good and real, like a car or a house, that nothing like this would ever happen to her. And here she stood, without a doubt pregnant, and in love with a little Dublin gurrier who'd equally doubtless bedded half the women in the metropolitan district and was busily embarked on corrupting the rest. And what was she? Merely another notch in his gun, which he'd lost, she reminded himself.

She'd heard of such things; in fact they'd been told to read about them in police training—the psychological ramifications and whatnot. Plainly, Hughie Ward had a Don Juan complex. It was the conquest that mattered to him and no more, and once he had that, there was nothing left. He simply couldn't love, and his involvement with women was just an attempt to prove himself as a man. And wouldn't you know—tears of self-pity now gushed from her eyes—she'd fallen for somebody like that, and she felt she was going to be sick.

Until a knock came to the door. "Are ya comin'?" Ward asked.

She wondered what he meant. "Comin' where?"

"Hogan's. If you don't get a wiggle on we'll be late.

You know how Bernie is with rounds. He'll stick us with two and then leave."

With both hands on the basin and looking at herself in the mirror, Bresnahan said, "Let me understand this completely—you want me to go with you to Hogan's for the gargle."

"Well—you don't seem to be one to say no to a drink. I mean, the *proper* drink. And Hogan's serves wine, I know."

"*With* Detective Sergeant McKeon and the others."

"That's his rank. Superintendent O'Shaughnessy'll be there, and maybe the Chief, if he gets back from that book thing in time."

"And you'll go in one door and me in the other?"

"No, no—what are ya talkin' about, Rut'ie. C'mon, get your clothes on. We go in together."

Suddenly the door opened and her uniform and shoes were tossed in. The door closed.

She examined the tears streaming down her face, which now looked worse than her body. "And what are we to do about this afternoon?"

There was a pause, and then, "I don't understand."

"How do we . . . approach people? McKeon. The Chief."

A longer pause. "I dunno—that's up to you, I guess."

"And not you?"

"Well—I won't let on, if that's what you're worrying about, and why all the questions? Why don't we just ramble on and see what happens."

Bresnahan watched her head move to one side as she assessed what he had said. She nodded. Don't be heavy, be light. Granted he bore an even half of the responsibility for what had gone on, but if he was going to leave it in her hands, so much the better. They were capable ones. She now raised and pressed them on the mirror, then watched the prints evaporate.

In the medicine chest, among a veritable chemist's shop of emollients, shampoos, after-shaves, colognes, and dental flosses, Bresnahan found some eye drops. God bless yuppies, she thought. Or, rather, this yuppy. She scrutinized what skin that could be seen above her collar for monkey bites.

And then her hands and her legs. She couldn't remember where all he'd been, but she would, given a minute.

16

cGarr walked from Dublin Castle to St. Stephen's Green and the Shelbourne Hotel where the book-launching party for Kevin Coyle's *Phon/Antiphon* was being held. As he expected, the event had attracted people from every part of the country; the entire area was jammed with cars, media vans, uniformed police, and a gaggle of raucous press persons who scurried hissing and clicking to every large car that pulled up in front of the hotel.

There were brilliant camera lights on stanchions on the footpath and stairs of the hotel, and a new red carpet below. Somebody—presumably Catty—had even arranged for a massive klieg light that, driven by its computer, was trying to burn through the leaden skies that had rolled in over Dublin with the change in weather. McGarr wondered if the book launching would have been so well attended if not held posthumously. He half hoped it would rain.

For out of their vehicles stepped the smart, trendy people who inevitably gathered at such occasions. They were Lord and Lady This or Baronet That or the sons and daughters of arriviste shopping-center moguls or plumbing-supply heirs with not much more to do of a day than haunt their property or, once or twice a month, haunt places like the Shelbourne. They ate too well and drank too much and, as expected, had little to say

apart from tiresome chat about dogs and horses or inane
drivel about the small circle of people they called friends.

"Oh, Pegeen—didn't I see your picture in the *Times*
the other day?" With a blasé smile Pegeen would then
reply, "But I saw *you* as well. You remember Dermot
or Damian or Darryl, don't you?" who was her latest,
her husband being conveniently absent among the com-
modes and pipes of a warehouse or the featureless streets
of his new housing scheme. How could she forget?
There wasn't much else to remember and—who knew?—
Darryl might well be making the rounds, which was
what persons like Darryl—McGarr now saw one—did.

He was tall and thin with outsized shoulders and a
great mane of black, curly hair. He had a long face
with a drooping nose to match; his dark eyebrows had
grown together. In all, he was an unsightly thing, the
gaunt height of whom a black tuxedo only emphasized,
and he virtually loped toward the marquee of the hotel
with a youngish, busty woman in a satin, emerald gown.
McGarr imagined that he was as ignorant as cow pie
and probably hadn't cracked a book—much less Kevin
Coyle's *Phon/Antiphon,*—in years, yet for all his rude-
ness, he carried himself with a certain panache.

Unself-consciously he strode forward, turning the
charm of long, imperfect teeth to the cameras and of-
fering his hand easily to Catty Doyle and the manager
of the Shelbourne, who were greeting people inside the
lobby. He made the grand entrance seem so terribly
usual that McGarr was rather envious of his aplomb.
But then, he had arrived in a glorious, ancient Daimler
the color of an antique, ruby gemstone, and the black
tie meant that he had been invited to one of the several
smart cocktail parties and dinners that the papers were

reporting had been arranged to follow the "fete/wake for the lamented auteur Coyle."

McGarr had enjoyed what he now appreciated as the Joycean touch in the phrase "fete/wake." Now he waited until the Rolls of the "blond," self-made publisher of several of Ireland's most popular magazines pulled up, and he saw his chance. When the cameras rushed forward to engrave for posterity the image of the fortunate man who was her escort for the night, McGarr pulled the brim of his linen-covered hat over his eyes. Taking the stairs two at a time, he moved quickly past Catty Doyle, still in deep coo with earlier entrants.

The reception itself was being held in the largest of the Shelbourne's public rooms, into which it did not fit, and the invited guests had already spilled out into the wide hall. A waiter bearing a tray of champagne offered a glass to McGarr, who only knitted a brow and, using a shoulder, plunged into the smoky din. McGarr had only once drunk champagne in depth—lamentably, it had been on his wedding night—and he now had a pet theory that lightly alcoholic, deceptively acidic, Gallic, sparged water did not react favorably with the Celtic personality or corpus. Instead of warming the Irish and making them happy and libidinous, as advertised, it sparked flame and illuminated the other, darker side of the tribal personality. After only a few glasses they became argumentative and pugnacious and not infrequently sick for days. Or at least his and his wife's kind of Irish.

And there she was at the drinks table, glass in one hand, book in another, beaming up at the young man with the black, curly mane and long face that McGarr had disparaged from afar only a few minutes earlier.

"Oh, Peter—just who I was looking for," she said when after a good minute she finally noticed her husband by her side. "Do you know what Diarmuid just pointed out? You know Diarmuid Cox, don't you? He's at the Institute for Advanced Studies. This is my husband, Peter."

So much for ignorant suppositions, thought McGarr, taking the tall man's hand, which engulfed his own.

"He too has read *Phon/Antiphon*," she announced, her nostrils flaring superiorly as she surveyed the crowd, only a few of whom were also holding a book, "and he's called my attention to the most remarkable parallel between Kevin's death and an attack upon Samuel Beckett that Kevin mentions here. Tell him about it, Diarmuid." She looked around for someplace to put her empty glass; unfortunately, another waiter was just passing with a tray. "How felicitous. We must be on the same wavelength, you and I." She picked up another, and the waiter glanced at both men before departing.

Said Cox, "Coyle's not the first to report it, but the parallel between what once happened to Beckett and how Coyle met his end is startling."

McGarr turned his head slightly.

"A stabbing."

"Beckett?"

"Yes—right in the chest, for no apparent reason. You see, little in a personal nature is known about Beckett. We know where he was born and went to school and university, and that, like Joyce, he left Ireland shortly afterward and settled in Paris, where he began writing.

"But unlike Joyce, he didn't develop a theory of the artist as a special person, as 'seer' or—"

"Priest of external experience."

Noreen lowered the book, which she had been pretending to read, and turned her head abruptly to McGarr. She blinked several times, as though trying to clear his image. She was wearing a new plum-colored dress that swathed her like a second skin and was split up the side. He wondered to whose cocktail party and which dinner they had been invited.

"Exactly. Beckett contends that nobody's especially gifted with sight or tongues, and no experience, no matter how seemingly dramatic or unique, is so particularly notable that it should demand narration. In other words—and again completely unlike Joyce—the specific and myriad details of human life, all the objects and myths and ideas that Joyce wrote, for example, into *Ulysses* and *The Wake,* can't tell us much about who we are as individuals, because those things are named as words, which are—"

"The creations of Others."

Again a pair of eyes devolved upon McGarr and seemed to see him anew. McGarr was not very literary, but he was a good listener. Before exams in school, he had always made it a point to visit the first boy and coax him to expound at length; McGarr imagined that with Coyle's death, Fergus Flood—whom he could see in a far corner of the room—was again first boy.

"But if the thrust of literature, as we've known it since the Renaissance, has been the attempt—"

"—to define oneself as an individual in one's own terms, then using the words of Others makes it impossible. The second problem is that we think—"

"*Conceive,*" Cox corrected, "of the persona as being an essential—"

"Blank slate."

"*Néant.*" Cox's gaze was now stony. "And finally, modern philosophers tell us that—"

"—words don't work."

Cox nodded. "The naming process is too general, and essentially flawed. The only way to name a thing truly specifically is to negate everything else in the universe, which is absurd."

"But we are forced to try, since, poor tools that they are—" McGarr waited for Cox to carry on.

"—words are all we have. But try minimally we must," Cox added, if only to have the last word, it seemed to McGarr. "Since the entire process of confirming our existences—and therefore being human—is a just a nasty little joke that is being played upon each of us individually. Beckett calls it the *risus puris*, 'The laugh down the snout at that which is—silence please—*cruel.*' "

Noreen lowered her glass, which was half filled, looked into the pale, sparkling liquid, then set it on a table nearby.

Smiling slightly, McGarr asked, "The stabbing?"

"Oh, yes." Cox seemed to blush, and he cleared his throat volubly. "I'm unsure of the date or time, though Kevin—consummate academic that he was—has footnoted it in *Phon/Antiphon.* But at some time in his Paris experience, a man simply walked up to him, plunged a knife into his chest, and walked away. The man was apprehended; when Beckett recuperated, he insisted upon visiting him in prison. There he asked but one question, '*Pourquoi?*' The man replied, 'I don't know.' Kevin interpreted the incident as experiential proof to Beckett that we're merely motes living by chance in a purposeless universe."

"Tell me," asked McGarr, "was the knife ever found?"

"I don't understand."

"The thing. The object. The knife itself—was it ever found?"

Seemingly astonished at the question, Cox's eyes scanned McGarr. "I'm sure I don't know. If you'll excuse me now, I really must—Pleasure," he said to Noreen. "Oh, Deirdre, I was hoping I'd see you here." His hand caught the elbow of a passing woman.

Said Noreen to McGarr, her brow nettled, "Where'd you get all of that?"

"That what?"

"About *néants* and words. Beckett, for Jesus' sake, and don't play games with me."

McGarr again picked out Fergus Flood in the crowd; he took a step in his direction. "It's in the air," he said. Or the water.

Flood was in fettle, surrounded by a brace of young women, not a few of whom McGarr recognized as emissaries of the Fourth Estate. He was wearing a charcoal-gray suit with a black bow tie; a black band was wrapped around his right arm. His smile fell as McGarr approached.

"Ah, Fergus Flood," McGarr said, nodding to the others as he stepped up to them, "professor, author, businessman, academe, and liar. Enjoying yourself while you're still on the loose?"

Flood's eyes moved from McGarr to the women and back. "Please—do you wish to speak to me in private."

McGarr shook his head. "Already have, and pleasantly, with no result. I now have you placed definitely at the scene of the murder at the time of the murder. When you got to the Drumcondra Inn, Kevin Coyle was just coming out. You seized upon the opportunity of denying your wife—"

"Can't we step into another room?"

One of the reporters had snapped open a small, spiral notebook. Another was digging in her purse.

"Me take you out of here? How would that look? And then I wouldn't want to ruin your fun. Great crack, what?" McGarr asked the women, reaching for a glass from a waiter's tray. He handed it to Flood. "As I was saying—you saw it as a double chance to strand your wife, whom you thought was driving the Fiat, and to deny her her assignation with Coyle."

"Would you excuse us?" Flood said to the young woman whose hand was now moving furiously across the page of the notebook. When she said nothing, he took her arm.

"Let go," she complained, shaking him off. "Did you see that?" she asked McGarr, pushing back her eyeglasses on the bridge of a long, bony nose. They were thick and made her eyes look like two dark orbs swimming in a hazy medium.

Said another, "We're just trying to do our job."

"But how did you get in here?"

"Somebody tell him it's a party for the press."

"Ready with the truth?" said McGarr.

"I am, yes, but—" There was discomfort in the features of Flood's dark face. "Can't you understand that I've merely been trying to protect my wife and daughter?"

"What makes you think your wife and daughter need your protection?"

Flood's eyes swept the group, then turned back to McGarr imploringly.

Said McGarr, "Would you excuse us, ladies? I should have something for you by the end of the day."

"No—why? We were invited here. Were you? And get this, McGarr—we're not ladies," she managed, "we're—" But the rest was lost in the din of the others' complaints.

When McGarr finally got them to leave, he said, "You first. And your lies."

"I was confused and couldn't imagine what had happened. I'd driven Kinch—I mean Kevin—up there to remove him from the hotel and, you know, make it difficult for Maura to get to Foxrock. I assumed it was she who was driving the Fiat. But I then had the problem of getting him close to the back gate of Catty's house, and it wasn't until he was out of the car that I realized how drunk he was. He complained and shouted, and—not wanting to make a scene—I left him propped against a wall with all his impedimenta—the hat and ashplant stick. Then to have him turn up dead *and* with the murder weapon under the seat of the car I'd driven away from there, *knowing* he was alive when I'd left him . . . well, I knew I didn't kill him, and I thought maybe—"

"Your wife had. Why?"

Flood twisted his head, as though looking for her along the line of the ceiling. "She's the most possessive—I mean, like most women—" He broke that off too. "What I mean to say is, it's been my experience that some women are possessive. They want not only what they've got but what other women have too, and they'll do— I don't want to say that either.

"It's just that my wife is the jealous type and—"

"She was of Catty Doyle?"

"Certainly. Most assuredly. Elemental jealousy. Dark. Incomprehensible. Capable of—"

"But she said—" She hadn't actually left Foxrock, McGarr meant to say, but of course Flood was right. She *said* she hadn't left the neighborhood. "How could she have gotten there and back before you returned?"

Flood hunched his large, sloped shoulders. "Taxi? A lift from a friend. She might've borrowed a car from a friend."

What was McGarr hearing here, a man implicating his wife? The Floods, like Catty Doyle and her mates and David Holderness, were complicated people, and he wondered if all along the lie had been a ruse to divulge to the greatest effect what was now being said.

"The Fiat is dead slow, and it took me an eternity to get it between the pillars in that laneway."

Dead slow, to be sure.

"In a fast car she could have come and gone easily. And then I didn't actually know that she was in her room when I got back. One thing, though—she'd been drinking. There was only an inch or two left in a bottle of gin on the sideboard in the sitting room when I got in. A glass. Melted ice. And when she's drinking—"

"Then you think she could have brought herself to murder her lover, Coyle?"

Flood cocked his head, "It was my thought . . ." In lying to them, he meant.

"And what about your daughter?" McGarr turned his head toward Hiliary Flood, who was standing just inside the doorway with David Holderness, chatting with a number of people who had turned to them readily as they entered.

"I'm afraid she's daft on yer mahn," Flood said,

meaning Holderness, his accent suddenly unmistakably Dublin in tone and inflection. "And Kevin was a one-man roadblock for David. He would have gotten nowhere at Trinity with Kinch in his way."

"Why? What had Holderness ever done to Coyle?" McGarr continued to watch Hiliary Flood and David Holderness, who now seemed very much the center of attention. A brace of lights had flashed on, and a camera crew from RTE were filming them as they moved into the room, nodding and smiling, accepting a hand here and there. They made a handsome couple, tall and thin, and Holderness surely enjoyed the natural command that McGarr had envied in the others of his class earlier.

"I don't know, though I've thought about it, and often. David was like Kevin's Achilles' heel, the one thing in his tenure at Trinity that seemed arbitrary and even wrong, since by any standard apart from Kinch's, David's work is more than simply competent."

"Something personal, like Catty?"

Flood considered that for a moment, and even turned toward Catty, who was now speaking to a group of musicians who were just about to begin to play. "I don't think so. Kinch's extramarital involvements were wholly recreational and at his convenience. I think it was more a matter of"—Flood's eyes returned to McGarr—"class and style. Analogies are often inaccurate or obtuse, but Kinch's approach to literature and life was indeed Joycean. It was inclusive and encyclopedic and sometimes even rough and banal, though studiously so. Like Beckett's, David's is exclusive, elegant, and nearly minimalist in viewpoint. Each considered the other's position a dead end. Kinch, though, held power over David, and he used it."

"Could Holderness have murdered him?"

"You're asking for an opinion?"

McGarr nodded.

"I certainly hope not." Again Flood's eyes had moved to his daughter and Holderness.

"Why didn't you tell us that where Coyle was murdered was called 'murderer's ground' in *Ulysses?*"

"Well—I thought of it, certainly. But I considered it a mere coincidence and not very important, the book being fiction and—"

"Who of the people we've just mentioned would have known that Samuel Beckett had once been stabbed in the chest just as Coyle was?"

With what appeared to be definite surprise, Flood's head went back. "I never thought of that. I knew, mind, but it didn't occur to me to put the two together."

"Even though you read the proofs of *Phon/Antiphon*, when, six months, a year ago?"

"But I didn't. After his thesis, Kinch never let anybody go over his work. He even managed to arrange his book contracts that nobody—editor, copy editor— could change a word." Flood thought for a moment. "I suppose anybody well acquainted with Beckett and his work. It's not something generally known."

"Who would have had access to copies of *Phon/Antiphon* before Coyle was killed?"

Flood hunched his shoulders. "You'll have ask Catty. While Kinch was alive, she put an absolute lid on the book. At his insistence. He didn't want a single copy leaked to a reviewer or the press until"—Flood waved a hand at the crowd—"in theory, today. The publication date. For all his"—Flood searched for a term—"informality, Kinch was a consummate tactician who understood how to both arouse interest and discourage any possibility of a negative early word blunting the thrust of the book. He used to say there's no accounting for taste or ignorance, to which I always added jealousy, spite, and prejudice."

"I'll ask you one final time—how do you think that knife came to be found under the seat of your Fiat?"

Flood looked down at the full drink in his hand. "I have no idea."

"Your wife here tonight?"

Flood shook his head. "She and Catty . . . and when Maura drinks—"

"Ever get back?" McGarr said, turning toward the musicians.

"Back where?"

"Burlington, Iowa. Your hometown."

Flood reached for McGarr's sleeve.

"Bloke from the *Boston Globe* told me. Said he'd like to do a feature, you know, fellow American making good in Ireland and that class of thing. Wouldn't be surprised if he turns up here."

Flood's eyes darted to the door.

"Rabbi Viner sends you his best, but wonders if you've not been avoiding him."

Catty Doyle tried to duck McGarr. She kept moving through the crowd ahead of him. When he finally caught up with her in a group of people, she spoke first. "Gina—this is Chief Superintendent McGarr. You've probably read of him in the papers. And this is—" With the last introduction she broke away, slipping back into the crowd, and when McGarr finally worked himself free, Mary Sittonn placed herself stolidly in his way.

"Mary!" McGarr said. "How pleasant to see you. And in a dress." He reached out his hand, which she hesitated taking, but when she did, he applied pressure. "Let's make this meeting as brief as we can. Tell me quick exactly when you got Catty home on the night of the murder." He squeezed harder, then a bit more.

Sittonn returned the grip for a few moments, but then snapped her head down at their hands. "You're hurting me."

"Thanks for the acknowledgment. When?"

"Early, you miserable suck." Again she tried to return the pressure, the flesh of her upper arm quaking. The dress was black and rather formal and heavy for summer; McGarr imagined it was one of a kind. For her.

And when she again relented, McGarr only put more into it. "The hour. As close to the second as you can remember. If you swing at me, I'll knock you on your arse. That's a promise."

Through her teeth she said, "When I pulled away from the curb, I rolled down the window to make sure nobody was coming and I heard church bells ringing in the hour. One, exactly."

Still McGarr didn't release her hand. He thought of how she and Katie Coyle had crossed Dublin in her horse-drawn cart to retrieve Coyle's corpse. "Goodness—you have a car? A Fiat perhaps?"

"It's a Jag, left to me by my father, and very special. It doesn't carry stiffs, if that's what you mean."

"Only Cattys. By the way, where is the vixen?" he asked, turning Sittonn so he could move by her. "Ah, I see her now."

She was standing near a dais that supported stacks

of Coyle's book. Behind was an immense, brilliantly-lit blow-up of Coyle standing on the Ha'penny Bridge with the Liffey and quayside Dublin in the background. Around Catty were a group of media people. One was applying makeup to Katie Coyle's face. When the technician turned to Catty, she raised a hand in horror.

"Always ready for any occasion," McGarr remarked, then, to Mary Sittonn, "I do thank you, Mary. You've been most helpful." Thrusting his arm forward, he moved Sittonn away from him and plunged into the crowd that was gathering before the dais.

"Can't we deal with this later?" Catty asked, glancing down nervously to straighten her dress. "Don't you think the mike is too high?" she asked somebody over McGarr's shoulder. "I don't want to have to toy with it."

"Nor me with you, though I will."

She glanced at him, her light blue eyes icy.

"I'll take you out of here right now," McGarr threatened.

"Ready, Catty?" a technician asked. "We really must hurry if we're to make the evening news. They'll want to edit to make the clip fit the time slot."

She started to turn from McGarr when his hand fell to her wrist. "Try me."

"But why? What d'you want from me? I've told you everything from the start."

"Mary Sittonn says she dropped you off at one. How long was it before Holderness arrived?"

Her nostrils, thin and delicately fluted, flared. "Can't this *wait?*" she demanded, loud enough to turn the heads of most near them.

McGarr kept hold of the wrist.

"Catty?" the same voice asked.

"Need some help?" someone else asked, and McGarr turned to the speaker, then back to Catty Doyle.

"I don't *know*, really. I'm not a clock watcher, especially at that hour of night. Not long, I'd imagine. I know I had to"—she lowered her voice, turned her body back toward McGarr and glanced at the others— "bathe and change. Half an hour. A little more. Why? I hope you don't think I or"—lower still—"David—"

"Why not?" said McGarr. "Think of the cachet. One of *your* writers murdering another *over you*, or at least you could make it appear that way."

The blue eyes blinked. "I hope you know what you're doing. A loose, a scurrilous remark like that could ruin me, and I swear to you that if it did, I'd have you in court for a decade, win or lose, and I wouldn't." She was angry now; color had seeped into her pale cheeks and her temple was pulsing.

She then seemed to pause and collect herself before she said, "It was half-one exactly when David got to my house. I remember, because he asked me what Fergus Flood could possibly be doing in the neighborhood at that hour. I was in my bedroom, waiting for him." Defiant eyes clashed with McGarr's. "I turned to the clock by the bed. David said he'd missed all but the last bus to Phibsborough and walked from there. He said he'd seen the car, the little Fiat, heading up the Finglas Road."

"Catty—spare us, please," implored one of the film crew.

"I said, maybe it's Hiliary. No—he'd seen Flood clearly on the driver's side, and there was another figure in the car. I thought nothing more of it or"—she waved a hand in a dismissive manner—"anything else for I don't know how long, until Kinch began barking, which woke me up. We then heard some noise out in the back garden, near Kinch's house and the back gate. It sounded like knocking. David said he'd go down and find out what it was, or at least quiet Kinch so the neighbors wouldn't complain. He's good like that, David." Her eyes rose to the crowd beyond the lights, as though looking for Holderness. "Attentive. Sober."

"Well, Christ—let's pack up and beat it."

"No, please. I won't be a moment." She glared at McGarr. "Where was I?"

"Holderness. Down at the back gate."

"He returned, saying it was just some punks out in the alley. He had Kinch with him so he wouldn't bark anymore. Punk singular, I thought to myself. The mysterious fellow who lives over the wall."

"How long was Holderness gone?"

She shook her head. Her dark hair shimmered in the strong light. "I dozed off until he returned. And afterward I fell asleep for good. I was exhausted."

McGarr didn't doubt.

"What time did you get up?"

"Really now—as I first told you, rather late for a working day."

"And Holderness?"

"David was gone by then. He knows that I prefer to awake alone."

"Don't like to be reminded?"

"Something like that."

"How would he have gotten back home?"

"I don't know. You'll have to ask him. Taxi. Or

hoofed it. He doesn't drive, and he's a great walker. Incredibly fit."

He would have to be to walk to Bray, which was at least a dozen miles distant from Glasnevin. More likely he would have walked down to O'Connell Street and gotten a cab or taken the first bus or train to Bray, if, say, he'd left the Bengal Terrace house at five or so. "Where was the dog, when you got up?"

She had to think. One of the camera crews had actually begun to pack up its gear. "In his house in the garden. David must have let him out when he left."

By the back door, though McGarr couldn't be sure of that.

To the crew, she said, "Hang on a moment. I'll be right with you."

"Tell me about the knives in your kitchen, and I'll let you go. How many days was it before your filleting knife reappeared?"

Her eyes widened. "Wasn't that the most curious thing? How'd you know?"

McGarr waited.

"I don't know, really. I can remember missing it a day or two after Kevin—I mean, Kevin's death. I'd bought a ton of food for Katie, what with the kids and all, and thought I'd prepare something that she could just pop in the oven. But when I turned for the filleting knife to bone out a roast, it was gone. I looked every-where, but—" She shook her head. "David found it that evening. I must have dropped it, and Kinch must have carried it out the open door into the back garden. David said he found it in front of the dog house. The handle has a few tooth marks on it. David wants to get me a better set."

"Do you see that much of Holderness?"

"Not really. Like most men, he's really pretty much of a bore. Always going on about himself and his project, which is not without merit, mind, but . . . and then with the death and the book launching, I think I've seen him just that once."

"When he found the knife?"

She nodded.

"What about Kevin Coyle? What were your impressions of him?"

"Kevin? Kevin had genius, and he was amusing. You never knew what he'd come out with. And then, when he put his thoughts on paper . . ." With a hand she indicated the milling crowd.

McGarr took a step toward the crew, which was preparing to leave. "Kinch—did you name him?"

She shook her head as she turned toward the dais. "David did. He gave him to me. It's what Mulligan called Dedalus in *Ulysses*."

And Flood called Coyle. The name of a dog, according to Holderness, who knew his Joyce but whose area of specialization was Beckett.

"Can't you see that I'm trying to listen?" Hiliary Flood complained as Catty Doyle's voice—introducing Coyle's widow—barely filled the large, packed room.

"And you'll hear more if you answer the question," said McGarr, speaking into her ear. "Between Bloomsday evening and my arriving at your house the day you drove out to yer mahn's digs in Bray, did you use the Fiat at all?" Holderness was standing on the other side of her.

She nodded, her eyes still on Catty.

"When?"

She turned to him. "Every day."

McGarr smiled.

"David is my lover, *as you know*, and I'm to help Catty with the books."

"Really? Are you that friendly with her?"

The girl's eyes strayed to Holderness. "I wouldn't say that. I *work* for Catty. University is expensive, and I don't expect my father to foot the entire cost."

"And how long have you been working for her?"

"On this project? Six weeks now."

"Daily?"

"Nearly—university is closed. It's summer holiday now, as you may have noticed."

"Do you drive in?"

"I used to." Before her car was confiscated, she meant. She moved off.

Standing on the other side of Holderness was an even taller man with a long, pleasant face; McGarr recognized Seamus Donaghy, a successful, if unscrupulous, barrister.

"Planning a legal action?" McGarr asked as he moved toward the door.

The lenses of Holderness's eyeglasses flashed as he turned his head away toward the stage.

"Paranoid, McGarr?" Donaghy declaimed jocularly in the voice he was known for before the bar. His hands were clasped behind his back, his head slightly raised. "Or have you been further invading privacies. Here. As well as there."

"Directly. Count on it."

From the dais Katie Coyle was saying, ". . . enjoy the crack. I'm plannin' to meself. After all the slaving he did on the book, Kevin would've wanted it like this."

Noreen met McGarr at the door. "I hope you're not leaving."

"Where can I meet you?"

"Nowhere. I mean, you don't expect me to go on without you."

It was a leading question, and McGarr glanced down at the glass in her hand, which he righted. "No, you can come with me." He took her arm.

"Where?"

"A little drive out to Glasnevin."

"I can't. There's the cocktails after and dinner at Whites."

"I'll hazard she won't miss you at all," said McGarr. And then, it would look so much less unusual for a man and woman to be entering Catty's De Courcy Square residence from the street than it would a lone man from the rear.

It was nearly tea time in the working-class neighborhood when McGarr pulled up before Catty Doyle's door.

"*This* is where Catty lives?" Noreen asked.

"Well, she owns the house. No mortgage. And I don't see how it differs all that much from your own, m'lady, apart from size."

"You *don't?* Then you've not an eye in your head. It's so meager."

"But consider the advantages. It's quiet, I'd say, once neighbor's kids are put to bed. And private, especially in the wee hours of the morning when everybody else is sleeping."

McGarr opened the door for Noreen and helped her out of the low car.

The skies were still leaden and turbulent, and what with the sudden change in temperature, it felt more like fall than high summer.

"But how . . . ?" Noreen asked him.

"Allow me," McGarr replied, opening the wrought-iron gate and stepping toward the lace curtain that blinded the window in the front door.

There he pushed the bell several times. From deep within the house, most probably from the back garden, they heard Kinch's faint bark. Unobtrusively McGarr raised the pick on his key chain, which had not left his hand, and worked the lock briefly until the bolt slid over. He stepped over the threshold, saying in a loud voice, "Ah, Catty—how are ya this evening. Ah, grim. Yes. Desperate change. It feels more like October than July." And to Noreen, "Say something. Sound like Catty."

She looked blank. "Like what?"

"I don't know, anything. Warble." The walls between the attached row houses were thick, and McGarr knew from experience that all one could hear without the aid of, say, a stethoscope, was the tone of what was said next door.

"Why *warble?*" Noreen asked. "Does she have a bird?"

McGarr closed the door and threw the bolt. "You'd make a heck of a cop, Frenche," he whispered as he moved her down the hall to the kitchen.

"Why? I've helped you in the past, you've said so yourself."

At least she was talking, McGarr thought, and loud enough to be heard. And hearing her, even the dog out in the back garden had stopped barking.

He switched on the overhead light and moved straight toward the cutting board and the brace of knives in the rosewood sheath above it.

The filleting knife was a trifle stuck, and McGarr had to tug to free it from the sheath. And no wonder. Unlike the murder weapon, with its high-carbon, blue steel blade, sharpened so often it was thin, the knife in McGarr's hands was new and made of a titanium alloy (attested to by a stamp on its heel). It still carried the shape that, he imagined, the first knife had borne when new. He pulled the other knives from the sheath. They were all older, with the same high-carbon blades as the murder weapon.

McGarr did not know what to think beyond the obvious conclusion that the murder weapon had most probably been taken from this kitchen. The knives in Jammer's shelter across the wall had been new as well, and made of titanium. Could the missing filleting knife from that set have found its way to this?

Why and how? What was the connection—of Catty to Jammer?

He replaced the knives in the sheath, and in turning around, found that Noreen was no longer in the kitchen. Nor the hall. Nor the sitting room off it.

He took the stairs to the second floor two at a time, only to discover his wife standing in a doorway, her hand to her mouth. She turned to him, her eyes wide in shock.

"What is it?"

"God bless us—who would have thought. Catty?"

Apart from the windows, which were sheathed in black vinyl blinds, the room was completely mirrored—floor, walls, ceiling. A kind of trapeze hung from the ceiling in one corner, and a variety of stools, low couches, and cushions filled the room. Painted on the mirrors in the center was a circular logo. It was the same as the tattoo on Mary Sittonn's shoulder—of a coy-looking cat with green eyes and a long, curling tongue.

A long closet with a bare-bulb makeup table was filled with negligees and every type of night attire: dozens of silk stockings in several patterns but only three colors (black, peach, and the blue of Catty's eyes); tall, spiked, sequined high heels; lacy brassieres with the nipple ends open; tutus with crinoline flounces; a whip; chains and handcuffs; a device that looked to be part of the trapeze, and if employed as McGarr imagined, would hoist a person, like a drawn crab, into the air, where—

"What's this?" Noreen asked. She had opened a drawer and was looking down into its shadows.

It contained nothing but a large—an enormous— dildo, black in color, shaped like an erection, and replete with straps and stiff positioning stays. The sequined letters that ran up its shaft read, LE MULE.

"How could Catty, the little thing that she is . . . ?"

McGarr closed the drawer. Ask Mary Sittonn, he thought. Or David Holderness or Kevin Coyle, were that possible. Kinch of the noose, or—was it?—the trapeze.

In the closet in her actual bedroom McGarr discovered among another great array of garments a pink wig, punk in cut, stylish pantaloons, and several jackets with exaggerated padded shoulders. In a jewelry box they found a pair of pink earrings, swastika-shaped and the size of McGarr's palm.

"Do you suppose she and that Jammer fellow . . . ?" Noreen asked.

McGarr didn't know. He would ask her, for all the

good it would do, but it was Jammer they needed, for several reasons, all vital. The surveillance of the shelter on the other side of the cemetery wall was still being maintained, but McGarr had little hope of his man turning up. The natty clothes that he had found there suggested other options, and Jammer—now involved in murder, grievous bodily assault, and the theft of a lethal weapon, all felonies—was too smart and deceptive to chance a return, for what? A few odds and ends.

Noreen's step faltered before the open door to the mirrored room. As if to herself, she said, "You hear or read of these things, but you think, well, if they exist it's in New York or in Paris or in Los Angeles. *Never* in Dublin and *never* somebody you know."

In the car McGarr checked his wristwatch. "The affair at the Shelbourne must be winding down. What say we canter on to the cocktail party or the dinner."

"Take me home," she said.

"What?"

Shock and dismay widened her eyes and furrowed her brow. "Surely you don't expect me to speak to the woman after what we just saw? Perhaps you, what with your occupation—"

"Profession," McGarr corrected.

"—and all are jaded and come upon that sort of thing every day, but not me. If I see that woman on the street, I'll cross to the other side. We're quits, and that's final."

"But remember, you didn't see anything at all. We weren't even—"

"You expect me to forget that?"

"What?" McGarr struggled not to smile.

Bright patches of indignation now colored his wife's

cheeks. "That—that *thing* in the drawer?" she demanded.

"I don't know—" He tried to say, I suppose that's up to you.

But she spoke over him. "It and that whole place and that woman and anybody, including Kevin Coyle, who ever had anything to do with her is ugly.

"Now. Belgrave Square, and not a smirk, if you know what's good for you. Ooh—" She leaned back in the seat and pincered her temples. "I've a splitting headache."

17

When McGarr got to Dublin Castle the next morning, he found a report on his desk about the murder weapon in the Coyle case. Another report—preliminary—concerned the discovery of a body floating in the Royal Canal sometime in the early hours of the morning. McKeon had dispatched Delaney and Flynn. Also, there were three requests for further information on cases pending before the courts.

He sipped from the hot mug of coffee that Bresnahan placed on his desk, then topped it up with fermented, aged malt from the bottle he kept in the lower left-hand drawer of his desk. Superintendent O'Shaughnessy was sitting in the chair by that side, reading the papers; he reached down and kept McGarr from closing the drawer. McGarr handed him the bottle, and he added a good three inches to his tea cup.

"Hard night?"

"Jammer. I thought I saw him." He raised the paper again and peered into it.

"Whereabouts?"

"Near the Shelbourne, of all places. Tuxedo, black tie. Long black wig curling in the back. But it was him, all right. I'd bet on it."

McGarr would too. O'Shaughnessy had a rare memory for faces, and the artist's mock-up of Jammer had been posted all over the office.

He wondered if Jammer had actually attended the book-launching ceremony or some of the later festivities. To what point? To taunt the police? Theft? Could he too have been involved with Catty? McGarr thought of all the modish clothes and the pink wig that they had discovered in her closets. The swastika earrings.

"Rut'ie?" O'Shaughnessy called out of the cubicle, then raised the paper again.

"Yes, Super?" she answered almost immediately, appearing in the doorway.

O'Shaughnessy said nothing. She picked up the tea cup. "A chaser, Chief?"

McGarr raised his head. It was the first time she or any subordinate had inferred that the substance added to his coffee in the morning was something other than what should be found in a Garda facility. And what was he seeing? There was something different about Bresnahan, but he couldn't tell what—her smile, her tone of voice, her manner? Perhaps.

He lowered his head to the report, and she left.

It said that the knife that had killed Coyle was an Everdur, a quality item that had been manufactured in Coventry up until seven years ago, when a multinational corporation had purchased the company, closed down the plant, and begun producing a different version in Taiwan. The new product differed only in its blade, which was stamped from a titanium alloy not forged from blue steel. None of the latter was available any longer in the Dublin area, or for that matter, anywhere else. The newer model, however, was stocked by two well-known kitchen- and restaurant-supply shops.

Eleven sets had been sold in the last week, and when the artist rendering of Jammer had been shown employees, one shop girl had said that she was almost certain he had purchased a set. "Very conservative type, though nice," she said. "Brown tweed suit and storm coat, like a solicitor." He had paid cash.

McGarr made a note in the margin to the effect that front facial photos should be obtained or taken of Fergus, Maura and Hiliary Flood, Katie Coyle, Mary Sittonn, Catty Doyle, and David Holderness and shown to the same employees, though he held no hope for that.

Conclusion? Jammer had bought the second set of knives to replace the missing filleting knife, which had been the murder weapon, in the sheath of the knife rack in Catty Doyle's kitchen.

Why? What was his relationship to her? Lover? Friend? Relative? Simple neighbor? McGarr made another note directing McKeon to obtain a bio of Catty Doyle, particularly indicating the whereabouts of any siblings.

And if Jammer did know her, how had he replaced the knife in the kitchen? With her concurrence? Was she a party to the murder? Had she lied to them?

Either she or Holderness had. And Flood.

At the cocktail and dinner parties, which McGarr attended alone, Catty, when asked, assured McGarr that she did not know Jammer. Twice while sunning herself in her back garden she had seen a man who looked like him steal over the wall of the cemetery, which she assumed he'd done to save the long walk around, and then a few other times while she was waiting for the bus. "Oh—I noticed him, certainly, as I would any other interesting young man. Or, man," she had added coyly. "Pity your wife took ill. I hope it wasn't the champagne."

Holderness, however, had said outright that she had

lied about him. If there had been some knock on the back garden gate that night, as Catty had said, they wouldn't have heard it, dog or no dog. "You see, we were in another room in Catty's house that's sound-proofed. If you ask properly, perhaps she'll show it you." He smiled. "And after our exertions, I'm afraid I fell fast asleep until about five or so, when I rose and walked back into town and took the first bus out to Bray and to some blessed rest. Catty's best taken in small parts." The smile grew fuller. The round, wire-rim glasses flashed in the light of the chandelier over-head. Donaghy was still standing by his side, listening intently now.

McGarr wondered if Holderness knew he had been in the house. But how? And why would Catty say what she had about his having gotten up to investigate the knock on the back garden gate if it weren't true—to implicate him in murder? "Could she be lying, then?"

"Lying's such a harsh term. Perhaps she dreamed it, or she's in shock—to have had such an ugly thing happen to an acquaintance so close to one's abode. And to somebody so"—he had opened his empty hands to mean the gathering—"noted as Kevin Coyle."

Then what of what Bang had said of Jammer: that Jammer, considerate as he was, had made a bargain with the drunken Kevin Coyle. The ashplant stick, blazer, and hat for safe passage down the alley to Catty Doyle's back garden gate? Would Jammer have knocked? McGarr would have, if only to get the man in. The hat: drunk or sober, Coyle would not have relinquished that to anybody, especially for something so slight as getting himself to a back door on a night that had been described by everybody concerned as fair.

And when McGarr had asked again if Donaghy and Holderness were planning some legal action, Donaghy replied in the affirmative, saying that they had only that afternoon initiated a suit against Trinity College to release Holderness's thesis—which Coyle, as thesis advisor, had rejected and sequestered—to an ad hoc faculty reviewing committee headed by Fergus Flood. "Kinch was so dogmatic in his antiquarianism, when in fact all that was required of him was an assessment of the academic merits of the paper, which are beyond reproach."

"Kinch?" McGarr asked.

Yet again the thin, unpleasant smile appeared. "I've grown fonder of him in death." McGarr thought of other references: to "murderer's ground" in *Ulysses*, where Coyle had been found; to the parallel between Beckett's and Coyle's stabbings; to Catty Doyle's little dog, the one that Holderness had given her; and the meaning of the word kinch. Noose.

"What about a man named Jammer?" he asked.

"Named *what?*"

"Jammer. You've heard it before."

"I have? When?"

"He's one of Catty's *friends*. A tall fellow. Modish in dress."

Holderness shook his head.

"Lives over the wall in the Glasnevin Cemetery."

"Certainly you don't mean he's a *shade?*"

"You've seen him plenty of times in the early morning, skulking out of the lane."

"Me or this Jammer?"

Donaghy had interrupted, "Fishing here, McGarr?"

McGarr had turned to a waiter who was dispensing

smoked salmon with capers and onions from a tray. "I like fish. Wouldn't mind if we had some tonight."

But the entrée had proved to be veal swimming in a champagne sauce, and, claiming he had a phone call to make, McGarr slipped out. Given his duties, he found people usually made excuses for him; then, actually, he had reports to write.

Now, with the staff filing in for the morning briefing, he raised the mug of coffee and took a long swallow. Pushing himself away from his desk, he let the hot malt trickle down his throat. He put his feet up on the edge of the dustbin and looked out the open window.

There, past the eaves of the Castle, past the spires of Christ Church and St. Audeon's in the Liberties, was a solitary patch of blue sky, dotted with a puff of cloud. It looked like a solitary, inquisitive hoary eye perusing the city. He thought of Catty Doyle's eyes, which were just about that color, and then the tattoo on Mary Sittonn's arm, and finally of the mechanisms and devices and whatnot in that mirrored room.

And he decided—taking another touch of liquid fire— that, considering the corpse that had been found overnight floating in the canal and the other murders that were sure to be committed as time went on, they had done about as much as they could for the moment to bring Kevin Coyle's murderer to justice. The investigation had come down to a small amount of physical evidence, a handful of potential suspects, and one person's word against another's. And even if, say, Holderness had admitted to answering the knock on the back garden gate, what then?

The problem was they were understaffed and would

soon have to end the surveillance of Jammer's kip inside the walls of the cemetery in Glasnevin. Sure, Ward had come back to work—he now entered the cubicle and was asked by Bresnahan *(Mirabile dictu!)* if he wished tea or coffee. But Ward was only good for paperwork, and that with one hand, and failing the reappearance of Jammer, they were stuck.

Said McKeon, wiggling his cup, "As long as you're going that way, Rut'ie."

"La—I'll have me hands full," she replied so pleasantly that McGarr turned his head to her, "and tell me, Sergeant, where's your rank?" And when he began to complain about Ward, she added, "Or your sling. Or were you crippled beyond the call of duty last night?"

McGarr blinked.

Some of the staff, which had filed in and taken their positions, chuckled.

What was it about her that was so odd? McGarr wondered. When she came back with the two cups (one for herself), he took another close look. Her hair? No. Yes—somehow it was thinner, or she'd brushed it back from her temples. And it was sort of curly and a bit spiked on top. And then, was she wearing makeup? He thought so, though what with the poor light and him only half awake, he couldn't tell.

He was about to take another satisfying belt from the mug when he snapped his head back. Bresnahan was out of uniform. That was the difference, and she looked—what was the word Catty Doyle had used?— *interesting* for the first time in his memory.

Said O'Shaughnessy, "Sinclaire and his crew need a break. I thought Rut'ie and Hughie might spell them for the next few days until—"

They could no longer afford to give the case such attention, he meant.

McGarr hadn't taken his eyes from Bresnahan. She was wearing a tight, sleeveless blouse that was open rakishly to, well—his eyes kept descending—and a wide, shiny plastic belt that made her waist seem tiny for a woman of her size. It emphasized the flare of her narrow hips, but more particularly, the expanse of her shoulders and the radical angle of her chest. Her skirt was tight and short and also black, and she was wearing flat shoes to match, which made her long legs look girlish and thin.

For the first time, McGarr began thinking of Bresnahan as something other than a spare who'd been borrowed from the uniformed service. If she could continue to make herself look more noticeably "Dublin," as it were, he might have continued use for her, and not just in the office. The way she'd handled Katie Coyle, Mary Sittonn, and Catty Doyle in the antique shop had been quite professional.

With most eyes on her, she now said brightly, "It all comes down to motive, doesn't it?" When McGarr said nothing, she continued, "We have four people that we know about who had the opportunity. Fergus Flood, though he was seen to leave the area, might've returned. Jammer, who was last seen with Coyle, and on the report of one of his mates, returned shortly after with the ashplant stick, the boater, and Coyle's blazer. Holderness, who Ms. Doyle reported left her company to investigate some noises they were hearing from the back garden, though he says not. And she herself. Ms. Doyle, that is.

"As for means, we have Flood in possession of the

murder weapon four days later. We have Jammer and his companions in possession of Coyle's stick, blazer, and hat. We have Jammer as well in possession of a set of knives like those in Catty Doyle's kitchen, but newer, and with the exception of the filleting knife itself which—again we assume—somehow found its way into the slot of the murder weapon in Catty Doyle's kitchen, *if* indeed the murder weapon was taken from her kitchen, and we have no way of knowing that. We have Holderness with access to that knife and to Coyle, *if* we can believe Catty's story that the considerate Holderness got up in the middle of the night to investigate some noise or knocking down at the back garden gate. Then there's Catty, who, if Holderness slept through some of the night, as he said, had the same chances with the knife and victim as he. And finally—to complete means—we have the knife itself, which turned up in the Fiat to which all of the above-named, apart from Jammer (and we don't know about him), had access: the Floods near total, Holderness on at least several occasions, and Catty on the occasions in which Hiliary drove down to help her prepare for the book-launching bash.

"Motives? Floods are several."

McGarr's eyes went from Bresnahan to Ward, who, seated on one of the tables, had leaned back against the cubicle wall and was watching her intently, a small smile puckering a dimple on his right cheek. Curiouser and curiouser, McGarr thought. Even down to Bresnahan's sudden loss of the most distressing aspects of her Kerry accent. Had she been taking elocution lessons? he wondered.

"Flood's wife was having an affair with Coyle about which Flood knew. Worse, it was rather public—the

Drumcondra Inn and that man Cathcart, and so forth. Coyle also had passed Flood by professionally and was likely, with the new book, to leave him in the dust entirely.

"Jammer?" She cocked her head from side to side as though assessing the boy. "I suspect that somebody like Jammer wouldn't need a motive, but why murder Coyle, who'd just made a deal to surrender what he had on him anyhow? Money? Coyle had needed none that day, and whatever little he'd had, I'd hazard was long spent by then. And would Jammer have come equipped with a filleting knife nearly a match for the one in Catty Doyle's kitchen, or, to reverse the scenario, the filleting knife from Catty Doyle's kitchen, which he would then carry all the way out to Flood's house in Foxrock and secret into the Fiat? And then be so astute as to find a look alike for, and replace it in the sheath in Catty Doyle's kitchen? And finally, after having done that, not gotten rid of the other knives in the new set, and him living just over the wall from Catty's and the murder scene?" Bresnahan shook her head. "Either he didn't know everything that was going on that night and/or later, or Jammer is stupid, and we're thinking by the way he's avoided us he's not.

"Holderness—he despised Kevin Coyle, who had denied him the advanced degree he was seeking. And then, what was it you wrote in yesterday's report, Chief?"

McGarr said nothing. She had the ball and was running well. He would let her continue. How many others of the staff had already read yesterday's reports? McKeon, perhaps. Maybe Ward.

" 'Kevin had genius, and he was amusing.' I wonder how many times Catty said that in Holderness's hearing?

She's manipulative and, I'd say, not a little bit nasty, when all's said and done. Might she have been 'playing' Holderness on the night in question? Might she have worked him up enough about Coyle that when the knock came to the door—and her, knowing it was Coyle and how drunk he was—she feigned sleep so that he could slip downstairs and complete her design? Coyle could have phoned her, the way he phoned Maura Flood, from the Drumcondra Inn."

"But *why* would she have wanted that to happen?" asked McKeon, looking sourly into his empty cup. "What did she have to gain?"

Bresnahan hunched her large shoulders. "I'd be hard-pressed to answer that. Something dark maybe that we don't know about. Could be she suspected that both of them or men in general looked upon Catty Doyle as somebody fun to be with in the small hours of the morning, and she was searching for some corroboration that that fear was unfounded. Could be that she secretly despises men, or hated Coyle in particular for the way he treated his wife. Or maybe even—who knows with her?—a murder that night might have seemed like an interesting diversion or added a certain—"

"Piquancy," McGarr mumbled.

"Thank you, Chief—to the book launching. I don't know, but there's the literary aspect to all of this—the reference to 'murderer's ground' out of *Ulysses,* and then the parallel to the Beckett stabbing in Paris—that shouldn't be ignored. But if I know anything about women," Bresnahan went on, her eyes narrowing a bit, "that Catty's game is control, and for her control is everything: *her* writers and *her* lovers and *her* friends and *acquaintances* even, like Hiliary Flood, for Jesus' sake, who was *working* for her and *continued* to work for her even after she knew of Catty's goings-on with Holderness!"

"Which is power," said McKeon.

"What?" Bresnahan demanded, again stopped in mid-stride.

"Down, girl. Down. I was just making the observation that control is power and *that's* what that . . . *woman* is after. Which is the animal that eats her mate, hoofs and all, after they've done the dirty boo-gee?"

"The dirty *what?*"

"The dirty boo-gee," said McKeon, rolling his eyeballs. "Like in boo-gee woo-gee."

"Why *dirty?*"

"I don't know, it's American."

"I think he means boogie-woogie," Delaney chimed in. "Something like, 'Beat Me, Daddy, Eight to the Bar.' "

"It's not an animal but an insect," Bresnahan announced in an attempt to regain the floor. "The praying mantis."

"Wouldn't you know it'd be American. They've every class of thing going on over there."

"Sure, you'd be praying too, if you knew you were going like that. I wonder—can it be pleasurable? For the male."

Which was how the Castle Murder Squad left the Kevin Coyle case.

Months went by. The hot summer mellowed into a fall of extended fair weather that did not harden into winter until November. Then, however, the days grew short, the skies darkened, coal was burned for heat, and with a sudden air inversion around the first of December, night seemed to extend right through the day.

It was on one such gloomy afternoon that Sergeant McKeon, having worked a fortnight without a break, was taken to lunch at Hogan's by McGarr and O'-Shaughnessy and ordered not to return to the office for at least three days. After they'd left, Hogan asked McKeon if he'd care to remain in a snug through "holy hour," an atavistic, Victorian licensing invention that forced Dublin tipplers into the streets between two-thirty and three-thirty each weekday afternoon.

But McGarr and O'Shaughnessy having done their duty, McKeon had already imbibed snootful enough to warrant a breath of air, such as it was, and he remembered suddenly that it was Ward's day off as well. His digs—a bachelor "pad," if the singularly married McKeon had ever ogled one—were merely a stagger away on the quays. Humming himself a little ditty and feeling free as a bird who'd be willingly recaged in an hour, McKeon, the father of twelve children, set off.

There he knocked once and, as was his custom with all friends, subordinates, or suspects, entered the old, battered, commercial building. Wondering why on the good, green earth that he once knew in his native County Monaghan, a young lad, like Ward from Waterford, would want to live in a shambles like this—unless it was to keep the cries of elation, the transports of joy, the screams of ecstasy from reaching innocent ears—he hauled his fifteen stone to the landing, where again he simply opened the door.

And there it was, much like he had left it—when was his last visit?—nearly a year ago Christmas, when he'd also been in his cups, apart from the plants. Jesus, could Ward be moonlighting as a horticulturalist? he wondered. He pushed past the fronds of some jungly palm in an immense pot and turned to a shelf of orchids, dozens of them, that scented the air like the perfume counter in a chemist's shop. They lined the entire long divider that led into the living area of the loft.

And distracted, turning this way and that, he failed to notice Ward in bed, bare from the torso up and a forearm covering his eyes in sleep, until he was nearly upon him. Checking his wristwatch, McKeon thought he'd just turn on his heel and go back out, since it was three and he'd return to Hogan's just as the doors were opening. It was then he heard the click of a plate on the stove in the kitchen area and smelled—was it? Coddle, he bet!—bubbling in a pot.

"Live-in" maid? he thought. The little dodger. But with the plants and all, he wasn't able to see what she looked like until he stepped around the counter that functioned as a serving table.

"*Rut'ie,*" he nearly shouted. "What are *you* doing here? I thought you were—" In Kerry on holiday, since they'd arranged the schedule such that she'd work through the Christmas holidays.

"And—" His eyes descended. Bresnahan was wearing a flowered a Japanese robe that extended only to her upper thighs and was belted—loosely was not the word—at the waist.

Plainly surprised by the visitor, she lowered the pot and tried out a smile. "Sergeant."

McKeon did not smile back.

She hunched her shoulders and placed her hands on her hips. The smock was nearly transparent. "I could tell you five lies that you'd not want to hear and you'd not believe. Instead, can I offer you a drink and something to eat? Excuse me while I get my robe."

And whether it was what he'd already consumed or the heat of the place or the shock at having much of what he knew of two people who were close to him so radically altered, McKeon felt suddenly drunk or tired. "Oh—oh, no *thanks*," he said, lowering himself into a chair in the kitchen area. "I—I t'ink it's beautiful," he crooned. "Bee-yoot-i-ful!" And all the more so when a glass was filled and tears came to his eyes. "I couldn't think of anything better." Or more surprising.

It was during the same week that McGarr opened the *Irish Times* and discovered two articles that pertained, albeit obliquely, to the still-unsolved Coyle case. One was a reprint of a long *Boston Globe* article about an interview with Professor Fergus Flood of Trinity College, in which he cited his humble beginnings in Burlington, Iowa, his training in various obscure American universities, and finally his arrival at Trinity College on the strength of his published work on Joyce, Yeats, Synge, O'Casey, and Beckett.

"You see, up until coming here I'd thought of myself as more writer than teacher. Here, however, teaching is my focus, if only because of the excellence of my peers. In particular, I mean the late, lamented Kevin Coyle, who was a brilliant chap altogether, and now people like . . ." He named several other Irish, academic writers, including David Holderness, "who has a book coming out, based on his thesis, that should make quite a stir."

Flood was candid about how quickly he'd become "acculturated"—"I'd had an Irish mother, you see, and things Irish just come natural to me, I guess"—and expressed no wish to return to his native land. "Everything's so much more accessible here." Like fame? the interviewer had asked. "In a country of four million people? Let's call it notoriety instead."

The second article was a report that the suit of David Allan George Holderness, M.A., against Trinity College either to release his thesis or grant him his doctorate had been settled out of court. Holderness agreed to drop his demand for punitive, monetary damages in return for the granting of the degree, as well as the college's pledge to examine without prejudice his further application for the position of Lecturer in English and Modern Languages.

> . . . a post that has been vacant since the death of the internationally respected Kevin Coyle. Holderness's volume, "Less and Less, Yes: A Study of Style and Narrative Voice in the Novels of Samuel Beckett," will be issued in March by the London publisher Hollis & Murken. Holderness was represented by Mr. Seamus Donaghy, Esquire.

When McGarr got home that evening, Noreen poured two frosted pints of lager and raised hers in toast. "This is by way of congratulations. It seems you're not as old and . . . used as you would have me think, and you've done your job." She clinked glasses and drank until she nearly choked. She set the glass down. "That's me last bit of booze for a good while. The doctor tells me I'm pregnant, and I'll be thanking you to keep none of it in the house."

After congratulating her as fully as he thought decorous, McGarr took himself out for a few solitary jars to consult his real feelings about the extraordinary news.

A few weeks closer to Christmas, Detective Inspector Hughie Ward was given by chance the very best of early presents. He was walking along Grafton Street, window shopping, when out of the corner of an eye he glimpsed something familiar and important in the throng of people before him.

Turning as though to look in at a shop window, he used the angle of the glass to scan the street which, closed off during shopping hours, became a mall. What? Or who?

The clutches of women, some speaking together, others window shopping? The tall, bearded man who, as always, was selling the latest issue of *In Dublin* in front of Bewley's coffeehouse? The woman bearing down on him with a pram in one hand and a toddler in the other? Two nuns, one lame with an aluminum walker? The gang of punks who, having taken the middle of the street with hoodlum bravado, were causing milling shoppers to break before them like froth from the bow of a ship?

No. The step. The walk. The bounce, cocky. It was one of the things that McGarr had taught Ward when he first joined the Squad and began surveillance work. New clothes, a different hairstyle or color, a disguise—it didn't matter. One thing few suspects could change for very long was the way they walked. And the tall man in the deep blue, three-piece pinstriped suit, wearing a bowler hat and carrying a long, spiked umbrella, bounced so on his shiny, black, wing-tipped brogues that Ward could see the soles were still beige.

He did not need to check the narrow nose flaring to wide nostrils, the close-set hazel eyes, the high cheekbones and forehead. In bitter gall that cocky strut had been etched on his memory.

Jammer.

Ward felt almost nauseous, knowing that he had at last found him, and he did not pause to think what to do.

Jammer himself had stopped to look at something a few doors distant, and in three quick strides Ward entered the boutique in front of which he was standing. A woman looked up and Ward said, "This is a police emergency. Phone this number. Tell them Ward has found Jammer near Bewley's in Grafton Street. He needs backup." Before he kills him, he thought.

"Got that?" He tossed his I.D., which also listed the Castle number, on the counter near the cash register.

"I think so. Who?"

"I'm Ward," he tapped the I.D., "and I've found Jammer."

"Jammer," she repeated, as he ripped off his topcoat and his suit coat, placing the weighty Walther that McGarr had loaned him—until they retrieved the Beretta—on a shelf beneath the counter.

The woman's eyes widened.

Ward raised a palm to calm her. He felt constrained by clothes; he never exercised in anything but tights and athletic shoes. He imagined he would look to Jammer like some shop boy hurrying back to business at closing time. And then there were far too many people about for the Walther. Or the Beretta, which he would have to get off him first. If he still had it, and Ward didn't doubt that he had.

"*Now*, please."

Jammer was now walking on jauntily, using the tall umbrella with its straight handle—something meant for golf, Ward judged, or to shield a group at the races—like a swagger stick. Looking this way and that, the bowler set down on his eyes, he was—and Ward knew he knew he was—collecting stares from the girls and young women passing by.

What were they seeing? Banker, businessman, solicitor, financier. At least a clothing-shop manager. And all at such a young age. Which was? Twenty-five, twenty-seven. Nearly Ward's own age, and much older than he had originally thought. But a felon packing a handgun? Nobody would have guessed, apart from Ward, who now stepped out of the shop.

Ward himself was twenty-eight and had spent a good bit of sixteen years in the ring. He weighed 148 pounds and was in splendid condition. His left wrist? Well, he'd undergone therapy—prescribed and his own—and it still felt dicey after an hour or so on the bags.

His left ear? With a surgical operation to remove dead tissue and blood from near the inner ear, his doctors had managed to save 10 percent of the hearing he'd had five months earlier. Ward had not managed to overcome the anger he felt about the loss, not that he had tried very hard.

And finally, of course, he was missing his service weapon. Sorely. It was that that rankled most—the injury to his pride and the constant reminder, whenever he learned of a crime committed with a handgun, of how he had erred. Ward eased the door of the shop closed.

He waited in the entry, which was darker than the street and shielded by glass, so he could see Jammer, but not Jammer him. No chances here. No warning. No regulation announcement. Ward was thinking revenge. He could taste it.

Jammer was maybe twenty feet away and closing.

Ward sucked himself up, the way he did in the ring, and shuffled a step or two. But muted; nothing to give himself away, no flurry of punches, no bobbing, no weave.

Ten.

Ward made himself realize that this was more than a vendetta, that beyond the personal score he would settle, Jammer had in some direct way been involved in the murder of not simply a citizen, which would be enough, but also a man who had made Ireland proud and could have made her prouder still, had he lived.

Five.

But Jammer broke suddenly. In a few quick steps he was off the curb and across Grafton Street toward the swinging doors of Bewley's, which was always packed but especially at this hour and time of year, when it bustled with weary shoppers and retail personnel refreshing themselves before heading home.

He was quick and agile for somebody so tall—could he have copped on to Ward's presence, as he had before? Ward wondered. No. There'd been no way Jammer could have seen him, his face having been averted when he had first noticed Jammer's stride.

Jammer bumped through the swinging doors into the wide foyer of Bewley's, a baked-goods and candy-sales area, and held the door for an old woman who was toddling out with a pushcart and a small, ancient dog on a leash.

Ward lowered his head and kept walking. He even

said, "Ta," when Jammer waited until Ward had the door before releasing it. Slowing his step, Ward pretended to take interest in a display of Christmas cakes while Jammer moved toward the main tea room and the lift and stairs that led either to a second floor dining room or to the toilets in the basement.

He chose the stairs up, mounting them two at a time as though in a hurry. Ward decided he'd give him a minute lead, since the upstairs dining room had only one emergency exit, which was rigged with an alarm. And a good thing he waited, for Jammer now appeared out of the lift and walked quickly into the main tea room. Careful. He consulted the reflection off the bakery display cases and glass doors to see if he were being followed, making Ward wonder if something had spooked him, like his own distinctive walk, some gesture, the one word he had uttered.

The main dining room was a turn-of-the-century relic with tall ceilings and large, multicolored, leaded-glass windows. It was divided into two sections: the smaller served by waitresses; the other cafeteria-style, with tables and deep, red-plush wall sofas distinctive to Bewley's and much favored by students and the elderly, who nursed single cups of coffee for hours while reading newspapers or chatting. Ward knew which section Jammer would choose: the larger and more anonymous, with no waitress to stare into his face and mark him.

But there was a long line at the sandwich, salad, and dessert cases, a longer one still at the hot-meal, steam-table service section. Only the four women at the tall, chrome coffee urns that dispensed Bewley's renowned brew seemed to be filling orders quickly; when Jammer moved in that direction, Ward decided what he would do. Pushing through the throng, he quickly made up the distance between them, so that when Jammer picked up a mug of coffee and turned toward the registers, Ward stood directly behind him.

Jammer had not taken a tray when he first walked into the dining room; he would have to release the umbrella to pay for the coffee. Then, with one hand around the mug, his other in a pocket, and his back turned to Ward, he would be exposed and vulnerable.

Jammer ordered a coffee white; it was dispensed in a hiss of steam from the urn, and by pointing to the cup and nodding, Ward ordered the same without having to speak. As he'd suspected, Jammer was too involved with the things in his hand and the coins he would need to pay for the coffee to turn for a look at him. And when, at the register, the left hand leaned the umbrella against the metal bars of the tray slide and slipped into a trouser pocket, Ward acted.

Raising his mug of coffee chest high to extend his elbow, he plunged into Jammer, striking him with his forearm just below the shoulder blades. The coffee sloshed over the rim onto the blue, pinstriped suit jacket, and Ward released his grip on the mug.

As it fell, he pulled up a vent of the jacket and discovered what had been causing the slight bulge there at Jammer's waist. His other hand clamped down on the butt of the Beretta, which had been stuck under his belt at the small of his back; he pulled it free. The mug, hitting the floor, broke into bits and splashed hot coffee over their shoes and trousers.

"Sorry," Ward said in the Dublin equivalent of pardon me. "Jammer," he added, smiling. "I believe this is mine." Ward tucked the Beretta under his own belt. "Or would you fancy trying to get it back?"

Jammer's eyes, still hooded under the narrow brim

of the bowler, darted to the exit door, then back at Ward, and finally to the cup of coffee that he was still holding daintily in his hand.

"Rachel!" The woman at the register began shouting. "We've got a spill. Over here at register one."

Two spills, as Jammer released his own mug and snatched up the umbrella. Jumping back, he raised it in front of him with arms extended, like a defensive brace.

Said Ward in a loud voice, "I am a police officer, and you are under arrest."

Taking a step forward with his fists tightened over the long umbrella, Jammer began backing Ward into the corner formed by the counter of the steam service area and the coffee urns, which was acceptable to Ward. The ceiling dropped down there, and any attempted blow with the umbrella from overhead or from the right would prove impossible.

Ward had one palm—the right—outstretched, and somebody not far from them had begun to scream. Beyond Jammer's wide shoulders he could see people beginning to leave hurriedly in panic, as was common now in Ireland when violence was threatened in a public place.

"I repeat—you are under arrest for assault, for inflicting grievous bodily harm, and in connection with a murder investigation."

Jammer struck out. His left hand slid down the handle of the umbrella and he swung it like a long, tight bat at Ward's head.

Ward ducked, then sidestepped quickly; the umbrella shot over him and over the serving counter and clipped through a steam pipe on a coffee urn. It struck the tall, metal reservoir with a resounding roar that raised further shrieks. A funnel of bright steam jetted toward the ceiling, and Ward, loading all his weight into his right fist, struck Jammer a stinging blow to the ear that made him cry out. "Ya fookin' bastard, ya. Ya *cop!*"

And again.

Jammer's head smacked into the glass of a food case, cracking it, and his derby and dark wig fell off. He was bald or had shaved his head, and infuriated now, he swung the other way, again missing Ward. The momentum carried the umbrella—which, Ward guessed, had been weighted—into the second register, which toppled to the floor, spilling change everywhere.

Ward hit out again at Jammer's other ear; the force of the blow spun Jammer around. Now the dining room was in full flight, and Ward stepped into the man.

Below the belt first, with punches shoveled up from knee level—once, twice—the belly softer with each blow, until with the third punch Jammer's fingers lost their grip on the handle and the umbrella slipped to the floor.

Ward stepped back and kicked it out of the way. He could hear sirens now, and he wondered how much time he had.

That was when Jammer's hand moved into a back pocket of his trousers and came out in a fist that sprouted a long, thin blade.

"Ah, now," said Ward, "we're to stop the fun and play serious, are we?" He looked around, hoping there might be a witness.

One: a stout woman across the counter in a kitchen doorway. She had a red face and a spotted apron and was holding in one, meaty hand a length of lead pipe.

"Do you see that?" Ward asked her.

"A knife," she replied.

"A stiletto," said Ward. "I don't like knives. Sometimes they kill people."

"Mind yourself now," she advised, as Ward reached for the umbrella and Jammer lashed out.

Ward snatched it up and, pivoting, swung the umbrella up from his heels and caught Jammer on the side of the jaw, the ear, and the head, which snapped around. It was indeed weighted. It was heavy and tight, its heft and point more like that of a spear than a support.

The second blow fell on the wrist that held the knife, which clattered out of Jammer's hand and which Ward kicked under the counter to the cook.

Ward hurled the umbrella toward the sofas and moved in again, beating the taller, larger man with combinations, hooks and uppercuts, toward the door of the dining room. He beat him over and through tables, a glass divider, the open doorway into the foyer, and along the glass-covered cake and pie cases, sliding Jammer along with his fists, turning him, rolling him, raising him with punches and drubbing every part of his upper body but his face, which he was saving for last.

They were near the doorway when he saw the two unmarked police cars nose through the deep crowd in front of Bewley's, and when, spinning Jammer around, he launched a flurry of hard, sharp blows at the small, fragile ribs—mere cartilage—each side that broke easily and would ache and remind him of Ward for at least a fortnight with every breath he drew. And then the pectoral muscle over the heart, the chin, the other side and the chin.

And then the chin and the ear, and the chin and the

other ear, and the chin and the chin and chin, and
finally, with a shot that he felt from his shoulder to his
back and even down in his legs, Ward shattered his
nose.

It drove Jammer through the glass divider behind
the display area of the front right window and into the
great chrome coffee grinder with its hopper of black
beans, which had been a feature of Bewley's since anybody could remember; when McGarr stepped out of the
staff Rover, he was showered with glass and cascading
coffee beans, was nearly struck by the falling hopper
and by a tall, bald man who fell roughly to the pavement
before him.

Then Ward appeared in the open window, shaking.
He tried to look down at his hands, which were now
galling him, but he couldn't hold them steady enough
for a clear view. They were raw and bleeding, and he
felt like he did after a long fight—giddy and nauseous
and suddenly very, very tired. He looked round and
wondered if Rut'ie was among the patches of blue uniform that now surrounded them. "This man is under
arrest," he said.

McGarr glanced at the Beretta, stuck under Ward's
belt. "Right. The Richmond, with him," he said to
McKeon. He meant Jammer and a hospital that special-
ized in emergency care.

"And the charge?" McKeon asked in a plain voice.

"Accomplice to murder," McGarr said for the crowd.
"Place a full guard on his room and keep him sequestered."

A week and a day later, McGarr again found himself
in Catty Doyle's kitchen. It was nearly seven in the

evening, and dark in the house, the only light filtering dimly through a curtained window that looked out on her back garden.

McGarr was actually pleased with the foul weather that had iced roads and footpaths and kept most people at home with their blinds drawn. It had made his second—albeit warranted—entry into the De Courcy Square row house all that much easier. There had been no neighbors to assuage, no uniformed Guards to deal with. And now with his feet up on the hob of the cooker, which burnt coal, he contented himself with the ticking of the clock in the sitting room, the occasional gurgle of a drain from the house next door, and once only with a low, muffled voice that issued from the spare room that Catty used as a pantry.

He wished he could smoke, but that might spoil things. And his mind strayed to the newspapers that had been filled with the beating Ward had given some ". . . respectable-looking man who has as yet to be charged or released." Bewley's had also complained about the damage incurred and their loss of business, until it was revealed by their own employees that the man had attacked Inspector Ward with a weighted umbrella and then pulled a knife. A gun as well earlier, some other employee said, though the allegation was never corroborated by the police.

Said the head cook, who had watched the entire altercation, "It was the single most complete beating I've ever had the pleasure of seeing one smaller man give another, in the ring or out. The little fella skint him, so he did. It was only later I learned it was Whipper Ward did the job, which I'm proud to say makes me one up on fight fans the country over." Through his family, Jammer—who turned out to be something more than they thought—had immediately contacted a solicitor who told the press that he planned to lodge against Ward the charge of assault with a dangerous weapon. Ward's hands, he meant.

But Kinch, Catty Doyle's dog, had now begun to bark, quieting only when the back-garden gate door was banged shut. McGarr lowered his feet to the floor, straightened up, and waited while the key was fit in the lock. The kitchen door opened and a form appeared, silhouetted against the gray stone of the cemetery wall beyond the lane. The door was closed, and McGarr waited while the light switch was fumbled for.

At length it was switched on, nearly blinding him, but still he said nothing. He only kept watching while a wet coat was shaken out and hung up, a pair of Welly's kicked off, and long, dark hair pulled out from under a collar and raked back with fingers.

Even when a tap was turned on and a teapot filled, McGarr wasn't seen. Not until a moment later, from the stove.

"Don't move," said McGarr. "Stay where you are. Bernie," he called to the door leading to the spare room.

It opened, and after a short pause a figure appeared in it. He was tall and his face was patched with bandages. The cast on his right arm was supported by a sling.

"This the person?" McGarr asked.

Jammer's eyes shifted from the figure at the stove to the floor. He nodded.

"Say it!"

"Yes, it is."

Said McGarr, "This is the person into whose care you surrendered Kevin Coyle on the night of his murder?"

McKeon, who was standing by Jammer, nudged him.

"Yes."

"At that point Coyle was well?"

"He was drunk."

"But he was conscious?"

Jammer nodded.

"What did this individual say to you?"

" 'Ah, Professor Coyle,' or something like that, 'how surprising to see you here and in this condition.' "

"And you?"

"I left with the things Coyle had on him."

"He gave them to you?"

"No—I took them, like. For having gotten him there."

"And did you see this person again?"

"A day later, he came to me in my kip."

"The shelter over the wall?"

Jammer nodded.

"And what was said to you then."

"I was asked to go out and buy a set of knives. I was given money for the knives and for a set of clothes so I wouldn't look like I was."

"And you were given other money?"

Jammer again nodded.

"How much?"

"One hundred pounds."

"Didn't you think it extraordinary?"

Jammer hunched his shoulders. "What's ordinary? It was a hundred pounds. It seemed legal. And then I'd have the suit and all, wouldn't I?"

"And so you did as you were asked?"

McKeon, who was standing near Jammer, said, "Answer, please," and adjusted a dial on the machine he was holding.

"Yes. I bought the knives, like I was asked, in

McNabb's in D'Olier Street. I paid cash and was waited on by a girl."

"Then what did you do?"

"I brought them back here, like I was told."

"To this house?"

"Yes."

"And you handed them over?"

"Just one. There was somebody coming down the alley, which is where we were, and I was left with the rest. I took them back to me kip. I thought maybe I'd use them, or in a pinch get a few quid for them."

"Did you see this person again?"

"No. We don't get on anymore. A couple a days later, that thing with the cop happened in Merrion Square, and I began asking after—"

"What had happened to bring the law down on you?"

"Yes."

"And you learned . . .?"

"That a bloke name of Coyle had been stabbed."

"Murdered."

"Yes. I guess it'd been in all the papers, but—"

"Had you ever seen this person before?" McGarr meant the person standing with the teapot in hand.

"Of course."

"But recently?"

"At the bus stop. Mornings. And sometimes—you know—at night."

"Had you spoken?"

"A nod. Like I said, we don't get on now."

"For the record"—McGarr pointed to the machine in McKeon's hands—"what is your name?"

"James Harrold Geoffrey Holderness. People call me Jammer. Me mates."

McGarr stood. "Please place the teapot on the table." That done, he continued, "David Allan George Holderness, you are charged with the murder of Kevin Coyle." Nearly a month earlier Holderness had moved in with Catty Doyle. "Do you have anything to say for yourself?"

"Certainly. This man lies. He lied as a child, as an adolescent, and now as an adult. He is a criminal with a record and a history of having done violence to others.

"On the night of Kevin Coyle's murder, he had Coyle in tow when he knocked on the back gate. We've never gotten along, not even as children, and then Coyle was drunk and abusive. I refused to let him in, but this man insisted. He pushed Coyle into the kitchen and then began taking things: the ashplant stick, which he smacked on the table, threatening both of us. He picked a clock— there, you can see by the paint where it used to hang— right off the wall.

"When Coyle objected to the rough way in which he was being handled, he began pulling Coyle's blazer off him, he snatched at the hat. Coyle objected to that even more strenuously, saying, 'The stick and the blazer I said you could have, but *not* the boater.' This man proved quicker, however, and got the hat off. Coyle, summoning himself, went for him. Coyle is—*was*—a man about my size, *his* size, and strong, especially when impassioned. Before Trinity he worked in the brewery. He kept going on drunkenly about it being Joyce's hat and that he'd paid four hundred and fifty pounds for it. They grappled and wrestled until this man, having been clipped in the face by Coyle, reached back, seized the filleting knife from the set you see there, and plunged it into Coyle's chest.

"He died instantly. Right on the spot. He was dead

on his feet and hadn't yet fallen before this man had the hat on his head. He turned to me and said, 'You too?' Or, 'You want some of the same,' or some such thing, and I stepped into the hall there. I've always abhorred violence. It's so senseless. I locked the door and waited.

"I heard some moving about. I heard Kinch, the dog, bark. And when—after, say, a dozen minutes—I heard nothing more, I unlocked the door and found them gone, apart from a single bloodstain here between the cutting board and the fridge." He pointed to a narrow gap between the two objects that looked as though it would be difficult to clean. There was a small dark spot on the tile. "I left it there for just the eventuality that has confronted me this evening. With genetic matching, I'm sure you'll find it's Coyle's definitely."

McGarr was surprised that Holderness would know of such a procedure, but then Holderness prided himself on his intelligence and on being informed. It had been the point of contention between him and Coyle. "Why didn't you tell me this before?"

"This man is my brother. The child of my parents. And then I was not—I *am* not—sure of what good it would have done anybody involved: Catty especially, or me, people knowing how Coyle and I had quarreled. As I said, Coyle, with all his early experience, was strong and fierce, and he was drunk. And finally, it wasn't as though it had been premeditated—at least that part of the crime."

McGarr only waited. Holderness had something more to tell them.

"The other part—the knife appearing under the seat

of Hiliary Flood's car—was pure Jammer. Ever since he's been a child, he's had to have somebody to blame. This time it was to be me and my woman friend."

Or her father, McGarr thought. How would Jammer have known it was the Flood's Fiat 500 and not some other? How would he have known where the Floods lived?

"He'd witnessed Flood dropping Coyle off, and he knew where the Floods lived since he'd been to school with Hiliary. This knife"—Holderness pointed to the new filleting knife in the rosewood sheath—"he replaced a few days later. If you check his police record, you'll find illegal entry to be one of his specialties. Jammer is, to his pride, a 'second-story' man of no mean ability. I also think you'll find that he recently purchased a set of knives somewhere in the Dublin area. Then—let me see—the clock is still missing as well. I bought another for Catty. He pointed to a smaller clock hanging below the circle of brighter wall. "She says she'll have to get the painters in. She has to have everything just so, don't you know."

Did McGarr see a small smile flicker across his thin lips? He thought he did.

McGarr reached into his jacket and shook a cigarette from its packet. He tapped it on the stove, then lowered his head to light it from the gas ring. He felt the hair of his eyebrows crinkle in the heat of the flame.

Exhaling, he glanced at Jammer, as though to say, Your turn.

"He met me and Coyle at the gate. I'd already taken the blazer and stick, but Coyle said I should know that the hat was his and his alone, until somebody more deserving, or something like that—he was drunk—could take it from him.

"When David here saw us, like I said, he knew yer mahn, who called him 'the sober solipsist,' whatever that means, and told him to tell Catty that sensibility, wit, intelligence, and something for the human . . . something or other had arrived, and it was time to chuck something that sounded like minimalist bullshit and 'incompetently incompetent, at that'—I remember that part—out on its arse. 'Well, if you can't think your way into' something like 'the collective unconscious,' says he, 'you might as well fuck it. Or'—here the bloke began laughing—'a motto for you for the nineties, Holderness: fuck it, I'll fuck it. You can call it Incompetence at its Rawest, or simply, Incompetence in the Raw.' I remember that 'specially, since it stuck in me mind later on."

While he was in the cemetery with Sweets? McGarr wondered.

"The fella was witty. David tried, but he was never really witty. It was then David invited him in, offered him a drink. He took the hat from his head, as though he would hang it up, but when I'd gotten Coyle onto a kitchen chair, he slipped it to me and pointed to that door, like he wanted me to leave. I had . . . someplace to go, so I left, David closing the gate after me. That was the last I saw of him—Coyle—until me mates and me were coming back through the laneway maybe two hours later. That was when we saw him up against the wall, like I told yous earlier.

"The clock *he* brought me when he came 'round to ask me to buy the knives in McNabb's and to give me the hundred pound. Would I have kept the clock or the knives if I'd a known, much less done it? And why? Hiliary Flood and I went to school together, yes. But that was years ago, and she was maybe four forms below

me. Just a wee girl then, and now . . . ? I have no
idea where she lives.

"The bloke—Coyle? I'd seen him, sure, around here
now and again. But for me there was always a nod or
a wave, and we had a jar together onc't in the Brian
Borimhe when we were both walking across Cross Guns
Bridge and it began pelting out cats and dogs. And
come 'ere while I tell ya, it was almost like he *gave* me
the stick and the blazer, because he said that was it.
He was tired of 'cloning' or 'clowning' Joyce to a bunch
of 'fallow'—I heard—drunks and foreigners, that after
his new 'fookin' book came out' he wouldn't 'fookin'
work for 'fookin' tips again ever.' It was how he was
talkin'. To me.

"And let's get another thing straight—it wasn't me
who was always having to blame things on others, it was
him." Jammer jabbed a finger at his brother. "He was
the oldest and best, and they believed everything he
ever said about us. Always."

McGarr drew on the cigarette. Noreen had told him
he'd have to give up the butts, that no daughter of
theirs was going to be "invested at an early age" in any
"sordid habit." His drinking, of course, would be next;
he could see it coming. And did she say daughter
because she *knew?* When he'd asked, she had only given
him a clever, knowing smile and said they'd see how
he came along with not smoking in the house. She
wouldn't insist on total abstinence.

He exhaled the smoke, and thought of how quickly
relationships, like things, could change. Change was the
order of things, at least on the surface of life. He thought
of *Ulysses,* and at once of how much and how little
Dublin had changed over what now amounted to nearly

a century. "And where was Catty all this time that Jammer here was struggling with Coyle?"

"Asleep, I believe," David Holderness replied.

"Through the stick being cracked on the table and Coyle complaining and finally falling to the floor?"

"In the mirrored room. As I said to you before, you really must see it. It's insulated so completely no sound can get in or out. She was exhausted, and fell asleep there. I myself went into the bedroom. Catty prefers to arise alone. Perhaps she mentioned that herself."

She had and she would again. McGarr motioned to Ward, who opened the door to the sitting room. Catty Doyle was standing in the doorway, having overheard the entire exchange.

Said Holderness, "Tell them about your room, Catty. Maybe they'd like a peek themselves."

Her eyes met his directly. "I won't lie for you, David. Months ago I told Superintendent McGarr how it was, and I won't change the truth. For you or anybody."

"Not even for yourself? Think before you speak. Think of your room upstairs and of Mary Sittonn and even of the Coyle volumes the three of you hoarded against the day that they'd rise in value. Then there's your relationship with Coyle while ostensibly you were so friendly with his wife. It'll all come out in the press, I promise. You'll give publishing and Hollis and Murken a bad name, to say nothing of Irish arts and letters. Why—you might even lose your job."

Catty Doyle turned her eyes to McGarr. "As I told you in the Shelbourne on the day of the book launching, Superintendent, it was half-one to the minute when David got to my house. I remember because he asked me what Fergus Flood could possibly be doing in the neighborhood at that hour. I was in my *bedroom*, waiting for him. He said he'd missed all but the last bus to Phibsborough and he had to walk from the quays. He said he saw the car, the little Fiat, heading up the Finglas Road. He said he saw Flood clearly on the driver's side, and there was another figure in the car.

"I remember nothing more of the night until Kinch's barking woke me up. We then heard some noise out in the back garden, near Kinch's house and the back gate. And knocking. David said he'd go down and find out, and I put a pillow over my head and went to sleep.

"I woke up when I again felt his presence beside me in the bed. He said, and I quote, 'It was just some punks,' and he had Kinch with him so the dog wouldn't bark anymore. When I woke up, he was gone. David. Kinch was in his house in the garden."

McGarr turned to Holderness. "Well . . . ?"

"Well, what?"

"Don't you have anything to say?"

"I don't know *what* to say, except that we'll see how it plays in court." Holderness even managed to flash his smile.

18

With a feeling that was much like loss, Bresnahan read the last words and closed the book nearly a year after first having begun. It had taken her that long to finish *Ulysses*, but at least now no know-it-all American exchange student or Japanese tourist who could scarcely speak the language, or worse, a pint-sized pugilist detective inspector, could presume to explain to her one of the high points of the country's culture.

It was Sunday, and she was sitting up in bed in her new "mews" apartment off the fashionable Morehampton Road, which she had *bought,* mind, with her own money and a small mortgage on the idea—cunningly formed in childhood in her native Kerry—that a woman should possess a place of her own and not be kept unless and until there arose a binding contract which also entailed a change of name.

Ward himself had been gone from the bed when she awoke, and had left a note saying he had jogged into town to the gym for a workout, after which he'd probably have a jar with the lads and "catch the action" while he was at it. He meant the boxing on the telly, which was a feature of nearly every weekend; she'd thought she'd like it, but had actually found it boring when Ward wasn't in the ring, pointless when he was and risked getting his lovely body or head smashed, brutal when he did, which—thank St.Alyoisius, patron saint of the thick and dumb—wasn't often. It was also a Nelson's Pillar–sized pain in the bottom every bleeding weekend, though she'd never let on and had never seen it. Not a "cute" culchie like her.

It—the pillar, which was mentioned at least a half-dozen times in *Ulysses*—had been blown up by some anti-British patriots as a "symbolic gesture" when she was still a little girl, and she understood that if she let Ward have his way in a few big things, like boxing and anything else "physical"—he always had to be moving, the little tyke—she could toss him around mostly on the rest, which was gratifying.

Hefting *Ulysses,* she fanned the pages. All those words in so many different voices of so many characters. As the paper flowed under her thumb in a white-edged blur, she thought of water tumbling over a weir, of streams and rivers, of the Liffey and Dublin Bay and the Irish Sea beyond. And of the ocean, and how the book was like an island in the river of the mind. She had read somewhere in one of the innumerable trots she'd bought to get through the thing that to read and understand even a part of *Ulysses,* but mostly to enjoy it, was to become a Dubliner, the experience marked and stayed with one so.

But was the experience of the book different from the Dublin she lived in every day? She thought for a while, looking out the narrow-paned casement windows onto the flagstone courtyard with the imminence of the grand house—of which her apartment had once been the stable loft—in the distance, and decided that it was. Everything in the book seemed constantly moving, changing, flowing, and wasn't her life that only a year before seemed like something out of Gerty MacDowell, now more the class of thing that a Mrs. Bandman Palmer might enjoy, what with the way she was now being accepted by the Squad and all Ward's up-market friends?

And then, just as it was hard to get a hold on the characters in *Ulysses*—they seemed so slippery—so too were the people she knew in the here and now, and what they did. The reality of things—*how it was*—kept changing right before her eyes almost as much as though to make her out a fool or, worse, an ejit who *couldn't* know what was going on. She pushed herself up in the pillows and reached for the thermos pitcher of hot coffee that Ward had left on the night stand, the imp.

Take the Coyle case, for instance, which had been in court the past five weeks and was now awaiting a verdict. She herself had been called to testify, and was astounded at how Mr. Seamus Donaghy—aped slavishly in the papers—could make David Holderness out to be an innocent university intellectual and pacifist, and his brother Jammer a lout and a thug of the type who were making the city unlivable for law-abiding Dubliners, especially after dark. The Holderness she knew of wasn't the Holderness that was presented in court, and Donaghy then proceeded to raise three other veils of illusion. Bresnahan glanced down at the book and smiled, congratulating herself on the felicity of the thought.

Donaghy made it seem as though Jammer were such a vile wretch that he was now fingering his own brother to save himself from being convicted of a murder which was without a doubt only one of his many. Hadn't he beat Ward over the head with a truncheon and left him for dead? Hadn't he later pulled a knife in a public place and tried to finish him a second time? Hadn't Jammer's "mates" desecrated St. Michan's church? And weren't there three other unsolved murders in Dublin this year alone?

Second, Donaghy made it seem that it wasn't so much a man who was on trial but rather Trinity College itself, which had been doubly wronged by the—what were Donaghy's words?—"scum and *canaille*" of the city, first in the loss of Coyle and then in the "attempted character assassination of his colleague and friend, David Holderness, which I shan't allow to continue."

The third veil was Donaghy himself. He was a big, handsome, winning man who, after one look, you said to yourself you'd like to know. And he made it seem that in a very direct way he, not Holderness, was on trial, charged by Jammer through the State with an even higher crime than murder—that of false perceptions in regard to the reality of the murder of Kevin Coyle. In such a way Jammer and his accomplice, the easy-to-hate-and-always-suspect State, were impugning Donaghy's motives. As well, they were standing in the way of the progress of his career, and it would be a world-darkening miscarriage of all that was right and holy were Seamus Donaghy (that is to say, David Holderness) convicted of anything.

He even stated that he would bring a civil action against the state to compensate Mr. Holderness for the way "his name has been dragged through the mud," thus promising to further attenuate the Coyle affair to the delight of the press and Donaghy's purse. One million pounds was the asked sum, which nobody thought fantastic coming from Donaghy, "the ballocks-befriending barrister," as McKeon called him. "He's a bigger liar than Shames Choice, and the bard's modern-day equivalent more than Kevin Coyle ever thought of being. Sure, we don't have poetry anymore, we don't even have literature. All we have is the theatre of the law. When Donaghy comes to write his memoirs, one guess what he'll call it. Not *Ulysses* but . . .?" None of the staff had a clue. "*Y'all-asses*. Donaghy's from the South. Cork, I believe."

The State was no match for him. Under the weight of his tongue, Catty Doyle, whom Bresnahan had thought sophisticated, capable, and worldly, appeared a confused, immature person who had recently been sacked from her job and was probably a consort of Jammer's. Donaghy pointedly asked her about the pink wig and leather items she had in her wardrobe. No mention was made of the fact that she had lost her coveted position with the publishing company *because* of her relationship with Holderness.

Then there was Katie Coyle, who had seemed so plain and matronly. Well, sir (and ms.), wasn't she now on tour with her husband's book, continent-hopping from one talk show to another and appearing at the trial looking like a refugee from the West End. She was being heralded as a veritable Molly Bloom. To be fair, she could talk, but so could everybody else in Dublin, and the drill was to sit her down and let her babble in Libertese.

Who else had changed? Mary Sittonn? Well—there was really no changing Mary, who was committed, but she surely established herself as a good friend to Catty, too good perhaps. She accompanied her to and from court, shoving the press out of the way, parking her immensely filmable vintage Jag up on the footpath, where it got ticketed and finally towed away, and with her short haircut, denim jacket, and infantry boots, generally "butchering the prosecution." (McKeon again.)

Flood? Because of the murder and the thunderous reception of Coyle's book, Joyce's Ireland and Bloomsday Tours had received much free publicity at home and abroad and was thriving. Flood was divorcing his wife, and rumor had it that he would marry a former student who was employed as office manager of Blooms-day Tours. She was a dark little thing who looked no older than twelve. The difficult wife and daughter were presently on a long holiday in France. Her family, it seemed, had money which had recently passed to her, and she told the *Sunday Tribune* that she was tired of "things self-consciously Irish," which was interpreted to mean her immigrant husband himself.

Even Chief Super McGarr had changed. Far from suffering through the trial and all its distortions, he actually seemed to enjoy it. Even though his wife had given birth to a baby girl a month or so before, he seemed almost glad to have to be in the courtroom, waiting to testify, and he insisted on having lunch in places where there was no phone.

Hers now began ringing.

"Rut'ie—getcha out of bed, did I?" It was Ward.

"You must have a crystal ball."

"I thought for sure you'd be up by now."

The implication was that he had already put miles on his Pumas and hours on the small bag and the big bag and on somebody's baggy frame. She could tell from the elation in his voice he had just given somebody a good drubbing.

"Look—for tonight, something's come up."

She didn't allow herself to suspicion what. Like emotional rot, jealousy was insidious, and once begun, it corrupted everything. And then other tactics worked better.

"Could I meet you later—say, around half-eight for a drink?"

"Sure. Or why don't we leave it that I'll see you at the Castle tomorrow?"

Bresnahan savored the pause, before he said, "Why?" There was a certain sweet note of consternation in the question.

"Well, I might be tied up."

He waited.

After counting to five, Bresnahan went on. "Maire called." She was a new stylish friend to whom Ward had introduced her. "She thought we might slap on the war paint and trot over to Sachs for the afternoon." A nearby hotel which for years had presented jazz bands in its lounge bar on Sunday afternoons, Sachs was frequented by post-match ruggers and other sportsmen and -women.

"And . . . ?"

"Well, who knows? We thought we'd ramble on to that tidy little Moroccan restaurant she likes so much." And the tidy, not-so-little Moroccan restaurateur Maire had told everybody she liked even better, though after Sachs they might have other offers to dinner. Ward, of all people, was acquainted with the possibilities.

"Suit yourself." The tone was harsh. He hung up.

Bresnahan debated waiting for his second call in bed or actually getting up and bathing and dressing for Sachs. She decided on the latter course, since the date with Maire was real, and she didn't want Ward to think she wasn't a woman of her word.

Slipping *Ulysses* onto the shelf with her other books, she thought of Molly Bloom saying, "a woman wants to be embraced twenty times a day almost to make her look young no matter by who so long as to be in love or loved by somebody. . . ." Well, twenty times was perhaps asking too much, and Bresnahan wasn't sure she agreed with the "no matter by who." But it was the reassurance that was comforting, even if her "somebody" was a cagey little fella who had to be cajoled into admitting his true feelings.

Was that the phone? Bresnahan opened the door to the loo, where she was running the bath.

"Turns out it's off anyway."

"What's off?"

"Me bit of business," Ward said, as though she'd been privy to his every thought which he kept vague, ostensibly because of their off-again, on-again rivalry at the Castle. "Let's not go to Sachs." It was familiar turf, and he was known there all too well. "Hungry?"

Now that she thought about it, she was famished.

"Why don't we pop down to the Greystones Hotel. They've a brunch on Sundays I hear is excellent." He forgot that she too had overheard McGarr say as much to O'Shaughnessy. "Phone and ask for a table by the window, and I'll be by in about an hour."

Bresnahan didn't know what that meant, but she was learning.

"What about Maire?"

"What about her?"

"What do I tell her—about Sachs and all?"

"Tell her you have a legitimate date, and you've no need to go out collecting scalps. Oh, and I've got some news."

"About what?"

"The Coyle case."

"Have they decided?"

He hung up.

Men were too intense, she decided, setting the alarm

on the chair by the tub and slipping into her bath. They went at everything hammers and tongs or, in Ward's case, with fists clenched, when life was best approached on the carom—gently, obliquely, with some understanding of the movement of other spheres. The Coyle case was much in the news, and she could switch on the radio or the television, which were doubtless full of it, if she were of a mind. But where was the hurry? And more, the need? Would her knowing the verdict forty-five minutes sooner in any way change Holderness's fate, or alter the fact that Kevin Coyle was dead?

Again Molly's voice came to her,

I don't care what anybody says itd be much better for the world to be governed by the women in it you wouldn't see women going and killing one another and slaughtering . . . because a woman whatever she does she knows where to stop. . . .

Bresnahan let the hot water pool up around her breasts and, slipping deeper into the tub, closed her eyes and thought of all the things in her life that Ward would never know of: Kerry and the farm and the sea beyond the wall on the other side of the road where they still went for the kelp for fertilizer near the caves where seals mated and the strand where once a whale beached and died and, like a kind of miracle, got carried off on a high tide and was seen no more.

And the high pastures, every stone in the walls of which she once knew from helping her father lift and tug and rebuild the gray line that seemed to rise right up to heaven. And the mountain with the sheep they "left out to God" and collected every now and again and how on a good day on one spin of heel you could see Tralee, Castlemaine, Killarney, Cahersiveen, and Dingle.

Well, perhaps Ward could be made to know them. City fella or no, he *would* be made to know that mountain, she now vowed. She would see to it herself, personally.

Said Molly:

he said I was a flower of the mountain yes so we are flowers all a womans body yes that was one true thing he said in his life . . . that was why I liked him because I saw he understood or felt what a woman is and I knew I could always get round him and I gave him all the pleasure I could leading him on till he asked me to say yes and I wouldn't answer first only looked out over the sea and the sky I was thinking of so many things he didn't know of. . . .

Bresnahan met Ward at the door; she could see from his smile and the sparkle in his dark eyes that he had good news for her, good enough that they might be late for their reservation in Greystones. With both hands he held up the *Tribune.* Banner headlines read,

T W O F E R
T H E B R O T H E R S H.

David Convicted of Murder
"Jammer" Charged As Accomplice

Below was a picture of Seamus Donaghy scowling into a camera, with the advisory that the verdict would be appealed.

"Yes!" Bresnahan cried, raising her arms. Ward wrapped his own around her and raised her off her feet.

"Ya happy?"

"Yes!"

There was a pause, and then his smile changed, an eyebrow arched, and his eyes flickered toward the bed.

then I asked him with my eyes to ask again yes and then he asked me would I yes to say yes my mountain flower and first I put my arms around him yes and drew him down to me so he could feel my breasts all perfume yes and his heart was going like mad and yes I said yes I will Yes.